ADVANCE PRAISE FOR GOOD MAN GONE BAD

"*Good Man Gone Bad* is Gar Anthony Haywood's best work yet, keeping a tight focus on Aaron Gunner and his exploration of his city and the meaning of justice. More than a mystery, this book is a mirror held up to society and the world."

—Michael Connelly, *New York Times*—best-selling author of the Harry Bosch novels

"Haywood is in peak form, a classic hard-boiled mystery full of sly humor and street wisdom—but also a surprisingly tender treatise on masculinity and the futility of violence. A page-turner as engaging as it is deep."

—Attica Locke, author of *Bluebird, Bluebird, Heaven, My Home,* and *The Cutting Season*

"*Good Man Gone Bad* is bracing, heart-wrenching fiction from Haywood, and the best in his Aaron Gunner series to date. Gunner is by now part of LA's contemporary noir canon—cynical, compassionate, and tireless in his pursuit of stubborn truths. Hip and raw. Don't miss it."

—T. Jefferson Parker, *New York Times*—best-selling author of *The Last Good Guy*

"Aaron Gunner is back! And Los Angeles needs him now, more than ever. *Good Man Gone Bad* peels away the lies we tell each other to avoid our painful inner truths—the most powerful kind of detective story."

—Naomi Hirahara, the Edgar Award–winning author of the Mas Arai mysteries

PRAISE FOR THE AARON GUNNER MYSTERIES

"A masterful mystery writer.... Haywood's the real thing, all right, a formidable artist with something important to say about some of the most troubling issues of our day."

—Chicago Tribune

"Gunner yanks the sheet off the American nightmare of race, politics, and murder, LA style."

—Spike Lee

"The fresh dialogue, raffish atmosphere, and boldly drawn characters leave little doubt as to why Haywood's mysteries are fast becoming hard-boiled classics."

—Entertainment Weekly
(Page Turner of the Week)

"Haywood is particularly adept at sliding social commentary into his carefully plotted tales. And his descriptions of Southern California are sometimes worthy of Raymond Chandler."

—Los Angeles Times

"Haywood deserves comparison with Raymond Chandler, Ross Macdonald, and Walter Mosley. Each of these writers has given us a different Los Angeles, and Haywood adds another precinct to this protean city of dreams. If your mystery collection doesn't include the Gunner novels, begin to remedy the situation."

—Booklist

"Gunner is one detective you don't want to miss."

—The Atlanta Constitution

GOOD MAN GONE BAD

An Aaron Gunner Mystery

Gar Anthony Haywood

Prospect Park Books

Published by Prospect Park Books
2359 Lincoln Avenue
Altadena, California 91001
www.prospectparkbooks.com

Distributed by Consortium Book Sales & Distribution
www.cbsd.com

Library of Congress Cataloging-in-Publication Data
Names: Haywood, Gar Anthony, author.
Title: Good man gone bad : an Aaron Gunner mystery / Gar
Anthony Haywood.
Description: Altadena, California : Prospect Park Books, [2019]
Identifiers: LCCN 2019003319 (print) | LCCN 2019005639
(ebook) | ISBN
9781945551673 (Ebook) | ISBN 9781945551666 (pbk.)
Classification: LCC PS3558.A885 (ebook) | LCC PS3558.A885
G66 2019 (print) |
DDC 813/.54--dc23
LC record available at https://lccn.loc.gov/2019003319

Cover design by David Ter-Avanesyan
Interior design by Amy Inouye, Future Studio
Printed in the United States of America

For my children:

Courtney, Erin, Maya, and Jackson

The best work I've ever done.

THE AARON GUNNER NOVELS

GUNNER WAS SITTING IN TRAFFIC on the eastbound 105 when he saw the helicopter. The traffic was nothing new and neither was the police aircraft, the latter cutting and recutting a circle in the gray sky ahead like a boat with a broken rudder. This was Los Angeles, after all, and well east of the great class divide that was La Cienega Boulevard, so inertia and signs of law enforcement in action went hand in hand.

People in the hood called the LAPD's helicopters "ghetto birds," and if feathered birds filled the air over the city in greater number on any given day, it wasn't by a wide margin. At least, that's how it sometimes felt to Gunner. Day or night, rotors booming and/or searchlights blazing, the choppers were there, doing their part to tighten the noose that forces on the ground were trying to close around the neck of some poor runaway miscreant. They drowned out the sound of televisions and rattled the panes in windows, and when they shook you from a restful sleep at two in the morning, they didn't leave you in peace to drift back to base until all hope of finding sleep again was lost.

Still, like every other nagging inconvenience that came with being poor and of color in the City of Angels, a man eventually learned to live with the black-and-white flying machines. He could see them and yet not see them; hear the churning of their blades as little more than white noise. Gunner himself had long ago learned to marginalize them in exactly that way.

So this particular ghetto bird meant nothing to him at first. It was just a mild distraction from the gridlock that held him fast, only two exits away from the Wilmington Avenue off-ramp that would take him to his backroom office at Mickey Moore's Trueblood Barbershop on Wilmington and 109th. He was in a foul mood and this delay would do nothing to improve it. Another potential client had offered him a job this morning he couldn't do for twice what the person wanted to pay, and it had cost him $30 in gas just to hear the pitch and turn it down. The red Shelby Cobra he was driving today guzzled fuel like a wino drank Boones Farm, and Gunner was beginning to think it was an extravagance he could no longer afford. Garaging the car again was a thought that saddened him deeply, so few and far between lately were such small pleasures as getting behind the Cobra's wheel.

He sat in the convertible's open-air cockpit, inching forward on his side of the freeway like a child on an amusement park ride, and tried to clear his mind. He'd been a practicing private investigator for over twenty years now, operating out of the one corner of Los Angeles—what few wanted to call South Central anymore—that seemed to have no use for such services. He'd tried to quit a dozen times, a standing offer from his cousin Del to join his electrical maintenance business always on the table, but quitting never stuck. He couldn't explain why. Something about the profession—if you could call doing the invasive dirty work few people wanted to do for themselves a "profession"—met a deep-seated need in him that nothing else could.

He watched the police helicopter carve another ring in the sky above, now not more than a mile off to his right, and wondered, as he always did, how much the target of the bird's attention was worthy of such frenzy. Were the uniformed men on the ground pitted against a killer this time or just another fool? When he read the story in the paper tomorrow, or caught some TV news coverage of it tonight, would he find out all this drama had been caused by a convenience-store robber who'd murdered three people, or a drunken mother of four threatening her neighbors with a garden hoe?

Whatever the case, the media had finally deemed it newsworthy, because now there were two more choppers in the air, each bearing the colors of their respective news agencies. They respectfully hovered just outside the wide orbit of the circling ghetto bird, reminding Gunner of nothing more than vultures waiting for death to deliver their next meal.

Prior to this moment, he had given no thought to what location on the ground might correspond to the police chopper's flight pattern, but as he drew ever closer to his exit off the freeway, he found himself considering the question. By his calculation, it had to be somewhere in the vicinity of Compton Avenue and 118th Street, give or take a block or two. If he knew anyone who lived in that immediate area, their identity escaped him.

His thoughts turned back to more pressing matters.

He did a mental accounting of his finances, one of several he was doing on a daily basis as of late, and concluded that his situation was uncomfortable but not yet alarming. He had enough money socked away to survive the light trickle his workload had become for five or six months at least, and his bills were all paid up. He'd canceled his cable service a month ago and taken to eating all but a few meals per week at home, two legs of an austerity program that put a few extra dollars in his pocket if nothing else.

Things could have been much worse. He knew people for whom things already were much worse: ordinary people just like himself who'd lost everything—career, home, family—to the fallout of a federally mandated tax cut for the rich that could only be paid for in blood. Not blue blood but red, drained from the veins of the poor and the vanishing all-but-extinct middle class. That Gunner had work at all in the present climate put him well ahead of the game, and he knew it. If the end came for him tomorrow, if he never made another dime, that would still be more time than God or the fates had given many people better than he.

As for what the future might hold, it was hard to be hopeful under the thumb of the fools and madmen currently at the helm in the nation's capital. Empowered and emboldened by the last elected president, racists and misogynists and neo-Nazis—Nazis!—had emerged from America's shadows to take center stage, and men and women like Gunner were once again being forced to assert their right to life, liberty, and the pursuit of happiness on a regular basis. This wasn't America prior to the Civil Rights Act of 1964, by any means, but that was where the country seemed to be headed, following the lead of its commander in chief, a real estate huckster turned politician who made lying into the camera both an art form and a weapon of mass destruction.

Gunner's cell phone had to ring twice to draw him back from the depths of his growing funk.

The name on the phone's screen belonged to his cousin the electrician, Del Curry. He didn't have his Bluetooth headset on, and his first impulse was to just let the phone ring; wind noise made the device all but worthless in the convertible, and he didn't want to risk a ticket for driving with the phone up to his ear. Still, any man as short on paying work as Gunner was had to look for opportunity at every turn, and Del had sent prospective clients his way before, so he snatched the phone off the seat and answered it before a third ring tone was complete.

"Del, what's up?"

The man on the other end of the line was already talking over him. "Aaron? Cuz?"

It sounded like Del, but he couldn't be sure. The voice had been faint and all but drowned out by some kind of stuttering background noise.

"Man, I fucked up," Del said, and if the words themselves hadn't been clear, the way in which he had uttered them—through a despondency that had him crying like

a baby—would have been. And despondency wasn't Del
Curry's thing. "I really fucked up."

"Fucked up how? Man, what are you talking about?"

His cousin didn't answer; all Gunner could hear
instead was that same dissonant thrumming sound in the
background, vaguely familiar yet hard to identify.

"Del!"

"They're gone, cuz. My girls. They're both gone and
it's my fault," Del said, trying to pull himself together.
"Ain't nobody's fault but mine."

He fell silent again, and somehow Gunner knew he
had just heard Del's voice for the final time. He shouted
his cousin's name into the phone repeatedly, trying now
to steer the Cobra off the freeway by force of will alone,
but it was hopeless. The cell connection died and Del was
gone.

Just in time for Gunner to realize that the incessant
droning he'd been hearing over the phone, and the buzzing of three helicopters flying high above his head, had
been one and the same.

1

"AND THAT WAS ALL HE SAID?"

"Yes."

"He didn't—"

"No. He didn't say anything more than what I've just told you, for what? The fourth time now?"

"We apologize, Mr. Gunner," the detective said. His name was Luckman, Jeff, and his low-key manner was almost soothing enough to compensate for the freezing cold of the little police interrogation room and the rickety, uneven legs on Gunner's chair. "But we're just trying to understand what happened here."

"You've already told me what happened. My cousin killed his wife and tried to kill his daughter, then turned the gun on himself."

Even now, many hours after he'd first heard the news, it sounded more like a joke than a matter of fact. Del and his wife, Noelle, were dead, and their twenty-two-year-old daughter Zina was in critical condition out at Harbor UCLA. All of them shot at Zina's home with a 9mm handgun registered to Del. The detectives said the young woman's chances of survival didn't look good.

"Maybe you'd like to take a break," Luckman said.

"A break's not going to change anything. I've told you all I know. The man said he'd fucked up but didn't tell me how. He said his girls were dead and that it was his fault. Then he hung up. That's it. There is no more."

"He didn't say he'd just shot his wife and daughter?"

"No."

"Or that he was about to take his own life?"

More forcefully this time: "No."

"And you have no idea why Mr. Curry would have wanted to harm either person."

"None whatsoever."

"Were there any problems in the home that you were aware of? Were Mr. Curry and his wife getting along?"

"Yes. I mean, I think they were. Del loved Noelle. And I'm sure she loved him."

That had always been Gunner's understanding, anyway. Del didn't talk much about his family life, even with Gunner. When he did, however, it was usually to recount a story that made everything on that side of his world sound either funny or touching, Noelle in particular. On those rare occasions Gunner saw her, at family barbecues or holiday dinners, Del's wife—a tall, heavyset woman with flawless dark skin and a dazzling smile—gave him no reason to suspect she was anything but happy.

"What about money? Could Mr. Curry have been in any kind of financial trouble?"

"Money was always an issue, sure. And lately, more so than ever, I suppose. But was he hurting bad enough to do something like this?" Gunner shook his head, unable to fathom the possibility. "I can't see it."

And yet, something had driven Del to do what he'd done. Something larger and more pitch black than anything Gunner, prior to today, could have ever dreamt his cousin was coping with. Unless things hadn't really gone down the way the cops were saying they had. Luckman and his partner didn't seem to have any doubts whatsoever, but Gunner asked the detective again if there was a chance—any chance at all—that somebody other than Del had done the shooting.

"We can't answer that conclusively until we've completed our investigation, of course," Luckman said. "But right now? Based upon witness accounts and the evidence at the scene? I'd say there's little to no chance that anyone other than Mr. Curry was involved."

The "witness accounts" he was referring to were statements they'd received from two neighbors of Del's daughter, who'd reported hearing a loud argument taking place in the house, followed shortly thereafter by gunfire. One of these people had called 911, and paramedics and police had arrived on the scene just in time to hear one more shot, the one that had apparently ended Del's life.

The ghetto bird cutting circles in the air above Zina's home hadn't been interested in Gunner's cousin, at all. Its focus, and that of the news 'copters accompanying it, was another crime altogether, just blocks away. Which was how shit often went down in Gunner's world: one disaster after another, packed as tightly together as rounds in a magazine. The cruel coincidence only served to make Del's death just that much harder for Gunner to swallow.

As he was the last person to speak to Del before he died, Luckman and his partner were looking to Gunner for answers, and they seemed willing to lean on him all day and night to get them. If Gunner couldn't explain what had caused the bloodbath in Zina's home, and she died before she could make a statement, maybe there never would be an explanation.

They kept him down at the Southeast station for another forty minutes, Luckman finally content to answer more questions than he asked. In the end, both he and Gunner left the little interrogation room as confused as they had been going in.

Gunner drove out to Harbor UCLA hospital on automatic pilot, no more aware of what he was doing than a rock was of rolling downhill. A host of news reporters had tried to get a statement out of him at the station while he was sleepwalking to his car, but they would have had better luck drawing a quote from one of the wax figures at Madame Tussauds. He vacillated over which inalienable fact was more difficult to believe: that Del was dead, or that he'd killed himself after turning a gun on both his wife and daughter.

Either way, Gunner knew his world had just narrowed dramatically. Del hadn't been his only family, but he had been Gunner's closest. Gunner had lost contact with his younger brother, John, almost a year ago now—the last he'd heard, the retired Navy man had been living somewhere just outside of Portsmouth, Virginia—and his baby sister, Jo, was up in Seattle. He had a nephew here in Los Angeles—his late sister Ruth's son Alred—"Ready," as he was known on the street, was a bona fide gangster Gunner treated like a rabid dog on too short a chain. Del, by contrast, was someone he saw or spoke to over the phone at least two or three times a week. The only child of his mother Juliette's brother Daniel, Del was the nearest thing Gunner had to a confidant.

And yet, as Gunner thought about it now, he realized that their frequency of contact had dropped off precipitously over the last two months or so. He'd last seen his cousin only three days earlier, at the Acey Deuce bar where they often hooked up, but prior to that, the two men hadn't spoken in almost two weeks. As it was, that last night at the Deuce, they'd had almost nothing to say to each other; even the banter Gunner and Del liked to exchange with the bar's loud-mouthed owner Lilly Tennell had been decidedly muted and uninspired. Looking back, Gunner could see that a space had opened up between them, a wedge of silence and secrecy that had crept up on them like a ghost, and it shamed him that it had taken him this long to become aware of it.

He'd been too caught up in his own troubles to care if Del had developed any of his own. Maybe if he'd tried to talk to Del about the things that had been weighing on his own mind lately, his cousin would have felt obliged to reciprocate, giving Gunner a chance to defuse whatever it was that had driven him to murder-suicide. But men didn't open themselves up to each other that way, especially when times were hard and complaining just made you feel like an old woman. Pride shut you down instead and made you pretend all was well, feeding the false hope that, no matter the odds against it, you could fix whatever was broken all by yourself.

Still operating under a cocktail fog of guilt and reflection, Gunner parked the Cobra in the hospital lot and made his way up to the ICU where Zina Curry—assuming the girl was still alive—waited. He knew it would be some time before she'd be able to answer the questions he and the police had for her, if she ever recovered from her injuries enough to do so at all, but the girl was unmarried and childless and, as far as he knew, Gunner was her last living relative in Los Angeles. Somebody had to be there when she either opened her eyes again or passed on. It didn't matter that he and Zina were, for all practical purposes, strangers—he couldn't remember the last time he'd seen her, and what little Del used to say about her hadn't left him with anything more than a vague idea of what kind of foolishness she liked to watch on television or how much weight she'd lost or gained; she was family, and a man didn't let family go unrepresented in hospital waiting rooms. Ever.

When he found the nurses' desk on the third floor, they told him Zina had just come out of surgery and was still on her way to the ICU recovery room. They couldn't comment on her condition. He asked to speak with the doctor who'd performed her surgery and then followed the nurses' directions to the waiting room, which was every bit as claustrophobic and depressing as he'd feared it would be. The walls were bare, the magazines were all unreadable, and the muted television was tuned to a cooking show he would have traded for a cartoon had he access to the remote. The room's only other occupant, a fat white woman in a yellow blouse and gray sweatpants, sat in one corner crying the blues into a cell phone, making a mockery of a sign mounted directly over her head forbidding the use of such devices.

Gunner figured he could live with her ignorance for a good five minutes; after that, the lady was going to need a new cell phone.

He had calls of his own to make. Del's parents, Daniel and Corinne, had to be informed of his death and Noelle's, and the condition of their granddaughter. He would wait until he spoke to Zina's surgeon before contacting them in Atlanta. With any luck, they would absolve him of any further responsibility and volunteer to pass the word on to anyone else in the family who needed to be notified. It was a selfish wish, but that was what he wanted.

The big woman in the gray sweatpants and knockoff running shoes closed up her phone and waddled out of the room, leaving Gunner free to replumb the depths of his grief and confusion in relative peace. He tried the thought on for size one more time: Del was dead, and he'd murdered Noelle and tried to kill Zina.

It still made no sense.

It made no sense at all.

2

THE BACK DOOR OFF THE ALLEY at Mickey Moore's Trueblood Barbershop led directly into Gunner's office, but Gunner almost never used it as an entrance. Mickey was his unofficial secretary, and coming in through the front door enabled him to check for messages on his way to his desk. Today, however, whatever messages might be waiting for him could wait until hell froze over.

Today, the amusement he usually derived from walking the gauntlet of Mickey and whatever cast of fools, liars, and/or comedians was in the shop at the moment did not interest him in the least. He knew that word of Del's death—and the crimes he was suspected of committing—would have reached this place by now, hotbed of community gossip that it was, and he was in no mood to deflect all the questions those in attendance would no doubt rain upon him. He had no way to answer those questions, and his ignorance was becoming a greater annoyance to him by the minute.

Still, he had no illusions that sneaking into his office through the back door was going to save him from Mickey himself. His landlord had a sixth sense where the shop was concerned and could detect the slightest disturbance within it, whether the shop was filled to capacity or as empty as a tomb. Mickey didn't disappoint him. Gunner hadn't completely closed the back door behind him before the barber split the beaded curtain that divided the two halves of the shop and started toward him, moving like a white-smocked spirit in the dark.

"Not now, Mickey," Gunner said.

"I'm just checkin' to see if you're okay."

"I'm okay." Gunner fell into the chair behind his desk. "I just need a little time alone."

"They say—" Gunner's glare struck him silent. Mickey stood there for a moment, trying to decide how close to the edge of Gunner's patience he should let his curiosity take him. Finally, he said, "Just so you know, reporters been calling askin' for you all mornin', and a couple have actually come in here lookin' for you. I think one of 'em's still parked out front."

Gunner nodded. "Thanks."

Mickey went to the doorway, turned before passing through the curtain to return to the head of hair he was supposed to be cutting. "He was a good man. No matter what might'a happened today, he was a good man."

He walked out. Gunner watched the strands of walnut beads sway back and forth in his wake, and heard a host of anxious voices on the other side of the barrier welcome the barber's return. Gunner counted three voices in all, including those of Joe Worthy and Chester Hayes, two of Mickey's most regular customers—but it might have been four. He couldn't trust his instincts enough to be sure of anything today.

He sat alone in the dark and closed his eyes, summoning the strength to do what he had to do next. He had put it off long enough. He picked up the phone on his desk, only to put it right back down again, having forgotten the instrument was nothing but a useless prop now. As he had his cable TV service, he'd canceled the phone's landline a week ago, seeking one less bill to pay, and had been reduced ever since to being one of those people who lived and breathed at the mercy of a viable cell phone signal. It was a heartfelt loss. Maintaining a landline might have been ridiculously old school, even for him, but the comfort he found these days in things that were more reliable than fashionable could not be overstated.

Using his cell phone now, he called Del's parents in

Atlanta to give them the terrible news.

Daniel Curry answered the phone on the fourth ring, just as Gunner was about to lose his nerve and hang up. He hadn't spoken to his uncle in over two years, and it made him sick to think that this was how he was going to break that silence, by dropping a bomb on the old man he couldn't possibly see coming. Making every effort to be kind, he identified himself and got right to the point, not wanting small talk to give Daniel Curry any false hope that what he was about to hear was going to be anything less than devastating.

When Gunner was done and it was his uncle's turn to speak, Del's father reacted exactly the way Gunner thought he would. After letting the space of a few seconds go by, he said, "I don't understand."

And of course, Gunner couldn't make him understand, as unable to understand it as he was himself. All Gunner could do was redeliver the bad news, over and over again, and promise to do whatever he could to help Daniel and Corinne Curry survive the dark days to come. Naturally, his uncle expected much more of him—he was the one out in Los Angeles, seeing Del on a regular basis— how could he not know more about what had happened than he was professing to know? How could Gunner not have more answers to Daniel Curry's questions than he was offering? Wasn't he some kind of policeman by trade? How could a policeman be as ignorant of his own cousin's business as Gunner was making himself out to be?

And, most incredible of all, how could Gunner so willingly accept the authorities' explanation for what had happened to Del and his family as fact when such a thing was so obviously impossible?

Gunner didn't know what to say to any of this, especially the last, so he said very little. Apologies and condolences were his only recourse, and he offered up both until his voice was gone and his throat was dry. He let the call peter out with an exchange of sad goodbyes and hung up the phone, certain he had done all the damage his uncle and aunt—both well into their seventies—could endure.

They were going to fly out from Atlanta as soon as they could make arrangements, firmly convinced they were in a race against death to reach their only grandchild. Gunner had told his uncle what Zina's doctor had told him: though the surgery to remove a bullet from the parietal lobe of the girl's brain had been successful, and it appeared her injuries would not prove fatal, it would be hours yet before they could say what her long-term prognosis might be. She could suffer extensive memory loss, partial paralysis—or, God willing, she could recover completely. They were going to have to wait until the swelling in her brain receded and she regained consciousness to know.

As reasons to hope went, it wasn't much, but for Gunner at least, it was better than nothing.

Somewhere in Los Angeles, Noelle had a younger brother, and a father in a convalescent hospital. Gunner had never met either man, but he'd heard enough from Del over the years that he knew the brother spent his time in and out of drug rehab, and the father suffered from dementia. Assuming they were still alive, they needed to be notified of Noelle's death, as well, and Gunner would have felt obligated to make the calls now had he any idea where the two men could be reached. But he didn't. He was thankful for small favors.

Sitting motionless behind his desk, listening to the chatter of Mickey and his customers out front, he considered his next move. He had paid work to do and that needed to come first. It was bad form to put off a client in hand just to hustle for your next one or two, regardless of how dire your future prospects appeared to be. He was weeks into a legal defense case for Kelly DeCharme, an attorney who occasionally retained him, and he had both personal and professional reasons for wanting to keep

Kelly a satisfied customer.

On the professional side, he needed the work she gave him to keep coming; on the flip side, over the last fifteen days, he and Kelly had taken the first tentative steps into the muddy waters of a romantic relationship.

It was a romance long in the making, a surprising development neither had suspected was even possible this far down the road of their acquaintance. Physical attraction had always been part of the mix between them, ever since their first meeting over twenty years ago when the attorney, then on staff at the Public Defender's office, had hired Gunner to assist her with a case she didn't trust the city's own detectives to reliably handle. She was a striking, dark-eyed brunette, and he was an older, bronze-skinned giant with a shaved head and a wry smile. But he was also a black pretend-cop working from the back of a Watts barbershop, while she was a white defense attorney with Century City aspirations, and the discordance of that combination was clear enough to them both that they'd never let their lightweight flirting take any kind of serious turn.

Until two weeks ago.

They'd met for dinner to talk about a case and allowed the personal to creep into the conversation near the end. She told him that her marriage of four years to a Woodland Hills dentist had ended in divorce six months earlier, and he countered by describing how his last attempt at a long-term relationship had taken its final breath almost a year before that. Neither could explain why afterward, but something in this exchange gave them the idea that the next logical step for them both was to sleep in the same bed, and that's where they ended up that night.

Now they were gingerly going wherever that fateful evening seemed to be taking them. They'd had no regrets the morning after and were still waiting to see if any would ever develop. But they were taking it slow. Painfully slow. No multiple-night sleepovers, no talk about the future. She'd made no promises to him and he'd made none to her. If it all unraveled tomorrow, it wasn't going to be because they'd pushed too hard.

Their business relationship, meanwhile, continued unabated. Gunner was being paid by DeCharme—now working for a private law firm in North Hollywood—to do legwork on a complicated murder case, and he was obligated to make this his first priority. But it wasn't going to be his only priority. Finding out what had happened to Del, and why, was going to be a primary occupation for him, as well. Maybe it had been unfair of Daniel Curry to think his nephew should have seen this thing coming, and to have expected him to have all the answers to the questions Del had left his survivors to ask. But Gunner's uncle would be well within his rights to hold him accountable if he didn't seek those answers out now. He owed Del and his parents that much, at least.

Whatever the truth was, it wouldn't bring anyone back from the dead. And knowing it could prove to be more terrible than not.

But that was a risk Gunner knew he was just going to have to take.

3

IT WAS THE SPRING OF 1969. The war in Southeast Asia that America despised with all its heart was continuing to churn. Newly elected President Richard M. Nixon was giving lip service to peace but had yet to strike a deal with the North Vietnamese and Viet Cong that the nation's collective pride could accept. The draft was still sending eighteen-year-old kids into the heart of the conflict by the tens of thousands, and far too many were coming back in body bags.

Aaron Douglass Gunner was seventeen.

He could have waited to go until they came to get him. He could have run away to Canada or gone into hiding at college. He was in no hurry to make an enemy of the Viet Cong, nor to meet an untimely death in a foreign land he could barely find on a map. But college wasn't in his plans, and the role of a draft dodger was too laden with cowardice to suit him. More to the point, he'd seen friends go off to Vietnam who were better men than he, some with wives and kids and careers on the rise, and he couldn't see how their obligation to serve God and country had been any greater than his own. So one rainy day in March, he walked into an Army recruiter's office on Florence Avenue and signed his life away, pride all puffed up with the sense he had done something brave and noble, denied the Man the satisfaction of putting him back in chains by reentering into bondage of his own free will. It took him hours to win her over, but eventually his sister Ruth, who'd become his legal guardian after their father's passing just one year earlier, made the deal binding by putting her own name on the recruiting papers.

What neither Ruth nor Gunner could know was how idiotic his volunteer enlistment would appear in less than a year's time.

He had thrown himself headlong into Vietnam thinking there would be no avoiding it, that despite all the demonstrations and sit-ins and speeches made against it, this was a war destined to have no end. But America's patience for the conflict was in fact about to finally run out, pushed to the limit by the My Lai massacre and the senseless bloodbath of Hamburger Hill. Shamed into retreat by the fallout from his secret bombing of Cambodia, Nixon began pulling troops out of Vietnam as early as July, only four months after Gunner's enlistment, and by year's end the draft Gunner had been so certain would drag him overseas on its own terms was turned into a lottery, a game of chance he might have easily won.

It all made for a bitter pill to swallow, especially from the vantage point of a shallow foxhole on Hill 1000, Firebase Ripcord in the A Shau Valley, in July 1970.

Unlike Gunner, Kelly DeCharme's client had never been to Vietnam, but hell by any other name was still hell. Before his enlistment in the US Army, twenty-six-year-old Afghanistan War vet Harper Stowe III had been a sociology major at Cal State Dominguez Hills holding down two part-time jobs while earning a 3.5 grade point average. He had friends and family, the latter in the form of the father who'd raised him and one older brother. People who knew him described him as quiet but polite. He had a girlfriend with whom he occasionally discussed marriage and children.

Today, retired Specialist Harper Stowe III, Tenth Mountain Division's Second Battalion, 87th Infantry, bore no obvious resemblance to the man he had once been. He had come back home eleven months ago, after thirty-eight months in southern Afghanistan, damaged goods. He was broken in all the ways war can break a man, short of tearing his limbs from his body or rendering him blind. His injuries were the kind you don't see at first glance, the kind that live down deep beneath the surface of the skin. He had a bad back that pained him constantly and a left hand he could barely use, both reminders of a brush he'd had with a stray RPG in Kandahar, but his mind was where his real disabilities began.

Like so many other young men who'd fought in Iraq or Afghanistan, Stowe suffered from what doctors liked to call Post Traumatic Stress Disorder, a catchall diagnosis for a host of mental conditions that were often the consequences of time spent wandering the living nightmare that was war. In Stowe's case, these conditions included sleeplessness and migraines, deep depression, and an inability to focus—and a tendency to fly off into a searing rage with little or no provocation. It was a state of being that wreaked havoc on his private life and rendered him all but unemployable. Veterans of America's two most recent wars, in general, had a hard time getting a fair shake on the work front—employers tended to view them as one crazed and unreliable whole, rather than as individuals to be judged on a case-by-case basis—but those who suffered Harper Stowe's volatile mix of symptoms received the shortest shrift of all. Stowe's suffering left him with an almost permanent scowl on his face that people interpreted—correctly—as a warning to keep their distance, and the minute a prospective employer saw it, Stowe's fate was sealed, his resume discarded.

If he'd been less of a good man to begin with, or even if he were more of a monster now, the war's effects on him might have been less tragic. But Harper Stowe III had been a sweet kid going into the Afghanistan meat grinder, and that's what he was coming out of it, all his war wounds aside. Underneath his pain and insomnia and the fog a host of prescription meds kept him in (when he found the discipline to take them)—Ambien, Percodan, Effexor—he was his father's son, the one who still smiled at the sound of laughing children and held doors open for women, who said "Thank you" and "You're welcome" and spoke as if the whole world were a library. You could see that man clearly when the clouds of his condition parted, but the shame of it was, that parting was too infrequent for most to notice.

What people noticed instead was a moody young black man who walked with a slight limp and grimaced just taking a deep breath, whose eyes lay dead in their sockets one minute, then flashed white with outrage the next. This was the Harper Stowe III who now stood accused of murder.

He was charged with killing a forty-one-year-old white woman named Darlene Evans, his employer at an Empire Auto Parts store in the heart of downtown Los Angeles. Evans had been shot to death in the back room of her shop one morning before dawn three weeks ago, hours after firing Stowe for cause. He'd been late getting in the previous day, an offense he was prone to commit, and Evans had had enough. Eric Woods, a friend and coworker of Stowe's who witnessed their encounter, said Evans met Stowe at the door and proceeded to dress him down, unfazed to hear he'd been thrown off an MTA bus on his way to work for, according to the report the driver would file later, "creating a disturbance." Enraged by his employer's indifference to this excuse, Stowe became verbally abusive himself and was summarily terminated. Only after threatening Evans's life at least twice did he leave the premises, Woods said.

The next morning, less than twenty-four hours later, the shop's manager arrived to discover Evans's lifeless body and the gun that killed her: a .38 Taurus semiautomatic, Stowe's fingerprints all over its stock.

Now, Kelly DeCharme—and, by extension, Gunner, the investigator she'd hired to assist her—had the unenviable task of countering what police and LA prosecutors viewed as an open-and-shut case against Harper Stowe III. No witnesses to the crime had yet been found, and a faulty in-store security system had somehow failed to record it, but everything short of a confession seemed to point to Stowe being Darlene Evans's killer. This included Stowe's own memory, which he claimed could neither account for his whereabouts at the time of Evans's death nor how his fingerprints could have ended up all over the handgun she was shot with.

In fact, according to Stowe, the combination of being tossed from the city bus and losing his job in the span of two hours had reduced the remainder of that day and part of the next to a drug- and alcohol-fueled haze, one that appeared to come and go inside his head like whispers on the wind. Kelly was looking to Gunner to put the pieces of Stowe's tortured memory together just long enough to find an alibi that might save him, but Gunner had been at it for eleven days now and still had nothing to show for his efforts.

He was hoping that was finally about to change.

One of the few things Kelly's client claimed to know for certain was that he'd spent the night prior to Darlene Evans's murder at the home of Tyrecee Abbott, his nineteen-year-old on-again, off-again girlfriend of the last eight months. Abbott, whom Stowe liked to call Ty, had confirmed this was true in the course of the brief telephone conversations Gunner had managed to elicit from her, but the girl hadn't offered up much more aid to her boyfriend's cause than that. Trying to pin her down for a face-to-face, Gunner had been playing phone tag with Abbott for days, and he was finally all done. What she couldn't—or wouldn't—grant him out of the goodness of her heart, he had decided he was just going to have to force upon her.

"What you want Tyrecee for?"

"I'd just like to talk to her for a minute. Regarding her friend Harper Stowe."

"She didn't have nothin' to do with him killin' that woman."

"I'm sure she didn't. In fact, I don't think Harper had anything to do with it, either."

Tyrecee Abbott's mother stood in the doorway to their Panorama City apartment, measuring Gunner with the unabashed distrust of a jaded parole officer. She was a big woman with unruly brown hair and glassy eyes, dressed either for bed or a trip to the nearest Walmart, and if Gunner had been of a mind to try and bull his way past her into her apartment, it would have likely cost him the loss of a limb.

"You got a warrant?"

"No. I'm not a cop." He gave no thought to mentioning that a cop wouldn't have needed a warrant just to talk to her daughter, even if he'd been one. "I'm a private investigator. I'm working for Harper's lawyer and I think Ty can help us with his defense."

"How's she gonna do that?"

Before Gunner could answer, somebody behind the woman said, "Momma, who you talking to?"

Tyrecee Abbott stepped into view alongside her mother. Gunner had never seen the girl before, but he'd recognized the voice; her particular brand of pouty sensuality was hard to forget.

"Who's this?" She regarded Gunner as if he were an unmarked package someone had dumped on their doorstep.

"Nobody you need to talk to. Go back inside." Her mother tried to guide her back into the apartment.

"Aaron Gunner. The investigator working for Harper's attorney," he said. "We spoke over the phone a few days ago."

Holding her ground in the doorway, Tyrecee said,

"So? I already told you all I know." She tore her mother's hand from her arm and, with a glare, dared her to lay it upon her again. Her mother huffed, disgusted, and with a final glance in Gunner's direction, left the two of them to do what they would to each other.

"I'm just following up," Gunner said. "In case you might have forgotten something."

"Like what?"

She looked like a "Real Housewife of" dressed down for a day off. Gunner wondered if the department store bling and makeup ever left her body, even for sleep.

"Like what time Harper left here the morning after he got fired."

Stowe had said he couldn't recall when he'd left, or where he'd gone afterward.

"I don't know when he left. He was gone when I woke up."

"And what time was that?"

"What?"

"When you woke up." Gunner took a wild guess without stating it openly: 10 a.m.

"I don't know. 'Bout 10:30, something like that."

"And he was already gone?"

"Yeah."

"How about your mother? Maybe she was awake when he left?"

"Momma?" She glanced over her shoulder, checking for witnesses, and chuckled. "She wasn't home that night."

"So it was just the two of you here?"

It seemed like a simple question, but she had to pause before answering it. "Yeah."

"What about Eric?"

"What about him?"

"Eric says he was the one who dropped Harper off, somewhere around 10 or 11 p.m." In fact, Eric Woods claimed to have spent most of the evening beforehand with Stowe, trying to talk him down from the raging resentment he was continuing to harbor for Darlene Evans. "He didn't hang around a while afterwards?"

"No."

"Not even for a minute or two?"

"No."

"Okay. Getting back to Harper. You don't know where he might have gone that morning?"

"No. I told you—"

"You weren't awake when he left. I got that. But maybe he mentioned where he was going before he took off. Or has told you where he went since. You have spoken to him since that night, haven't you?"

"Once. On the phone."

"The phone? When?"

"A few days ago. Last week, I think. Why?"

"Well, he was arrested three weeks ago. I thought you might've gone down to the jail to see him by now."

"No. Not yet." If she felt at all guilty about it, she was hiding it well. "Any more questions?"

"Just a few. You said Harper never told you where he went after leaving here that morning."

"That's right. He says he can't remember."

"And you believe him?"

"Harper forgets all kinds of shit. He can't help it. Why wouldn't I believe him?"

"No reason. What did you two talk about the night before? Did he talk about his firing?"

"Of course. That's all he did talk about."

"So what did he say?"

"He said it was all that fuckin' bus driver's fault. If she hadn't thrown him off the bus, he woulda never been late and gotten fired in the first place."

"The bus driver? What about his boss? Didn't he blame her, too?"

"Darlene? Oh, yeah. He was pissed at her, too, hell yes. But it was that bitch on the bus he wanted to kill."

"I don't understand."

"I didn't neither. But Harp was like, Darlene only did what she had to do. 'Cause his bein' late all the time, he put her in that position, right? It was just business. But that driver, kickin' him off the bus for no reason like that—he took that shit personal."

What the girl was saying seemed to turn Eric Woods's testimony on its head. The Harper Stowe he had described both to Gunner and the authorities would hardly have developed such a forgiving attitude toward Darlene Evans so soon after his termination.

"Did Harper have a gun that night?"

"A gun? No." She shook her head to drive the point home.

"Are you sure?"

"Yes, I'm sure."

"Have you ever seen him with a gun?"

"No. Never. I don't like guns, and he knows it." She'd been shifting her weight from foot to foot, arms crossed, and now she stopped. "Look, mister, I gotta get ready for school. And I've told you all I know."

"Sure. I've taken up enough of your time."

"Yeah. If you talk to Harp—"

"Who was here with you and Harper the night before the murder?"

He'd let her think he hadn't noticed her hesitation the first time he'd posed the question, but now it was time to revisit the subject.

"What?"

"I know you told me you were alone, but I got the sense that may not be entirely true."

"You're callin' me a liar?"

"I'm not calling you anything. I'm just telling you your boyfriend—assuming you still think of Harper as your boyfriend—is in a world of hurt if we can't prove he was somewhere else, other than Empire Auto Parts, the morning Darlene Evans was killed. A good start would be to determine what time he left here that day and who he was with, if he didn't leave alone."

Try as she might, she still couldn't answer the question without taking a few seconds first to consider it. "Wasn't nobody else here that night but Harp and me. Okay?"

"Okay," Gunner said. It was either that, or invite her to go on lying to his face. "Anything you'd like me to tell Harper, the next time I see him?"

"No. Anything I got to tell Harp, I can tell him myself. But thanks."

She went inside and closed the door.

Just before Gunner turned to walk away, he caught a brief glimpse of the girl's mother, yanking the curtain closed behind her at a side window.

4

GUNNER HAD MADE ARRANGEMENTS to meet with Viola Gates, Del's part-time office assistant, at his cousin's office at 5 p.m., but he showed up a half-hour early to look the place over before her arrival. Del had given him a set of keys years ago, when Gunner had succumbed to all of Del's badgering and agreed to work for him as an electrician's apprentice. The career change hadn't lasted longer than a month.

The office now was as it had been then, just a small, two-room suite on the ground floor of what had once been a bank building on Vermont and Slauson. The building was the kind of place small businesses went to die, a dimly lit shell abandoned by its original tenant like a snake's shed skin. The uppermost floors were vacant, and the offices below, when they weren't equally empty, were home to a revolving door of disparate business professionals who came and went at the whim of their ability to pay rent: insurance salesmen, dentists, attorneys at law. The economy of late hadn't driven everyone away, but as he unlocked the door to Del's suite to let himself in, Gunner couldn't help feeling like a man trespassing on a movie set long after production had shut down for good.

Del had only really used the office as a place to greet customers and do paperwork, and it showed. You could almost count the pieces of furniture in both rooms on one hand: an old metal desk and wooden rolling chair in each, a filing cabinet, printer cart, and hard-backed chair for visitors to sit on out in the front. Both rooms were choked with stacks of magazines and catalogs, the desktops littered with open and unopened mail, order forms, and writing instruments. But the laptop computer on the desk and the coffee machine atop the filing cabinet were evidence enough that the anteroom was Viola's domain, the room directly behind it, Del's.

Gunner hit the overhead fluorescents, washing the suite in a light both yellow and sickening, and started poking around.

He began with Viola's desk. It was strewn with phone messages torn from a pink pad, handwritten notes to and from Viola and her employer, loose sheaths of printed invoices and written estimates. A paperback romance novel lay face down, open to chapter fourteen. Alongside the computer's mouse, an emery board sat next to two bottles of garish pink nail polish.

In lightly perusing the paperwork, Gunner thought he detected a theme running throughout, that of creeping disorganization and customer dissatisfaction. He found a few "please remit" and "cancellation of services" notices, and saw enough phone messages from the same two or three people demanding a call back to suggest that Del had in recent weeks been in some state of avoidance, as men with money troubles often were. It seemed, too, that Viola had been losing patience with Del, as her written conveyance of these messages to him were growing increasingly curt and imploring:

Please call Ms. Esposito back!!! She's called three times today!

Two things, in particular, caught Gunner's eye. One was a series of printed reviews someone had posted online trashing DC Electrical Services, the formal name of Del's company. Written by someone who identified themselves as A. Fuentes, all three reviews were one-star, scathing indictments of DC Electrical and its owner. Fuentes described an experience with Del's company that involved everything from shoddy workmanship to outright fraud, one that left readers little choice but to conclude that Gunner's cousin was both a liar and a thief.

The other thing of note Gunner found on Viola's desk was the draft of a termination notice for Glenn Hopp, Del's only full-time employee, effective three weeks prior. Gunner didn't know much about Hopp, a tech school grad in his early twenties he had never actually met, but his understanding had been that Del was happy with his work. At least, in the twelve months or so since his hiring, Del had issued no word of complaint about the man in Gunner's presence. If he'd been fired for cause, his letter of termination made no mention of it; it simply stated Hopp's services would no longer be required.

Gunner did a cursory inspection of all the drawers in Viola's desk, finding nothing of interest in any of them, then moved on to Del's room in the back. He had to pause a moment after sitting down in the man's chair, feeling Del's presence here despite his best efforts to suppress all emotion. Del is dead, he thought, once more remembering something he'd almost managed to forget. Never again would his cousin rock back in this chair with a phone at his ear, yell out orders at Viola, or fall asleep with an open newspaper in his lap, as Gunner had seen him do on numerous occasions. He was gone and this empty office was as close as Gunner would ever come, in this life, to being in his company again.

Gunner drew himself out of the descent he was drifting toward and began to subject Del's desk to the same examination he'd just given Viola's. Predictably, the papered chaos here was much the same, only worse: things were in piles sliding this way and that, like a moat surrounding his computer monitor and keyboard, no effort made to arrangement according to content. Invoices and notes from Viola were jumbled with receipts from fast-food restaurants and open magazines, rough sketches of electrical schematics, and direct-mail ads from suppliers. Gunner tried to recall if it had always been thus and found himself doubting it; Del had never been much for neatness, but this seemed to be a new level of disarray, even for him. Did it mean he'd had too much work to handle recently, or nowhere near enough? Gunner couldn't decide.

He picked up a framed photo from the desk, studied the three smiling people frozen in time behind the glass: Del, Noelle, and Zina. They were posing alongside some poor bastard wearing a Goofy costume, the unmistakable trappings of a Disney amusement park in the background. Zina appeared to be in her midteens, making the photo at least five years old. Everyone seemed to be genuinely happy, though Zina's grin could have been viewed as more artificial than the two her parents were wearing; it didn't have the look of being forced, just half-hearted. Or maybe that was just his imagination, Gunner thought, looking as he was for signs of Del's discontent everywhere.

He was rummaging through his cousin's desk drawers, discovering treasures no more meaningful than old coffee mugs and packs of gum, when the office door opened and Viola Gates walked in, a jangling keychain in her right hand and a look of surprise on her face. And it was surprise, not fear, Gunner noted; in fact, he got the impression she could have found him robbing her own home and not been more personally insulted.

"How did you get in here?" she demanded.

Gunner had met her at least twice before, long after he'd left Del's employ, but he took fresh stock of her now. What he saw was a middle-aged black woman of medium height, 140 to 150 pounds arranged in the shape of a teardrop vase, and a face chiseled in smooth brown marble beneath a Rasta's mane of beaded dreadlocks. A black mole the size of a small diamond drew attention to her left cheek, just beside her flat nose, like a lighthouse calls out to stray ships in the night.

"I have my own keys."

"I thought you said 5 o'clock."

"I did. You're right on time." With his right hand, he

slid closed the desk drawer he'd been rooting about in, not wasting the effort to be discreet about it.

Viola's eyes drifted over to her desk, seeking signs of invasion, as Gunner stood up to join her in the anteroom. "Is it really true?" she asked, and up close he was able to see her eyes were rimmed in red. "Mr. Curry's really dead? And he killed Noelle and shot Zina?"

"They were all shot, and Del and Noelle are dead, yes," Gunner said. "But we're still trying to find out how and why."

"We?"

Gunner ignored the bitter skepticism in her voice and said, "The police and I. Their investigation into what happened this morning is still open, and I'm just doing my part to help them with it. You don't have any objection to that, do you?"

Viola pushed past him to take her seat behind the desk, leaving him with the other so that he'd have no confusion about the pecking order in this room. "So why haven't the police called me yet? Shouldn't I talk to them first?"

Gunner sat down in the hard-backed chair across from her, accepting her terms of fealty without complaint. "To be frank? I doubt you'll ever hear from them. The detectives in charge of the case seem pretty satisfied that things went down exactly the way you just said they did—Del shot Noelle and Zina, then turned the gun on himself—so it's unlikely they'll look very hard for a reason to change their minds."

"What about Zina? What does she say happened?"

"She's in no condition to say. She hasn't regained consciousness yet."

Gunner waited for her to respond. Tears slowly pooled in her eyes and her head began to swivel from side to side, almost imperceptibly. "I can't believe it," she said.

"What?"

"He wouldn't do such a thing. He couldn't have!"

Gunner didn't push; he knew she'd get around to explaining herself eventually.

Viola yanked a tissue from the box on her desk and dabbed her eyes with it, expelling a deep sigh. "Things were bad. He was having a rough time. I could see how he might've wanted to kill himself just to put an end to his troubles, but killing his family, too? No." She shook her head more emphatically. "No."

Gunner let a moment pass, determined to tread softly. "How bad were things? Exactly?"

Del's assistant appraised him carefully. "I'm not sure I should answer that."

"I'm sorry?"

"I don't mean to be rude. But I barely know you. Why should I tell you all of Mr. Curry's business?"

"Because—"

"I know what you said your motives are. But that doesn't explain everything." She pulled herself upright in her chair, becoming Del's fire-breathing, outraged protector again. "Like why you broke in here before I showed up so you could go through this office, instead of waiting for me to let you in. Mr. Curry hasn't been dead a full day yet and already he's got relatives sniffing around his things, looking for their piece of what little the poor man didn't take with him."

"It's not like that," Gunner said, though he fully understood how she might have thought otherwise. He'd seen it himself too many times, the dead's so-called "family" picking over whatever riches had been left behind, desperate to be the first in order to get the best. No amount of wealth was ever too big or too small to fight over like hyenas over a carcass.

"No?" Viola said. "Then tell me how it is."

It incensed Gunner to be questioned like this, when he had more right to his pain than she had to hers. But he gave in and said, "Del was my first cousin. And the closest thing I have, I guess, to a best friend. I loved him. And it pisses me the hell off that I'm so goddamned clueless about what happened to him today. I'm the only family he had out here, and family's supposed to know when the world's turned so far upside down for somebody that they're thinking about picking up a gun and using it. So that's what I'm doing here, snooping around his office and talking to you." Gunner forced himself to stop and take a breath, before the train that was his guilt could accelerate beyond his control. "His parents are going to arrive from Atlanta tomorrow or the next day for his services, and when they get here, they're going to ask me to explain why their son and daughter-in-law are dead, and their only grandchild is the next thing to it. Assuming Zina's even still alive by then. I want to have answers for them when they ask their questions, Viola. And you can help me do that."

She took a long time deciding whether or not she wanted to help him. "How?"

"I asked you how bad things had gotten for him, and in what ways."

"I don't know everything. I only know what I've seen and heard in here, and I'm only here Monday through Thursday."

"Okay."

She sighed. "He had money problems. Business was down and he couldn't pay his bills on time. I think he was tapped out on all his credit cards."

"And you know this because?"

"Because I was taking the calls from people demanding payment. Banks, suppliers, utilities. We had the electricity cut off in here at least once."

"How long had this been going on?"

"I don't know. Three, four months, maybe."

Gunner couldn't believe it. Four months in debt and Del had never once asked him for a dime.

"How deep in the hole do you think he was?" he asked Viola.

She shook her head. "I really couldn't say."

"You weren't responsible for his books?"

"His books? Oh, no. I could have done them, if he'd let me, but Mr. Curry did his own books. All I do—" She immediately corrected herself: "All I did around here was answer phones and do paperwork." She picked up on Gunner's hesitation and read it perfectly. "I know. That's the kind of work any girl out of high school could do. What's a grown woman like me want with a job like this?" She smiled at an old wound, the twisted knife still in her back. "If that paper I got from Morehouse was still worth anything, I wouldn't be here. But it's not, and I've got to eat, so here I am."

Gunner could only nod, sorry for whatever he'd done to make her think such a painful admission had been necessary.

"When you say business was down, exactly how far down was it?"

"Way down. He still had work coming in, but nowhere near what he used to have. New business was down, especially. Somebody was spreading lies about him online, driving folks away."

"A. Fuentes?"

"Yes. At least, that's the name they used. How did you know?"

"I saw a few of his—or her?—reviews on your desk. What's the story?"

"There is no story. I never heard of any A. Fuentes and neither did Mr. Curry. The name, the call, the things they said Mr. Curry did—it was all BS. Every word of it."

The subject seemed to have touched a nerve with her.

"So who did Del think was writing these fake reviews?"

"He didn't have any idea."

The twist she'd put on the word "he" was an open invitation to a follow-up question.

"But you did," Gunner said, obliging.

"It was just a feeling I had."

Gunner waited.

"I think it was Zina."

"Zina?" Gunner couldn't hide his surprise. "Why Zina?"

"How well do you know her?"

"Not very."

"Kids, they throw this word around way too much, but sometimes it's appropriate: she's a little bitch. I'm sorry, I know I should have more consideration for her than that, considering her condition, but that's the word that fits. Poor Mr. Curry was on the phone with either her or his wife every day, trying to keep them from killing each other. That's why—"

She checked herself.

"What?"

"No. I'm not going to say it."

Gunner took a stab in the dark: "That's why you thought Zina had done the shooting."

"When I first heard about it—my mother called to tell me to turn on the TV—that was my first thought. That Zina must have killed her mother and Mr. Curry, then turned the gun on herself. I couldn't imagine it happening any other way. Kids these days are so crazy. But that's not possible, is it?"

"It wouldn't appear to be, no," Gunner said. "But that could change."

Viola's eyes welled up with tears again. The tissue was still balled up in her right hand, but she just sat there and let the tears come. "I hope it does. I hope to God it does. Because Mr. Curry didn't deserve what she did to him. He was a good father and a good husband, and just because he wouldn't let her have everything she wanted...."

"Like what?"

She shook her head. "I'm sorry. I don't want to talk about this anymore. I can't."

"I just need a few more minutes of your time."

"No. Please."

"Glenn Hopp. I saw Del had to let him go a few weeks ago."

Gates eyed him suspiciously. "That's right."

"Can you tell me why? Was his termination for cause?"

"No. Mr. Curry just couldn't afford to pay him anymore. Glenn didn't do anything to get fired. But what if he had? What difference would that make?"

"People who get laid off for financial reasons don't usually take it personally. But getting canned for reasons related to work performance sometimes bends folks out of shape, especially if they think the reasons given are bogus."

"Work performance had nothing to do with Glenn's termination. The money just wasn't there to pay him anymore. If you're thinking he blamed Mr. Curry for that, you're wrong." She stood up. "Now, I'd like to go, and I'd prefer to lock up behind me. Are you done in here?"

"I think so," Gunner said. Gates seemed awfully anxious to stop talking about Hopp for some reason, but asking her why now was likely to prove fruitless.

"Good. Let's go."

5

"**IT SHOULD BE DEUCY,** with a Y," the stranger said again, because nobody had acknowledged him the first time.

"Excuse me?"

"The name of the bar. It should be The Acey Deucy, with a Y at the end. Not The Acey Deuce."

He was a newcomer here, everyone could see that, so his ignorance was forgivable. But Lilly Tennell, who had been the Central Los Angeles bar's sole owner and operator since her husband J.T. had been murdered in it going on twenty years ago, did not always have patience for those who made this observation about its name. It was a slow and somber night at the Deuce as it was, owner and regular patrons alike dealing with the death of one of their own, and Lilly didn't need any added incentive to be uncivil.

"We lost the Y in a fire," she said, her mouth an angry red line against the inky black of her face. "Summer of '73. Some fool use' to rent the building next door burned up his top two floors and part of our roof, settin' an old space heater too close to a pile'a clothes, and the fire took the Y in our sign up there with it. 'Course, we didn't have no insurance, took us eight months to raise the six hundred the man said it would cost to put the damn Y back, and by that time, people were already callin' the place the Deuce and likin' the sound of it too much to change. Okay?"

Sitting at the bar two stools off the stranger's left elbow, Gunner had heard Lilly tell the story at least a half dozen times before, but never with such open resentment. Tonight, with all who knew him grieving for Del and the family he'd allegedly laid to waste, things the barkeep usually found only mildly annoying got a real rise out of her instead. She didn't know this chunky, red-haired brother in the Sears delivery truck uniform and had no reason to dislike him, but in choosing this moment in time to suggest she'd misspelled the name of her own establishment, he'd yanked on the proverbial tiger's tail.

To his credit, and to the relief of Gunner and the four other customers in the bar, the man recognized his mistake and just said, "Okay." Lilly's piercing gaze dared him to do otherwise.

The house fell back into quiet, sans the sound of Roberta Flack's voice floating at the outer edges of everyone's consciousness, until the stranger finished his drink and walked out. Then, amazingly, the bar grew quieter still. Lilly stood behind the counter of the bar just off to Gunner's right, drying a glass with a towel like somebody wringing a chicken's neck.

"It's called the Deuce 'cause I wanna call it the Deuce," she said under her breath, no more aware she was speaking out loud than she was of the glass she was torturing. "I gotta explain to one more motherfucka why there ain't no Y in the goddamn name, I'll lose my mind, I swear to God...."

"Lilly," Gunner said.

"This is my place. I'll call it whatever the fuck I wanna call it."

"Lilly," Gunner said, more forcefully this time.

The big woman swung her fat head around to face him, almost too fast for the wig she always wore to follow. "What?"

"Never mind him. I need to ask you some questions." He turned on his stool to regard the other four patrons in the bar, all people he knew as regular customers here: Howard Gaines, Eggy Jones, Jackie Scarborough, and Aubrey Coleman. "That goes for all of you."

"What kind of questions?" Jackie asked from the booth she was sharing with Aubrey. She was small and compact, a single mother of three with a pretty face and a dancer's body who worked as an RN out at Kaiser Hospital downtown, and she always came into the Deuce suspicious of everyone's intentions.

"You know what kind of questions," Gunner said with some irritation. "I want to talk to you about Del."

"If you're thinkin' we know something about what happened today..." Lilly started to say.

"Man, we just as much in the dark as you are," Howard completed the thought for her as he and Eggy Jones left their table in the corner to join Gunner at the bar. Aubrey and Jackie, having no such compunction, stayed in the booth where they were.

"Maybe so," Gunner said. "But I'm going to ask my questions anyway, and you're going to answer them."

He looked directly at Aubrey, he of the post-doctoral education and professorial manner, the one person in the house most likely to object to being bullied in this way, and waited to hear a complaint. Aubrey offered none.

"Okay. Go ahead," Lilly said. She stepped right up to Gunner's position at the bar and set the glass she'd been polishing down on the countertop in front of him, like a dare.

"You've all heard the news. You know what they say he did. They say he killed his wife and tried to kill his daughter, then shot himself to death." Gunner turned this way and that to regard each person in turn. "They say it couldn't have happened any other way, but I can't believe it. Maybe I'm a fool. Maybe one of you knows something, anything, that I don't know that could help me to believe it. Could Del have really done such a thing? Is it possible?"

"Anything's possible," Eggy Jones said. His Coke-bottle eyeglasses reflected neon light from the illuminated beer signs hanging at Lilly's back behind the bar.

"With all due respect, that's bullshit," Gunner said.

"We all have our limits and Del had his. The Del I thought I knew could never have hurt anyone, least of all Noelle and Zina. But maybe he'd changed without my noticing. I've been thinking about it a lot today and I realize it's been a long time since he and I last talked—really talked—about anything."

"And you think he would'a talked to us instead?" Howard asked. The career custodian was the oldest man in the room and the most visibly weary, and what he lacked in intellect he more than made up for in heart.

"I don't know," Gunner said. "That's what I'm trying to find out. When was the last time any of you saw him?"

When no one spoke up, he turned to Lilly.

"He was in here just the other night. You was here, you know," the barkeep said.

"You hadn't seen him since?"

"No."

Gunner looked to the others. "And you?"

"I saw him in here that night, too," Jackie said. "But we didn't talk."

"I hadn't seen him in over a week," Aubrey said. "And the last time wasn't here. I saw him pumping gas near the house. We said hello, and that was about it."

"I don't remember the last time I seen 'im," Howard said.

"Before the other night in here, you mean?" Lilly asked.

"Huh?"

"You was here Friday night, too, same as Gunner and Jackie."

"Oh, yeah, that's right," Howard said, nodding his head. "I was, huh?" Here at the Deuce, the man was always feeling the effects of a drink or two just short of his limit, so straight answers to even the simplest of questions were rarely expected of him.

"Did you talk to him?" Gunner asked, when Howard made no attempt to elaborate. He hadn't seen the two men together that night, but he'd left while they were both still here, leaving the possibility open they'd connected after he was gone.

"Did we talk? Yeah, I guess we did." Howard shrugged. "We must've talked. Me an' Del always got somethin' to say to each other."

"So what did you talk about, Howard?"

"I dunno. Just the usual. The Lakers. Movies. That boy got knifed to death at Home Warehouse. You hear about that? The security guard?"

Gunner had, though he couldn't see the story's relevance to the present discussion. The teenage guard had caught a thirty-eight-year-old day laborer trying to sneak a set of drill bits out of the hardware chain's Van Nuys location and died when the would-be thief attacked him with a box cutter. According to the news reports Gunner had seen, the guard's rate of pay was $9 an hour, while the cost of the drill bits was $13 and change.

"I heard about it. What else?"

"What else?"

"What else did you and Del talk about? Anything?"

Howard shook his head. "No. 'Least, I can't think of nothin' else."

Gunner finally turned to Jones. "What about you, Eggy? When did you last see Del?"

"I been trying to remember, exactly. But I can't. It's been a long time, Gunner, I can tell you that." His sorrowful expression was all but a plea that Gunner not press him on the matter.

Acquiescing, Gunner brought his questioning full circle and said to Lilly, "Okay. Here on Friday was the last time you saw him. What did you talk about? He must've said something to you."

" 'Course he said something to me. You was sittin' right next to him, you heard what he said just as clear as me."

"I'm not talking about while I was here. That was nothing, just the usual bullshit. I'm talking about before I arrived or after I left. What, does all conversation fucking cease in here when I'm not around?"

Lilly's eyes flared in the dark. "Say again?"

Gunner had let his impatience get the better of him and pushed the last person in the bar he wanted to alienate. Even taking into account all he was dealing with tonight, Lilly wasn't going to tolerate his disrespect for a minute.

"I'm sorry. I shouldn't have said that."

"You got that right. You wanna try again?"

Sufficiently humbled before the others, Gunner said, "Did you and Del talk, either before I came in here Friday or after I went home?"

"Yes. We talked after you left."

"About what?"

"He asked me if I missed J.T."

"J.T.?"

"Yeah. I don't know how we got started—I think he just asked straight up, out of the blue: 'Do you miss J.T.?' And I said hell, yes, I miss him. Ain't a day goes by I don't think about that man."

"He say why he asked?"

"No. All he said was, he didn't know how I do it. Go on livin' after somebody I'd been with all those years was gone. He said he'd never make it."

"If something happened to Noelle, you mean?"

"Yeah."

"Can you remember what he said, exactly?"

"Exactly?" Lilly braced her arms against the bar, let out a sigh befitting her considerable bulk. "I think he said somethin' like, 'I'd never make it alone, it was me.' And I said, well, God willing, you ain't never gonna have to. And then he just kind'a smiled and didn't say nothin' else."

"He smiled?"

"Yeah. I remember thinkin', 'What'd I say was funny?' I was gonna ask, but I got called away by somebody—" She turned to Gaines. "I think it might'a been you, Harold—

so I never got the chance. He must've left soon after that."

"Damn," Harold said. "You don't s'pose he was already thinkin' about what he was gonna do?"

"We don't know that he did anything, yet," Gunner said. But he only said it because somebody here had to, lest his faint hope it was true melt away to nothing.

"But if he didn't do it—" Howard said.

"I'll find out who did. You can bank that."

Gunner went around the room, giving everyone but Lilly, who had long ago committed his contact info to memory, a business card. "If you can think of anything that might help, anything you might have seen or heard that could explain what happened today, call me. Day or night. Understood?"

Five solemn nods told him it was. Gunner went back to his seat at the bar, and Howard and Jones returned to their table just as someone pushed the Deuce's door open and stepped tentatively inside. Kelly DeCharme squinted in the smoky dark, found the man she was looking for, then eased her way forward to join Gunner at the bar, every eye in the house moving right along with her.

"Hey," he said.

"Hey," she said, barely above a whisper, signaling her intent to treat him with the utmost care. He'd given her the news about Del earlier in the day, so she understood how fragile he was likely to be.

She started to take the stool beside his, but he stood up and said, "Not here. Let's get a booth."

They took one in the far corner of the bar, where they wouldn't be overheard and the curiosity the white woman still aroused here, even though she'd met Gunner at the Deuce several times before, would be easier to ignore. No sooner were they settled in than Lilly, as if tied to Gunner by a string, appeared to ask if Kelly would like something to drink. Kelly ordered a Rum and Coke, and Gunner asked for another Wild Turkey, wet.

"I still can't tell if she likes me or not," Kelly said as the barkeep walked away.

"Lilly? She likes you fine," Gunner said. "If she didn't, there'd be no doubt in your mind."

Kelly reached out to put her hand in his. "Any news on Del's daughter?"

"Not as of thirty minutes ago, when I last checked. She still hasn't regained consciousness, and her doctors remain uncertain that she ever will."

"And the police still think he did it?"

"Yes."

"But why? Why would he do something so horrible?" Having met Del on a number of occasions, the idea of him shooting his wife and daughter, and then killing himself, seemed almost as preposterous to her as it did to Gunner.

"I don't know. I wish to God I did. His office assistant says his business had been off for a while, but whose business hasn't been? And as for things at home, she says the only trouble there that she's aware of are some issues he and Noelle may have been having with Zina lately. Any of that sound like sufficient motive for a murder-suicide to you?"

"No. It doesn't." And then the lawyer in her added: "At least, not on the surface."

But the surface was all Gunner had at this point. He had hoped someone at the Deuce might know something he didn't, something to suggest there was an explanation for what had happened at Zina's home that didn't put the death of two people and the near-fatal shooting of another squarely at his cousin's feet, but the exact opposite had occurred. Lilly had Del talking about his wife three days ago like Noelle was already dead, and if that didn't suggest premeditation on his part, it at least pointed to the possibility of marital discord, which was almost just as damning. Had Noelle been about to leave him, Del would have hardly been the first man Gunner had heard of to decide his family would be better off dead than apart. Gunner still didn't believe his cousin was capable of murder, but so far, what evidence he had scraped together was only giving him greater reason to accept that conclusion, not less.

"Have you heard back from his parents yet?" Kelly asked.

"They caught a 7:30 red-eye scheduled to arrive at LAX tomorrow morning at 9:45. I told his father I'd pick them up and take them wherever they want to go." Anxious to change the subject, Gunner said, "But we didn't call this meeting to talk about Del, we called it to talk about your client. You want to go first or should I?"

"You go," Kelly said.

Gunner gave her the rundown of his interview with Tyrecee Abbott that afternoon, occasionally consulting the notes he had taken shortly afterward.

"Shit," she said when he was done.

"Yeah. A tower of support for her man, she wasn't."

"And she can't help us with an alibi."

"Not personally. But she might know somebody who can."

"Woods?"

"That would be my first guess. She insisted it was just her and Stowe at the apartment that night, but she was either lying to me or I've lost my capacity to judge such things."

"And your second guess?"

"Her mother. I got the impression Ms. Abbott keeps Tyrecee on a very short leash and doesn't miss much where her daughter and her friends are concerned. If I don't get anything useful out of Woods tomorrow, she might be worth talking to next."

Kelly downed the last of her drink in one gulp and nodded, endorsing Gunner's logic.

He had already spoken to Eric Woods once, over lunch four days ago, but he was anxious now to have Stowe's boy explain the discrepancies between his account of how Stowe had spent the hours before Darlene

Evans's death and the one Tyrecee Abbott had given him this morning.

"Cheer up," Gunner said, noting Kelly's despondency. "Little Tyrecee wasn't a total bust. Her shocking lack of affection for him aside, she at least stated without reservation that she's never seen your client with a gun."

Kelly nodded again, cheered not a whit.

"Of course...."

"Of course, we might have been better off if she'd said just the opposite."

"Well, sooner or later, we are going to have to put the murder weapon in Stowe's hands to explain his prints on it, and do it in a way that doesn't somehow prove he used it to shoot the deceased."

It was easily the most daunting aspect of their defense efforts. Stowe had no recollection of ever seeing the unregistered Taurus used to murder Evans, let alone handling it, and no one Gunner had yet spoken to could venture a guess as to how or when he might have come in contact with it. If Gunner and Kelly couldn't offer a jury an innocent explanation for his fingerprints being on the gun, even an alibi placing Stowe miles from Empire Auto Parts when Evans was killed might not be enough to win him an acquittal.

"I'm visiting Harper again Wednesday," Kelly said. "Hopefully, he'll have remembered a thing or two that will be useful to us since the last time we talked. His memory of those two days has to come back to him eventually."

"If it hasn't already, you mean."

She shot him a wary side-eye. "Excuse me?"

"Well, there is a chance he remembers more about all of it than he's been telling us, isn't there? I mean, if we're being honest about it?"

"No."

"I'm just saying."

"No, Aaron. Positively not. But if that's what you think—"

"I didn't say that's what I think. I'm just saying we'd be wise to consider the possibility that he hasn't been entirely truthful with us. Either because he did in fact commit the crime himself, or is protecting someone else who did."

"Harper didn't kill Darlene Evans, Aaron. And he's told us everything he knows or can remember about her murder. If I didn't believe that, I would have never taken his case in the first place." Gunner started to respond, but she pushed on: "You haven't spoken to him yet. I have. He's been telling us the truth. I know it and his father knows it."

Stowe's father was Harper Stowe Jr., the man who had actually retained the services of Kelly's firm. He was a sixty-six-year-old retired mechanical engineer who cast a brown bear's shadow and spoke like every word was a dollar out of his pocket, and both his bearing and physical appearance—from his well-tailored clothes to his trim white goatee—were unapologetically imperious. Gunner had met him only once, at a brief meeting with Kelly in her office ten days ago, but once had been enough to be suitably antagonized.

"Okay. I'm convinced," Gunner said.

"No. You're not. But that's okay. I didn't hire you to drink the Kool-Aid. I hired you to find out the truth."

"And if I find out your client's guilty?"

"Then Harper Junior is going to be one very unhappy man. When was the last time you called Samuel Evans?"

"He doesn't want to talk to me."

"Of course he doesn't. Nobody on our interview list does. But since when is that an excuse to stop trying?"

"Who said I was going to stop trying?"

"You'll call him again tomorrow, then."

"I already had plans to."

Gunner had been trying to question Darlene Evans's widower for days now, and only Tyrecee Abbott had proven more reluctant to cooperate. His reasons for wanting to talk to Samuel Evans were all too obvious, and being a likely suspect in his wife's murder, as the spouse of a homicide victim always was, helping Gunner along probably did not sit particularly well with the man.

"I'd like another," Kelly said, gesturing with her empty glass. Gunner waved Lilly over and ordered them both a refill, the bartender for once coming and going without her and Gunner exchanging any of their customary extraneous banter.

In Lilly's absence, Gunner and Kelly sat there in silence for a moment, each gripping the other's hand as if for the last time. Kelly studied Gunner's face in the bar's muted light, and asked, "Are you going to be okay?"

"No," he said, lacking any incentive to lie. "I don't think I'm going to be okay for quite a while."

He wanted to go on talking, to tell her everything he knew about Del Curry and everything he remembered about him. All the fights they'd had over things big and small, the laughter they'd shared first at one man's expense, then the other's, over and over, round and round, even when the target of all the levity had every right to be crying instead. He wanted to count for Kelly all the times Del had saved his ass, either by setting his head on straight when it was about to spin off or by having his back, both literally and figuratively, when Gunner was up against something or someone he couldn't take on alone. There were a thousand stories to tell, a thousand things to say about his dead cousin that Gunner wanted, needed to say.... But he couldn't bring himself to say them now. He was afraid of what might happen if he tried.

So he just held on tight to Kelly's hand and cried, instead.

6

AFTER A LONG, RESTLESS NIGHT, Gunner started the next day with a 7 a.m. phone call to Harbor UCLA to check on Zina Curry. He was due to pick up the girl's grandparents from the airport in a little over two hours and was praying he could greet them with the news she was still alive.

The nurse who answered the phone put him on hold for several minutes, a stretch of deadly silence he used to brace himself for the worst, but the word he ultimately received was all good. Zina had indeed survived the night. She had yet to regain consciousness but had suffered no setbacks, and her vital signs—for now, at least—were stable.

Encouraged, Gunner next placed a call to Jeff Luckman, seeking status of the LAPD's investigation into the murder-suicide his cousin had allegedly committed. This time, precisely what he thought might happen did: he was forced to leave Luckman a message when his call went straight through to voicemail. He knew Daniel Curry wouldn't like it, his having nothing new to report from the police, but Gunner figured that was soon to be Luckman's problem, not his.

He grabbed an egg sandwich and tall coffee at a burger stand near the house and headed out to Lilly Tennell's crib above the Deuce to pick up her car. Befitting a woman of her girth and general lack of humility, Lilly's ride was a late-model Chevy Tahoe that resembled a rolling battleship painted black, and as much as Gunner detested such monstrosities, it was far better suited to the duties of an airport taxi than his trunkless, two-seater Cobra. Kelly DeCharme couldn't drive a stick, ruling out swapping cars with her, so he'd asked to borrow Lilly's SUV last night, knowing full well he wouldn't like her conditions.

"Don't bring it back 'less it's got a full tank," she told him as he was pulling the car out of the Deuce's back lot. Still dressed for bed, head festooned with orange curlers, she was wearing the biggest terrycloth bathrobe Gunner had ever seen.

"But it's only got a half-tank now."

"I want it washed and waxed, too," Lilly said, as deaf to his complaints as a potted plant.

He drove off in disgust before she could up the ante any further.

Del's parents insisted on being driven directly to the hospital. They both looked like they hadn't slept in days, and Gunner suggested it might be more wise for Corinne Curry to get some rest at their Inglewood hotel while he drove her husband out to Harbor UCLA alone, but neither of them would hear of it. When their granddaughter regained consciousness—as they were determined God in all his mercy would see to it she did—they were both going to be there for the girl, right at her bedside. If they had to eat and sleep on the floor of her room for the next thirty days, that's what they were going to do.

"You can take me to the hotel later," Daniel Curry said. "I'll get us checked in, then go back to the hospital after I've rented a car."

He was doing most of the talking; Del's mother, Corinne, had very little to say to Gunner that a dull-eyed scowl could not convey. A tall, arch-backed woman who almost matched her husband pound for pound, she sat in the Tahoe's passenger seat and stared at the road ahead like something that had done her wrong. Daniel Curry sat in the back, using the car's rearview mirror as a cudgel to demand Gunner's undivided attention.

"I'd like to have the names and phone numbers of the policemen you've been talking to," he said. His square jaw was set such that his lips barely moved when he spoke.

Gunner was only surprised that the directive had been this long in coming. He had no sooner found his uncle and Corinne Curry in the airport baggage area than Daniel Curry had asked him what he'd heard so far from the police. Answering the question with what essentially boiled down to one word—nothing—had achieved the seemingly impossible in making the Currys even more irate with Gunner than they already were.

"Of course. And I'll be happy to let you deal with them from here, if that's what you want. Just know I'm not the problem. They aren't likely to be any more responsive to you than they have been to me."

"We'll see."

"Yes, sir."

They arrived at the hospital to find Zina Curry trapped in time, teetering on the same precipice between life and death she had been on for almost twenty-four hours now. Her head wrapped in layers of white gauze, she lay in her bed in the ICU as still as a photograph, the focal point of an array of machines watching over her like a grieving mother. The nurse at the desk said she was doing well, the standard euphemism for "not dead yet," and put in a call to the doctor on duty with little delay. The doctor only taxed the Currys' patience ten minutes before showing herself, a pretty young Asian woman in a white frock who could have passed through a cracked door without turning to one side.

As the next of kin who had signed all of Zina's paperwork, Gunner greeted her first. Her name was Carol Low. Gunner introduced her to Daniel and Corinne Curry and then stepped to one side, smart enough to know he had just served his uncle's purpose and his assistance would no longer be required. The Currys proceeded to pepper

Low with questions as Gunner followed their conversation in silence, tuning out everything but the most salient information Low had to offer.

Aside from the brighter outlook Low and Zina's surgeon now had for the girl's survival, he didn't learn a whole lot that was new. It would still be another day or two before the cerebral edema—the swelling in Zina's brain—receded enough for her to regain consciousness, and only then would it be possible to ascertain how critical her injuries truly were. Paralysis, loss of memory, limited motor function and speech—or a total and complete recovery—all were possibilities for Zina that could not yet be ruled out.

His wife sobbing effusively by his side, Daniel Curry absorbed it all with the stone-faced civility of a monk, liking not a word of what he was hearing but showing Low the courtesy of accepting it. The Currys thanked the doctor for her time and set her free, but only after she'd been made to understand that they were in charge of their granddaughter's care now, not Gunner, and that they intended to be within arm's reach of Zina Curry from this point forward, hospital regulations be damned.

Low turned to Gunner for counsel: should she insist these people adhere to the restrictions of the ICU or let them do as they pleased? By way of an answer, Gunner threw up his hands, palms out, reminding Low he'd been stripped of any rights here beyond those of a shadow on the wall.

Low bid them all a good morning and hurried off.

Just as he'd told Kelly DeCharme he would, Gunner made his first order of official business Tuesday another visit with Eric Woods.

Unlike Tyrecee Abbott and Samuel Evans, Woods had never forced Gunner to ask twice for an interview. Allegedly Stowe's closest friend, the twenty-five-year-old had known Kelly DeCharme's client since elementary school, and today he agreed to speak with Gunner between serving customers at Empire Auto Parts, where he and Stowe had only weeks ago worked side by side.

The parking lot of the shop on Central and 18th was the usual open-air garage for amateur mechanics such places always were. Gunner made his appearance there just before noon. Men in T-shirts and greasy overalls were folded over the grilles and front fenders of pickup trucks and beaters, lowriders and cargo vans, performing whatever surgeries were required beneath the raised hoods of their vehicles. Gunner pulled Lilly's Tahoe into a space alongside a tricked-out tangerine-colored Honda Civic SI, its owner and a uniformed store employee testing an air filter for fit in the car's engine bay. The nametag on the uniformed man's shirt was out of his view, but Gunner took a shot anyway: "Eric?"

Woods turned. He was diminutive at five-foot-five in his stockinged feet, his pale brown face dotted with freckles.

"Aaron Gunner. We spoke earlier this morning?"

"Oh, yeah. Harp's investigator. Gimme a sec."

He offered his customer a few more instructions, wiped his hands on a rag in his pocket, then greeted Gunner officially. "Okay if we talk out here? I could use a smoke."

"No problem."

Woods went around to the side of the building and Gunner followed. He watched as the younger man produced a pack of unfiltered Camels from his shirt pocket and lit one up, taking a hard draw and blowing the smoke to one side before speaking again.

"So how can I help you today?"

"I spoke to Tyrecee Abbott yesterday. Harper's girl?"

Woods nodded.

"She said a few things that seem to conflict with what you've testified to earlier and I thought you might be able to explain the discrepancies."

"I might. What'd she say?"

"She said Harper was a lot more interested in killing the bus driver who threw him off the bus the day he was fired than he was your boss Darlene. Yet you seem to believe just the opposite."

"I do?" He blew more smoke into the air, as unruffled as a newly pressed suit.

"Well, the statement you gave to the police, and the conversation we had earlier made it sound like Harper's only focus that day was on harming Darlene. In fact, I don't think you even mentioned the bus driver."

"I just answered the questions I was asked, and all the questions were about Harp and Darlene. If somebody had asked me about the bus driver, I would have told them Harp was pissed at her, too. Why not?"

"So how pissed was he?"

"Plenty. But the only one he talked about killin', around me anyways, was Darlene."

"You said you were with Harper most of that night, right? The Tuesday he was fired?"

"Yeah, that's right."

Gunner began consulting some notes he'd written in a small pocket notebook, knowing full well he had to look to Woods like a caveman pondering cryptograms on a stone tablet, Millennial that the kid was. "He showed up at your place around six and you left him at Tyrecee's mother's apartment around eleven. Correct?"

"Sounds right."

"What time did you arrive at the apartment?"

"Ty's? I dunno. Ten, maybe? I only stayed about an hour."

"So what did you guys do in between? From the time he arrived at your crib to the time you arrived at Tyrecee's?"

"Not a whole lot. Played a little C.O.D. Went out for some grub. Came back and watched a movie. That was about it."

"C.O.D.?"

"Call of Duty. Black Ops Two. It's a video game."

Gunner wasn't sure, but he thought he detected a hint of condescension toward the end of Woods's reply. He made a note of the game's title in his book.

"And the movie? You remember what it was?"

Woods took a final drag off his cigarette, crushed it under his boot, giving Gunner's question some thought. "Something on Netflix. It sucked, so we didn't even finish it. Transporter Three, or Two, something like that."

Gunner made another note in his book. "Anybody join you?"

"Nope. It was just me and Harp."

"Did he have a gun with him?"

"A gun? Hell, no."

"Have you ever known him to carry a gun?"

"No. Never."

"What about Darlene? Did she keep a gun in the office?"

"No. I mean, I don't know. Not that I ever saw."

"But it's possible."

"Sure. I guess so. I don't go in the office much."

"What about Harper?"

"What about him?"

"How often was he in the office? If Darlene had kept a gun in there, might Harper have come across it?"

"I don't know. Maybe." Woods's face lit up, the clouds suddenly parting. "Oh, I get it. You're thinking she got shot with her own gun. And if Harp had touched it before—"

"That would explain how the police found his finger-prints on it."

"Smart. But"—he shook his head—"I don't know if he did or he didn't. I don't know anything about a gun in the office. There might have been one, and there might not. Man you should talk to about that is Johnny."

"Johnny Rivera?"

"Yeah."

Rivera was the shop's manager and the man who'd discovered Evans's body. Gunner hadn't yet interviewed him and hadn't been sure up to now that he should.

"Is he here?"

"Now? No. He's on a parts run."

"Any idea when he'll be back?"

"About an hour. Maybe two. Look, Mr.—Gunner, right?" He waited for Gunner to nod. "Like I told you the other day, Harp's my boy. Nobody wants to help him more than me. But I don't know what I can tell you that's gonna do him any good. I wish I could say—hell, man, I wish I could prove—that he was with me when Darlene got shot, but I can't. He wasn't. Last time I seen Harp was the night before it happened, when I dropped him at Ty's crib. I don't know where he went or what he did after that, I swear."

"Okay. Let's just go on talking about what you do know. Like whether or not Ty was alone when you and Harper showed up, and how long you hung around after."

"I didn't hang around. I told you, I dropped Harp and bounced."

"And Ty was the only one there?"

"Naw. She had a girlfriend with her. A fat girl." Woods caught the look of surprise on Gunner's face and said, "And before you ask her name, don't bother, 'cause I don't remember it. Ty introduced us but I forgot her name soon as I heard it. Girlfriend was fat for real, and that ain't how I roll."

He checked his phone for the time. "Sorry, but I gotta go."

"Of course. The new boss in today?"

"The new boss? You mean Sam?"

"I understand he's taken over the business since Darlene's death. Is he in?"

Gunner was hoping he could kill two birds with one stone with this visit, but Woods shook his head and said,

"He hasn't come in today, and he probably won't. He's pretty much been letting Johnny run things around here."

Woods's head swung to one side as he finished the thought, his gaze drawn to a car racing into the lot: an emerald green, late-model Camaro that its owner had been treating like a drum that needed a daily beating. The driver slammed it into a space and stepped out, giving both Woods and Gunner a good look at a swarthy white man in his early twenties, as unshaven as a castaway and twice as resentful of his lot in life. He stormed inside the shop without so much as a sideways glance.

"I gotta be getting back," Woods said, addressing Gunner without actually facing him.

"Sure. I appreciate your giving me the time. And I'm sure your boy Harp will appreciate it, too."

Woods nodded, appearing to teeter on the brink of adding a final word, before leaving Gunner to go back to work.

7

DEL'S HOME SMELLED LIKE DEATH.
Gunner knew it was a false perception—his cousin
and Noelle Curry had died the day before at their daughter's place eight miles away, not here—but he felt it, nonetheless. The little two-bedroom bungalow on Halldale
Avenue between 94th Place and 95th Street was cold and
dark, and brimming with all the unsettling silence of a
closed casket.

As he had at Del's office, he let himself in with his own
key, the first time in memory he'd had any use for it. He
was only able to take five steps into the living room before he had to stop, unable to shake the notion that he was
trespassing on the living and not the dead. Everywhere he
looked, he saw Del: stretched out on his recliner, legs up,
reading glasses on his nose; standing at the open refrigerator in the kitchen; laughing at one of his own stupid
jokes as he salted a plate of greens at the dining table.

"Shit," Gunner said out loud.

He forced himself to move forward, slow and me-
thodical, head turning this way and that as he sought
out anything worth close examination. If this had been
the home of a man contemplating not only suicide but
the murder of his wife and only daughter, some sign of it
would have to be evident. Marital discord, financial hard-
ship, mental instability—something would leave a mark.
But in what form? Experience told him the answer was
disarray, evidence of a life slowly—or rapidly—going to
seed. A mountain of dirty dishes left neglected in a sink;
unwashed clothes scattered hither and yon; the broken or

bloody residue of some violent quarrel.

Gunner saw none of those things here.

What he saw instead was what he'd always seen at Del's: all the trappings of a good, simple man leading an ordinary life. Inexpensive department store furniture; flea market African art prints on the walls; the requisite large-screen flat-panel television dominating the living room. The mantle over the fireplace was crawling with framed photographs of various family members in assorted combinations: Del and Noelle together, Zina with them both or individually, Zina alone, Del's parents and in-laws. Even Gunner himself was represented in one photo, a memento of a wine-tasting trip to the Napa Valley he and Del had embarked on three years ago that had left them in stitches from first mile to last.

He took the framed photo in his hands, gave it a lingering look before quickly setting it down again.

He moved on to the kitchen, Noelle's domain, where he had found her more often than not, stirring a pot on the stove or dicing something up at the counter near the sink. Like his memory of her, the room was clean and bright, flawlessly organized and devoid of all ostentation. The appliances were either white or stainless steel, minor-brand-name stuff that worked forever but offended interior decorators. The sink was barren and only a pair of dirty dishes, and one drinking glass, occupied the dishwasher.

Gunner went to the refrigerator, glanced over the three brightly colored notes pinned to the door with little ladybug magnets. All appeared to have been written in the same hand by someone other than Del, based on the numerous examples of his cousin's illegible scrawl he'd seen in Del's office the afternoon before. One of the notes was a short grocery list, one a reminder to record a television show Gunner actively avoided watching, and the third was just a phone number in the 818 area code and a name: Lucy.

He slipped this last off the door and put it in his pocket.

He spent a few moments sifting listlessly through the folded dish towels, clipped coupons, and takeout menus that littered a couple cabinet drawers, then went back to the remaining three rooms at the rear of the house.

He started with Del and Noelle's bedroom, where the curtains were drawn wide, the bed freshly made. Two pairs of slippers, his and hers, sat on the floor on opposite sides of the bed. Del's slippers, larger than the other pair, were set at a cockeyed angle to each other, while Noelle's were in perfect alignment. That Del's were in here and not in Zina's old bedroom, or out in the living room near his recliner or the couch, seemed to further indicate that things couldn't have been too bad between him and his wife; they were both still sleeping in the same bed.

Gunner inspected Del's bedside table. On top were an old-school radio-alarm clock, a reading lamp, and the remote control to the small television sitting on a stand across from the bed. In the table's only drawer, Gunner found two men's magazines, a lined notepad, several writing instruments, and a bottle of nonprescription sleeping pills. The bottle was half-full and the notepad was blank except for the first page. There, Del had been crunching numbers of some kind, adding and subtracting dollar figures, in the hundreds and thousands, without indicating what they represented. He'd circled with great emphasis a total at the bottom: $48,208.

Like the Post-it note he'd pulled off the refrigerator, Gunner tore the page off the notepad, folded it neatly four ways, and stuck it in his pocket.

A reading lamp identical to Del's sat atop Noelle's bedside table, along with a romance novel, a pair of reading glasses inside a leatherette pouch, a wireless telephone and base, and a small, silver-chained rosary sprinkled with shiny black beads. Noelle and Del had both been Catholic, so the rosary wasn't exactly out of place, but Gunner couldn't recall ever seeing his cousin or his wife use one.

He opened the nightstand's drawer and did a quick inventory, hoping to find something that could lead him to Noelle's father and brother, her last living, local relatives as far as Gunner knew. But the drawer was home to nothing more revealing than one open bag of chocolate candies, a box of Kleenex tissues, a few bottles of nail polish and remover, one emery board, and two more paperback romance novels, bringing her bedside library to three volumes in all. An author named Serena Powers had apparently been Noelle's favorite.

Gunner looked through the closet Del had shared with his wife and came across nothing out of the ordinary: shoes on the floor and in boxes on a shelf, clothes for every occasion short of a black-tie dinner. Everything was perfectly appropriate for a middle-class couple on a budget.

The same could be said for the contents of the pair's joint dresser. Gunner sifted through every drawer and met with not a single surprise. Clothes and underwear, socks and stockings, a box of jewelry for her, one for tie pins and cuff links for him. Every item could have been paid for with a pauper's credit card.

He went to Zina's old bedroom next.

The girl had moved out of the house three years ago, by Gunner's estimation, but it could have been ten from the looks of the room in which she used to sleep. From the paint on the walls to the pillows on the bed, no obvious trace of Del's daughter was evident. This was a guest room/home office now, plain and simple, moderately inviting but totally gender neutral; and if anything in it dated back to the days when Zina lived here, Gunner was at a loss to recognize it.

It all had the look of a cleansing, as if Zina were a bad memory her parents had gone to great lengths to erase. And yet, she was far from forgotten these days, to hear

Viola Gates tell it. Zina had been fighting with her mother constantly, Gates said. But over what? Knuckleheaded boyfriends, some weed once discovered in the pocket of a backpack, school grades that rose and fell like the Dow Jones—all of Zina's sins that Del had ever mentioned while she was still at home were of the standard variety, things that every child or young woman her age who wasn't living in a cave went through as a rite of passage. What could she have been doing now, years after leaving home for college at Cal State Northridge, that would lead her and Noelle to such a state of discord?

Nothing here presented an answer.

Only the desk in the corner of the room, in fact, promised anything of interest. Gunner left it for last and made quick work of everything else, a closet stacked with boxes of what resembled garage sale junk, and three pieces of matching furniture: a pair of nightstands and a dresser. The drawer in every piece was filled with things only a pack rat would consider valuable: clothes catalogs and old greeting cards, used wrapping paper and ribbon.

The desk was a different story.

A glance was all it took to see that this was where the Curry household bills were paid. The checkbook for Del and Noelle's joint account was sitting right on top, along with a wooden inbox that held a few loose invoices and some unopened mail. Gunner flipped through the checkbook register, and the tale it had to tell was immediately apparent—and all too painfully familiar. Over the last eight months, Del and Noelle had had more money going out than coming in, and by a wider margin every week. Much of the outgoing had gone to Zina.

As of the ledger's last entry, which was four days old, Del and Noelle were in the hole to the tune of $8,000 and change.

It didn't sound like an insurmountable figure, except that the trend line the couple's finances seemed to be following would have offered them little hope of having such a sum in hand any time soon. Del's bimonthly deposits to the account had simply been getting smaller and smaller as their debt load remained static, bringing them to a point at which only a major reversal in fortune would have put them back in the black before the roof fell in.

Of course, Del and, to an even greater extent, Noelle, were the kind of people who believed in major reversals of fortune. They were optimists by nature and good, if imperfect, Christians by choice, and both liked to talk about miracles wrought by God as if there were no debate to be had about their existence. While some men would have panicked, Del might have viewed his mounting financial troubles as a mere test of faith that would eventually be resolved by divine intervention.

But that was assuming his troubles were only as vast as the state of his and Noelle's personal checking account would suggest, and Gunner already knew that wasn't the case. Viola Gates had told him the day before that Del's business was also in the red. By how much, she hadn't been able to say, but the picture she had painted was certainly no cause for optimism. Beneath the weight of mounting debt on both personal and professional fronts, Del's usual imperviousness to alarm could have failed him. The only question was, to what extent? Enough to leave him thinking death was his only way out, for not just himself but his entire family?

If Gunner still couldn't believe it, he was beginning to accept the remote possibility.

He went down the hall to the home's only bathroom and poked through the medicine cabinet above the sink and the storage cabinet below it. The medicine cabinet was stocked primarily with deodorant, toothpaste and brushes, mouthwash, hand razors, and shaving cream; the other held rolls of toilet paper, tissue boxes, cleaning supplies, and a plunger. The two drawers in the same cabinet revealed some unused bar soap, a first aid kit, and assorted feminine hygiene products. Gunner had yet to come across any medications in the entire house that weren't of the over-the-counter variety.

He returned to the kitchen with the specific goal of searching for prescription drugs. People over the age of thirty usually had a bottle or two of something prescribed by their doctor in their home, and Del and Noelle should have been no exception, especially if one or both of them had been dealing with a serious medical condition Gunner knew nothing about. Cancer, for example, would have compounded Del's financial woes exponentially and served to further justify the crime it appeared to everyone but his cousin that he had committed.

When Gunner found what he was looking for, however—four plastic bottles hiding in plain sight on a crowded patch of countertop beside the stove—it proved to be evidence of nothing quite so ominous as cancer. Three of the bottles bore Noelle's name and were for medications Gunner recognized as common treatments for high blood pressure; the other, written for Del, was for something called pantoprazole. This last was a little white, forty-milligram pill that, according to the label, Del was supposed to have been taking twice a day.

Gunner called the pharmacy that had filled the prescription and, after several minutes on hold, told the pharmacist who answered, "My damn wife's moved all my prescriptions and I can't find the one I'm supposed to take for my headaches. Is it the pantoprazole?"

"Pantoprazole? No sir. That would be prescribed for an ulcer or gastric reflux. If you'd give me your name—"

"Oh, wait, here it is. I found it. Thank you very much for your help."

He hung up.

It seemed to make sense. Among the nonprescription drugs he'd seen in the bathroom medicine cabinet had been various antacids in liquid and lozenge-like forms. So Del had likely been suffering from an ulcer or some other gastrointestinal or esophageal ailment. Yet another indicator he'd been under significant stress prior to his death.

While he still had his phone in hand, Gunner pulled the Post-it note he'd taken off Noelle's refrigerator from his pocket and dialed the number on it for Lucy. He got a voicemail message. A man's voicemail message:

"Hello, you've reached the offices of Lester Irving, family and marital counseling. I'm not available to take your call right now...."

Gunner hung up without leaving a message. Whether Del was concerned about their marriage or not, it was now apparent that his wife was.

Gunner had been in Del's house now for almost an hour, and his tolerance for its uncharacteristic silence was at an end. He had seen enough for the moment and wanted out, before his cousin's memory could bring him once more to the edge of tears. He was almost out the door when one last backward glance to check for something amiss alerted him to the fact he'd left a kitchen drawer ajar. It really shouldn't have mattered; there was no one around to care anymore. But such imprecision in Noelle's kitchen was as incongruous as a bloodstain on a wedding dress, and Gunner couldn't let it go.

He walked back to the drawer and tried to close it, only to find it wouldn't give. Something inside was holding it fast. He pulled the drawer all the way open and removed the stack of cloth napkins he'd halfheartedly flipped through earlier, thinking they needed to be refolded...

...and caught a glimpse of silver gunmetal.

The weapon had been pushed to the very back of the drawer where the napkins and a pair of pot holders could form a shroud around it. It was an old .380 Colt Mustang, so small and lightweight it almost felt like a toy in Gunner's hands. Its grips were worn smooth and its slide was heavily scarred, signs of a lifetime on the streets. There was a round in the chamber and six more in the clip.

Gunner studied the little gun as his mind began to whir, putting the pieces together. This wasn't likely to be Del's weapon because he already had one, the legally registered 9mm Glock he—or someone—had used to do all the shooting at Zina's home the day before. Since then, it had been all Gunner could do to wrap his head around the idea of his cousin owning one firearm, let alone two. And Del wouldn't have hidden another gun, unlocked and fully loaded, in the kitchen where Noelle could accidentally stumble upon it, in any case. He hadn't been that stupid.

The Colt must have been Noelle's.

It was the kind of gun a woman who hated guns would want, something light and compact she could fit in her purse or in the glove compartment of her car. It wasn't what Del would have given his wife for self-protection, however. Rather than a store-bought piece like Del's own, this was a Saturday Night Special, a chipped and scratched timeworn relic that had no doubt passed through many hands before reaching Noelle's. Del would have been loath to entrust his wife's safety to a firearm so inclined toward failure.

That left only one conclusion for Gunner to draw: Noelle had secured the gun herself, for herself.

He didn't know why, but he thought he might be able to guess how.

8

IF HARPER STOWE III HAD NO ALIBI for the murder of Darlene Evans, her husband Samuel Evans had the best. Multiple people had placed him 270 miles away at the time of his wife's murder, taking a persistent losing streak at the poker tables from one off-Strip Las Vegas casino to another, and any doubt his presence there was imaginary could be quickly dispelled by the mountain of receipts—airline, hotel, dining, etc.—he'd brought home with him.

Still, as the dead woman's spouse, Evans automatically qualified as a likely suspect in his wife's killing, his lack of opportunity notwithstanding. All he needed was a motive.

The police had obvious reasons to wonder if he had one, but Gunner's reasons were even more glaring. Establishing a motive for Evans to have conspired with someone else to kill his wife would go a long way toward undermining the prosecution's case against Harper Stowe III. It came as no surprise to the investigator, then, that Evans had so far flatly declined to talk to him, either by phone or in person. Gunner had hoped to catch him at Empire Auto Parts this morning, keeping the promise he'd made to Kelly DeCharme last night that he'd put an end to all of Evans's evasions, but it hadn't happened. So he was left to run him to ground, as he had Tyrecee Abbott the day before.

It was just after 2 p.m. when Gunner parked Lilly Tennell's SUV in front of Evans's two-story mid-century modern house in Northridge. This wasn't usually the best time to try catching someone at home during the week, but it was Gunner's information that Darlene Evans's widower was only a part-time cashier at a local Trader Joe's market, and the sudden inheritance of a thriving small business might have soured him on the idea of going in to work today, or any day ever again.

What sounded like an angry dog of little stature barked behind a side gate to the backyard when Gunner rang the bell. He took note of the weeds choking the grass out front and the telltale tilt of a broken garage door as he rang the bell again and waited for someone to acknowledge it. There were three yellowed newspapers taking up space on the porch, old deliveries gone ignored judging from the week-old date on one of them, and the porch light above Gunner's head was on for no discernible reason.

He had his finger on the doorbell, about to ring it a third time, when somebody on the other side of the door said, "Yeah? Who is it?" in a man's voice as full of sleep as it was hostility.

Gunner leaned in close. "My name's Aaron Gunner, Mr. Evans. I'm a private investigator looking into your wife's murder on behalf of the attorney for Harper Stowe." Silence. "I've left you several phone messages but you haven't returned them."

"Yeah, that's right. I haven't returned 'em because I don't have anything to say to you. Get the hell off my porch!"

"I understand your reluctance to speak with me, sir, but I only have a few questions that'll take you no more than ten, fifteen minutes to answer. At the most."

"I said get the hell off my porch or I'll call the police!"

Gunner stood his ground. He'd fought through the dense iron thicket that was the 405 freeway post–lunch hour to get here, and hell if he was going to leave without at least getting a look at Samuel Evans's face.

"I tell you what," he said. "I'll call them for you." He took out his cell phone so that Evans, on the chance he was watching through the door's peephole, could see that he was serious. "What should I tell them? That I'm trespassing? Harassing you? You're going to have to explain things when they get here, not me, so you may as well choose your story now."

The man on the other side of the door fell silent, no doubt weighing the relative inconvenience of talking to Gunner against that of talking to two inquisitive patrolmen from the LAPD, their squad car in his driveway instantly making him the center of his neighbors' attention. "Shit," he said with vibrant disgust, loud enough for Gunner to hear, before throwing the deadbolt on the door and yanking it open.

Samuel Evans was thus revealed to be a middle-aged white man with a double chin and a head sprouting unruly brown hair along the sides. He was fully dressed, but his feet were bare and his clothes looked slept in. His blue slacks were wrinkled, and the white dress shirt he wore was unbuttoned to the crest of his ample gut. There were food stains on the shirt's breast pocket.

"You're working for that asshole's lawyer. Trying to get him off. Why the hell should I talk to you?"

"Maybe because the asshole, as you call him, is innocent, and you might know something that could lead me and the police to your wife's actual killer," Gunner said.

"Bullshit. That's bullshit and you know it."

"Well, how about this: You should talk to me to relieve me of the notion you're afraid to talk to me. Because you're not afraid to talk to me, are you?"

Evans glared at him, wavering between spitting in his eye and slamming the door in his face. "Ten minutes, you said. Starting now."

Gunner glanced about, as if he gave a damn who might be watching. "Would it be possible to talk inside?"

He was pressing his luck but Evans let it pass. He allowed Gunner in and led him into the living room, a cool, dark cavern dominated by a giant flat-screen TV and a sectional set that screamed outlet store. Gunner had thought he'd see dishes and beer bottles everywhere, dirty clothes in piles, and drink glasses encrusted with dried milk; but much to his surprise, nothing in Evans's home matched the man's own physical level of disarray.

"I'm gonna tell you right now you're wasting your time," Evans said, taking a seat on the sofa without offering his guest a seat of his own.

"That's all right. Wasting time's part of the job description." Gunner lowered himself onto the leather recliner nearby.

"So ask your questions. Or better yet, let me just answer 'em for you, since I already know what they are."

"You do?"

"Of course. They're the same damn questions the police have asked me a dozen times already. You want to know where I was when Darlene got killed, and if the two of us were getting along before she died. That kind of crap."

"And what have you been telling the police?"

"I've been telling them the truth. That as a matter of fact, Darlene and I had been talking about divorce lately, and the morning she was shot, I was in Vegas."

"Proving you couldn't have possibly killed her. Personally, anyway."

Evans's eyes flared. "I didn't do it, period," he said.

"Which leads me to my next question. Maybe you can guess what that one is, too."

"Who else could have killed Darlene?"

"That's it."

"Nobody. Other than that dope fiend animal you work for, that is."

"You're telling me you and he are the only ones she didn't get along with."

"I loved Darlene. We got along fine. Stop twisting my words."

"Then there were others besides Harper Stowe who

might have wanted to hurt her."

"She was a businesswoman. She didn't take any shit from her customers or her employees. Of course she got on the wrong side of people from time to time."

"People like who?"

"You want names?"

"Humor me."

Evans glared at him. "Bill Duffy. A salesman for one of her suppliers. Until she got him canned, anyway."

"For what reason?"

"For having more interest in her parts than the ones he was supposed to be selling. Asshole couldn't keep his hands to himself."

"He was harassing her?"

"That's the legal term for it."

Gunner began taking notes. "What was the name of the supplier?"

"I don't remember."

"How about the line?"

Evans treated the question like a razor blade he was being forced to swallow. "Transmissions."

"And they fired him when Darlene complained about how he was treating her?"

"Yes."

"And that made him angry enough to want to kill her."

"Why not? It made him angry enough to show up at the store shortly afterwards and break all the windows in her damn car."

"Okay. Bill Duffy. Who else?"

"Who else what?"

"Who else had Darlene gotten on the wrong side of before she was killed?"

"Our psycho neighbor across the street. Julian Fischer. One of his fucking dogs went after me in our driveway last year, and Darlene reported it to Animal Control. He lost his mind. She made some enemies at church. A couple ladies who didn't care for the way she ran the white elephant sale at the carnival. You want their names too?"

Gunner gave it up. "Did your wife keep a gun in her office, Mr. Evans?"

"A gun? Not that I'm aware of. But if she had, what of it? Her store's damn near on skid row. She had crazies walking in on her there all the time. What was she supposed to scare them off with, a broom?"

"So the gun she was shot with might have been her own."

"I never said that."

"But it's possible."

"I never said that, either."

Not in so many words, Gunner thought.

"Why were you and Darlene talking about divorce?"

Evans showed him a wry smile. "So. We finally get to it."

Gunner just stared back at him.

"Well, you're getting paid to investigate, aren't you? To 'detect'? Why don't you tell me?"

"If I had to guess? I'd say money was involved."

"Bravo. Nicely done."

"So—"

"No elaboration should be necessary. The facts speak for themselves. Dar ran a successful retail store, while her husband bags groceries dressed in a Hawaiian clown suit every day." His eyes were suddenly rimmed in red, his voice quavering. He'd been angry since Gunner's first knock on the door, but now he was enraged.

"I haven't held a decent job in four years and Dar deserved better. I couldn't take her carrying me anymore, so yeah, we were talking about divorce." He stormed to his feet. "And now that you've got what you came here for, you can get the fuck out of my house."

"I wasn't quite done."

"But I'm afraid you are. Leave."

He couldn't have been less inclined to show Gunner out had his feet been nailed to the floor.

Out in Lilly's SUV, Gunner started the engine just to get some air flowing through the car and called Lester Irving again. This time he got a live body.

"Hello?"

He told Irving who he was and what he wanted.

"I'm sorry, but I don't know anyone by that name. Curry, was it?"

"Yes. Noelle Curry. She had your number on her refrigerator under an assumed name. Are you sure—"

"I'm quite sure. Maybe she intended to call but never did. Or called and didn't leave a message. That's quite common in my business, you know."

"Excuse me?"

"Admitting your marriage needs the help of a professional. It's one thing to have the number for one, and another to find the courage to use it."

Gunner conceded the point and let the man go.

Lilly Tennell had a problem with Little Pete Thorogood. Little Pete was the man you went to see in the Deuce's corner of the hood when you needed to buy a gun fast and on the cheap, with no questions asked, and Lilly didn't like him conducting his seedy business in her establishment. It didn't matter that he never really did—Pete only came in to the Deuce to drink and socialize, like everyone else. But just the sight of Pete set Lilly off. Illegal firearms were a chief contributor to the malaise of violence and fear she and her fellow residents of Central Los Angeles had been forced to endure for generations, so Pete's line of work alone was enough to earn him a sneer every time he chose to darken the barkeeper's door.

It was for this reason Gunner asked Pete to meet him in his office at Mickey's for a change. Lilly's grousing every time the two men hooked up at the Deuce never seemed to bother Pete very much, but Gunner was tired of hearing it. The little man's chosen profession ran just as counter to Gunner's sensibilities as it did Lilly's, but Gunner accepted it as a facet of inner-city commerce that wasn't going to change in his lifetime, and he had come to know Little Pete Thorogood as a man far less callous and without scruples than his profession might have suggested.

Gunner was sitting in the front of the shop waiting for him when Little Pete arrived. He'd been sitting there idly listening to Mickey, occupying the throne of his own barber chair, debate the superiority of Sam Cooke's singing voice to that of D'Angelo with one of his newest and youngest regular customers, an overweight college kid with an overbearing vocabulary Gunner knew only as Robbie. Little Pete entered the shop just as Mickey was telling the boy for the umpteenth time that D'Angelo was perfectly fine as crooners of his generation went, but Sam Cooke was a vocalist for the ages, a man who could turn a song into honey pouring from a pot. "I'll tell you what the difference 'tween the two is right now," Mickey said. "You want a woman to kiss you goodnight at the door, you play her some D'Angelo. You want her to let you in the damn door, you play her some Sam Cooke!"

That got a big laugh out of the barber and Robbie both, and even a small grin from Pete Thorogood, who'd caught the joke completely out of context. But Gunner was unmoved. It seemed no distraction was great enough to shift his thoughts away from Del for long.

He stood up from his chair. Mickey watched him and Pete pound fists and said, "Oh, no. Ain't nothin' I can do with that head!"

Unlike Lilly Tennell, Mickey had no qualms about welcoming the illegal arms dealer into his place of business. He had discovered many years ago that the barber who tried to be selective about whose head he would and would not cut was soon to starve, and where would one begin to draw the line, in any case? Pimps, shysters, drug dealers, and crooked preachers—brothers of every criminal stripe walked through Mickey's door. Who was he to say, Mickey wondered, that one was less deserving of a simple haircut than another?

"I ain't here to see you, you damn butcher," Little Pete told him. "I'm here to see G."

"Butcher? Who you callin' a butcher?"

"You, that's who. Last time I had you cut my head, I walked out of here looking like an old toothbrush."

Robbie threw his head back and laughed again. Mickey opened his mouth to defend himself, but Gunner chopped a hand in the air to silence him. "Save it, old man," he said. "Pete and I have business to discuss."

He rushed Little Pete out of the room and into the back before his landlord could stop them.

They sat on opposite sides of Gunner's desk, drinking from two glasses Gunner filled from a fifth of Wild Turkey he always kept on hand. They were silent for a long stretch.

"Really sorry to hear about Del, G," Little Pete finally said.

Only now did Gunner study him with anything approaching a professional eye. Pete looked the same as always—short and slight, with high-yellow skin and the facial hair of an adolescent—but the cool, quiet composure he was known for was noticeably absent. There was something on the man's mind today that had him resembling someone who, unlike himself ordinarily, was susceptible to the vagaries of emotion.

"Thanks, Pete," Gunner said.

"Any idea yet what set him off? You don't mind my asking?"

"I'm not convinced he did go off."

Pete raised an eyebrow. "Say what?"

"Let's just say I'm exploring all possibilities, including that someone other than Del was the shooter."

The idea seemed to shake Thorogood a little. "You mean like his wife or his daughter?"

Gunner answered the question with a simple gesture—removing the gun he'd found in Noelle Curry's kitchen from a drawer and laying it on its side atop his desk—and Little Pete all but fell from his chair onto his knees.

"Aw, Jesus," he said, staring at the little Colt like the body of a lifeless child. "That's not the one she used, is it?"

Gunner shook his head. "No."

Little Pete didn't say anything, but his relief was palpable.

"You sold this to Noelle."

"Me? No. But I almost did."

That wasn't the answer Gunner had been expecting. "Say again?"

"She came to me lookin' for a piece. 'Bout three weeks ago. But I told her no. I've never seen that gun before."

"So where did she get it?"

"I've got no idea. I told her if she needed a piece, she should ask Del to get one for her."

"He knew about this?"

"I don't know if he did or not. But I didn't tell him. She made me promise not to."

"Tell me what happened, Pete. Everything."

Thorogood's gaze moved to the Colt again. He took a deep breath and held it. "Cecil found me in the park one day. Said Del's wife wanted to talk to me."

The park was Enterprise Park in Rosewood, where Pete liked to conduct the majority of his daylight business; Gunner only knew one Cecil.

"Cecil? You mean Mr. Cecil?"

Mr. Cecil was a fixture at the Acey Deuce, an old homeless man Lilly had been paying to clean the bar's bathrooms and sweep its floors for as long as Gunner could remember.

"Yeah."

"Why would Noelle use him to find you?"

"I don't know. Maybe 'cause she thought he was the only one she could trust to keep quiet about it."

It made sense. What little Del might have mentioned to his wife about Little Pete and his services over the years was unlikely to have included how to reach him or where he could be found. Seeking this info from some mutual friend of her husband, the illegal arms merchant would have been Noelle's most logical recourse. But whom could she ask that wasn't almost certain to pepper her with questions or run straight to Del? Certainly not Lilly Tennell or Mickey Moore, and certainly not Del's first cousin Aaron Gunner. But kindly old Mr. Cecil, the Deuce's unofficial caretaker who knew every man or woman who'd ever stepped through the bar's doors—he might be willing to get word to Pete that Noelle had a need to speak with him, and do so with the promise to keep her interest in Thorogood a secret.

"Go on," Gunner said.

"I called her at the number Cecil gave me. Thinking this had to be a personal matter, 'cause I couldn't imagine she wanted to discuss business with me. Right? What would Del's wife want with a gun? But that was exactly what the girlfriend wanted. She said she needed something cheap and easy to use to carry around for protection. Man, I couldn't believe it."

"Protection from what?"

"She never really said. She just said she didn't feel safe anymore and wanted something that could help her feel safe again."

"So why didn't she ask Del to get her something she could register legally?"

"That was my first question. 'Why don't you ask Del to get you something on the real?' And my second question was, 'Why isn't Del talking to me about this instead of you?'"

"And?"

"She said he'd only tell her no. That he'd worry about her getting hurt, carrying a piece around. So this was something she had to do on her own, without his knowledge. She made me swear not to tell him anything about it."

"And you didn't."

The implied accusation wasn't missed on Thorogood. The downcast look he'd taken on when Gunner first set Noelle's handgun on the desktop between them returned to his face. "No. I never did. But I didn't sell her a piece, either. I told her if she was gonna get one on the street, she was gonna have to get it from somebody else, not me."

"Why? What made you say no?"

Pete shook his head. "It just didn't feel right. Somethin' was off about it, so...."

"You thought she wanted the gun to use on Del."

"No! It wasn't like that, exactly. But—hell, man, the thought had to enter my mind, right? Woman comes to me shopping for a piece and doesn't want me to say a word about it to her husband? What would you think?"

"I would've thought Del needed to know. Motherfuck what I promised his wife."

Gunner had checked himself as long as he could. If he was telling the truth, Little Pete hadn't put Noelle's gun in her hands nor Del's in his, but he carried some blame for their deaths just the same. At this moment, for the first time since they'd known each other, all Gunner could see in Thorogood was a petty criminal who pushed illegal firearms to their friends and neighbors for fun and profit.

"Come on, Gunner," Pete said. "I wanted to tell him. I was gonna tell him. Hell, man, I was gonna tell you. But when nothing happened the next day, or the day after that, or the next week...." He shrugged. "I just figured she'd done what I told her and forgot the whole thing."

"So you did the same."

"Yeah."

Gunner fell silent, so deep in thought that Little Pete

was left to wonder if his host still recognized his presence in the room.

"G?"

"You sure that was all she said? About why she needed a gun?"

Thorogood took a long time to think about it. "Yeah. 'I don't feel safe anymore,' she said. 'And I want to feel safe again.'" He paused, drawing the memory into focus. "Thing is, though—and thinking back on it now, I realize this is what put me off—she didn't sound afraid. She sounded...."

He couldn't put his finger on it.

"What, Pete?"

"It's kind'a hard to describe, man. But I guess the best word for it would be 'calm.' She sounded calm, like she'd made up her mind about something and was set on doing it."

Gunner wanted the man out of his office, now, before he could give his old friend something more to depart with than a well-deserved guilty conscience.

"Thanks for coming in, Pete," he said. "I appreciate the help and the kind words about Del."

Thorogood got up from his chair. "Sure, brother, sure. No problem." His eyes went to Noelle's little handgun again. "Sorry ass little Colt Mustang. The kind'a pocket piece I don't even try to sell anymore. Brothers take one look at a gun like that and just laugh." He met Gunner's gaze again. "But not the police. Policemen can't get enough of the little fuckers."

"The police?"

"To plant on a nigga when he's dead and inconveniently unarmed. Ain't no need to waste a real weapon under circumstances like that, right?"

Gunner mulled it over.

"Lady didn't have to get that one from a cop, but in my professional opinion—"

"I'll check it out, Pete. Thanks."

It took him a moment, but eventually Little Pete figured out he'd just been told goodbye.

9

"I WAS JUST CALLING TO THANK YOU," Jeff Luckman said. "And to make a small request."

"Thank me for what?"

"For giving my number to your friend Curry's father, Daniel. My message inbox might never be empty again; the man's called me four times just since lunch."

"You've got my condolences, detective," Gunner said, adjusting the wireless headset in his ear as he drove. "But Del was his only son, and his daughter is his only grand-child. Not knowing what happened yesterday is mak-ing him and his wife a little anxious, as I'm sure you can understand."

"He already knows what happened, same as you do, Mister Gunner. It's a difficult thing to accept, I know, but it is what it is."

"In other words, nothing's changed since yesterday. You still think Del shot the two women and then killed himself."

"It's not simply what I think, it's what the evidence supports. Three people in the house, all shot with the same gun. Mister Curry's gun. There was an argument, a struggle for the weapon ensued, and the women were shot before Mister Curry took his own life. We've done the math, Gunner, trust me."

"There was a struggle for the gun?"

"All three people had traces of GSR on their hands and clothing, Mister Curry most of all by a wide margin, and both his prints and his daughter's were on the mur-der weapon. How else would you interpret that?"

Stuck for an immediate answer, Gunner said, "You're sure there couldn't have been someone else in the house? Someone who could have done the shooting and then fled before the uniforms arrived?"

"Someone like who?"

"Noelle's brother. The one with the drug habit I told you about. Have you located him yet?"

"Lavar Long. Yeah, we've located him. He's out at LAC, serving a ten-year stretch for assault on a police officer. And before you ask about the father, he passed away two years ago."

"So that rules them out as the fourth party. But—"

"Like I told you yesterday, Gunner, none of the neighbors we've talked to have reported seeing such a person. And even if they had, a fourth party in the house might explain the injuries to the two females, but not those of Mister Curry, as his were most definitely self-inflicted. It says so right here in the coroner's preliminary report." Before Gunner could respond, Luckman added, "One might also wonder why, if someone else were in fact responsible for shooting his wife and daughter, Curry would call you instead of 911 before killing himself. Wouldn't one?"

Gunner had wondered about that but saw no point in admitting it.

"I know you'd like to think we're just mailing this one in," Luckman said, "but the truth of the matter is, we aren't. We won't really know for sure what happened in that house until the daughter regains consciousness and starts talking, but until then, we're going to do what we always do and base our conclusions on the evidence at hand. You have yourself a great day."

"Hold on a minute. You said something about a small request?"

"Oh, yeah. Tell your uncle to give it a rest. As soon as we have something new to report, we'll report it."

And with that, Luckman hung up.

Gunner arrived at Empire Auto Parts shortly after 4 p.m. This time he'd called ahead to see if Johnny Rivera—the store's manager and the man who had discovered Darlene Evans's body following her murder—was in, and Rivera himself had answered the phone. He hadn't sounded happy to take the call, but he'd agreed to talk to Gunner just the same.

Eric Woods was conspicuously missing among the other employees in the store when Rivera walked Gunner to the back office for their meeting. Gunner sized him up on the way, seeing a short, dark-skinned Latino in his mid-forties who filled out his uniform shirt with thick, tattooed arms and a broad chest, all more likely built on a prison yard than a padded gym floor. His slow, deliberate gait was that of a seasoned O.G. who never followed anyone anywhere. He either led the way or didn't go at all.

No surprises awaited Gunner in the late Darlene Evans's office. It was exactly the kind of cramped, lifeless place he would have expected, overstuffed while barely furnished at the same time. A metal desk, file cabinet, and two chairs fought amongst themselves for some share of the limited real estate. It was like Del's office only worse, the same magnitude of disarray jammed into two-thirds the space.

"Take a seat," Rivera said, plopping himself down in one of the chairs. He couldn't have appeared more at ease about Gunner's visit had he been asleep.

Taking the other chair, Gunner said, "So this is where you found Darlene's body."

"That's right. Room's all cleaned up now, so you'd never know. But she was sitting right here in this chair, slumped over the desk. Dead."

"And you think Harper killed her?"

"Me personally? No. But what do I know?"

"The district attorney says Harper's emotionally imbalanced. That he murdered Darlene in a fit of rage for firing him the day before."

"Maybe he did. The kid's got problems, that much is obvious. But until that day, he and Dar got along great. Harp got along with everybody here. So he said he wanted to kill her. You know how many times I've threatened to kill somebody without actually doing it?" He chuckled at the thought. "You should've seen me in here yesterday."

"So if Harper didn't kill Darlene, who did?"

"Man, it could've been anybody. We get a robbery attempt in here every three weeks. All those lowlifes you saw hanging out in the parking lot when you came in? Most of 'em don't go home at night; they're right there when we open up in the morning. Any one of 'em could've jumped Dar at the door that day and forced her inside. After that...."

"Except that no money or stock from the store was reported missing. That would seem to rule out robbery as a motive, no?"

"I guess." Rivera shrugged.

"I understand the store's surveillance system wasn't working that morning."

"That's right."

"So no video was recorded inside or out."

"Nope."

"And that didn't strike you as a little coincidental? The system being down that day of all days?"

"The system's always down. Two, three times a month, rats chew holes in the wiring. You should see what it looks like in some places. Got more duct tape on it than insulation."

Gunner glanced around the room, decided it took next to no imagination to visualize it.

"And that's common knowledge to everyone here?"

"How do you mean?"

"I mean, if someone on staff had wanted to kill the system the night Darlene was murdered, they would have known that's all it takes? Just yank on the wiring some-where to cause a short?"

Rivera was sharp enough to make note of Gunner's choice of words—"someone on staff"—and how he him-self fell under the umbrella of that description, but what-ever offense he took was well guarded. "I guess. We've all taken turns fixing the system at one time or another. Ain't no need to call an electrician to splice two wires together and wrap some tape around it, right?"

"Tell me about the new boss. Eric says he's been very hands-off so far."

"Sam? Oh." He nodded, catching on. "The cops asked about him, too. You wanna know if he and Dar got along."

"For one thing."

"As far as I know." He added another meaningless shrug.

"You see him around here much before she died?"

"Not much. He came around once, maybe twice a month, that's about all."

"And they were always cool with each other?"

"Cool? I don't know about 'cool.' How about 'civ-il.' They were always civil with each other when I was around."

"And when you weren't around?"

"I think she couldn't stand him, and he felt about the same for her. But they were keeping it together, hell if I could tell you why."

"She never talked about their problems?"

"Not with me."

"So you wouldn't know if they were bad enough for him to want her dead."

"That's right. I wouldn't know."

"Would you know if Darlene kept a gun here in the office?"

"A gun?" Rivera hadn't been expecting that question.

"You said she was warding off would-be muggers out in the parking lot every morning at opening. Surely she kept a gun on hand somewhere for self-defense?"

"None that I ever saw."

"You're the store manager. Wouldn't you know if she did?"

"Not necessarily. I work here, I don't live here."

"So if she kept a weapon in a drawer in that desk there—"

"Her office. Her desk. I only come in here to use the phone and do paperwork."

"And make repairs to the security system wiring."

"Right."

Gunner wasn't sold, but he wasn't going to call the man a liar on just his personal opinion.

"Does that go for all your employees, too?"

"What?"

"That they only come in here to use the phone and do paperwork."

"They're not really supposed to come in here at all. This was Dar's office, like I keep saying. But the door's always open, she never locked it, so...." He pulled off one more shrug.

"What can you tell me about"—Gunner consulted his notebook—"Bill Duffy? He's a salesman Darlene's husband says she once accused of sexual harassment."

"Duff? He's an asshole. And no, I never saw him put his hands on Dar, but I'm sure he did. Guys like that just can't control themselves, their dick points the way wherever they go."

"Samuel Evans says he vandalized Darlene's car out there in the parking lot after she got him fired."

"Sure did. Took out all her windows. But I wasn't here at the time. This happened on a Monday, my day off, and I don't think that was an accident. Fucker knew I would've kicked his teeth in, he'd have tried that shit while I was around." He added: "Excuse my French."

"You think he could have killed Darlene?"

"Duff? I can't see him having the guts to kill anybody.

But who knows? Man's in his mid-fifties and out of work.
That was probably the last job he'll ever get. It's for sure
he wasn't ready to forgive and forget, after she had him
arrested and filed suit to have him put all new glass in
her ride."

A young, plump Latina in an Empire Auto polo shirt
stuck her head into the room through the partially closed
door. "Excuse me, Johnny?"

Rivera turned.

"Louis needs help up front. Register one's not taking
his ID number again. I tried it, too, we don't know what's
going on."

"I'd better let you go," Gunner said, standing. He shook
Rivera's hand and gave him a business card. "Thanks for
all your help."

"No problem. Tell Harper I said hang in there. Unless
I'm wrong, and he really did kill Darlene. In which case,
he can kiss my ass."

Gunner's guess hadn't been that far off.

Yesterday, watching the ghetto and news birds circle
high above it, he had placed the focus of their attention—a
car thief's apprehension after a citywide pursuit, as it
would turn out—in the general vicinity of 118th Street
and Compton Avenue. Zina's house was in fact only a
few blocks away, on a quiet stretch of Alabama Street
just south of 117th Place. Gunner found it at the address
Jeff Luckman had given him the day before, a tiny little
one-bedroom sitting back from a perimeter wall that, in
between sections of peeling black wrought iron, was as
smothered in green stucco as the house itself.

Kelly DeCharme was waiting for him there when he
parked Lilly Tennell's SUV at the curb. It was well after 6
p.m. and the day was finally starting to cool, a bright yellow sun sinking into the horizon and taking the light out
of the sky along with it. A few houses down, an old His-

panic woman in a stained white apron swept dirt off her driveway while two small children rode bicycles in circles in her yard. None of them paid any attention as Kelly left her sedan to take a seat beside the black man in the gargantuan ebony Tahoe parked behind it.

She gave the car's interior a look of amusement, said, "People really drive these things?"

"In the absence of a tank available with nineteen-inch rims and tinted glass."

"Tell me again why I'm here?"

"To brighten my world for five minutes and hear about my day."

"Break it to me gently, please."

He told her about finding the gun in his cousin's kitchen and his talk with Little Pete afterward. He described his interviews with Eric Woods, Samuel Evans, and Johnny Rivera, and what all three men had in common: none could provide Harper Stowe with an alibi for the time of Darlene Evans's death, or explain how he could have handled the gun that killed her if he hadn't done the shooting himself.

"Shit."

"On the bright side, Evans admitted that his marriage to Darlene was in crisis. So despite his lack of opportunity and his denials to the contrary, he could have had a motive for murder-for-hire. It's for sure he's better off, financially anyway, with her out of the way. Three weeks ago he was a grocery store box boy; today he's a successful small businessman. Murders have been committed for much less."

"And Rivera?"

"He's a hard one to figure. He talks like someone who believes Stowe to be innocent, but if we put him on the stand, I don't think he'd bet on it. And I'm not convinced he's never seen a gun in Evans's office before, the way he claims."

"You think he's lying about it?"

"It's possible. Though what his motive would be, besides the obvious, I couldn't say."

"What about this fat girl Woods is talking about?"

"I'm going to try to run her down tomorrow. She probably won't know anything useful, but you never know. And I'm curious."

"Curious?"

"To see what it is about her besides her weight that Woods finds so revolting. The way he talked about her, you'd think she had three heads and a tail."

He heard a squeal behind them, turned in his seat to see one of the children in the old woman's yard chasing a gray tabby, bike tossed to one side, laughing as if she'd already caught the animal by its tail.

"Why do you think Noelle bought the gun?" Kelly asked with care, shifting the conversation to Del and his wife.

"To protect herself. Just like she said."

"From Del?"

"We'll see."

"You don't—"

"No. I don't think he was capable of hurting her. But then, I never thought he was capable of committing suicide, either." Before she could pursue the matter any further, he said, "You still scheduled to see Stowe tomorrow?"

"Eleven thirty. Why?"

"I'd like to go with you. Think you can get me in on short notice?"

"I think so. What do you want to talk to Harper about?"

"We need to ask him again about the gun. He handled it at some point, and we've got no shot of getting him off if he can't remember where or when."

Conceding the point, Kelly nodded and said, "Okay."

"That's all I've got." He leaned over to kiss her. "Now, get the hell out of here before the cops catch you trespassing on a crime scene."

Kelly glanced at Zina Curry's little green house. "I guess that is what this is, isn't it? A crime scene."

It didn't really look like one. Nobody had bothered to screen it off with the customary yellow tape, or so Gunner thought until Kelly departed. Inside the gate, he found a strand of the tape skipping about the dry grass in the front yard, dancing on the wind that had torn it from whatever moorings the LAPD had used to carelessly secure it. He rolled the tape up, jammed it into a pocket, and climbed the porch steps to the front door, hoping to get inside the house before all daylight was gone.

But the door was locked.

He went around to the back, acting like somebody entitled to do so in case the little Hispanic woman with the broom, or any of Zina's other neighbors, were watching, and found a windowed door there, standing off a small cement porch. That door, too, was locked.

As he came back down the steps, weighing the pluses and minuses of checking the windows for possible points of entry, his left foot kicked something off the porch. He glanced down to see a fragment of a small clay flower pot, the remains of which—along with the blue geraniums it had once held—lay in chunks on the walk below. Gunner studied the tableau, considering the possibilities, and made the calculated guess that someone had recently kicked the pot off the porch and neglected to clean up the mess afterward. Someone, perhaps, who'd come out the back door in too big a hurry to notice or care that the pot was there.

Gunner turned his attention next to Zina Curry's backyard. It was just a weed-choked patch of earth alongside a tiny garage, sprinkled with red pavers that had been scattered there like birdseed. Behind the garage and the dead grass, a rusty chain-link fence separated Zina's property from the alley that bordered it. Walking in a straight line, following the direct path he imagined someone would take in making a mad dash for it, Gunner approached the fence, eyes scanning the earth as he went.

The fence was a little over six feet high, warped in places but unbroken. There was a padlocked gate in the middle of it that looked like it hadn't been opened in years. As a younger man, Gunner would have scaled the fence to get to the alley on the other side, the thought of tearing his clothes or his flesh on the chain links' jagged upper edges no deterrent; but today he was more than content to settle for his view from the yard. The alley he saw was nothing unusual: just a narrow band of broken concrete running north and south, littered with old automobile tires and overstuffed trash bags, upended garbage cans, and discarded kitchen appliances. A stray dog prowled for food at one end, and a black cat dozed on a mattress at the other. The backyards on the opposite side of the alley within Gunner's range of vision were little more than mirror images of the one he was standing in.

There was no sign of another living, cognizant human being anywhere.

Gunner took it all in, decided his chances of fleeing Zina's home without being noticed, out the back and down the alley, would be pretty damn good, even in broad daylight.

But he wasn't in broad daylight now. Far from it. Night was rapidly falling, making him look and feel more like a thief casing the property, begging to draw a 911 call, by the minute. He walked back out to the street. Unwilling to break into the house, he had no choice but to leave its interior unexplored, at least for now; his time here would be a total waste if he didn't find some other way to make it pay off.

He scanned the street, first left, then right, and spotted a familiar car parked on the opposite side: Del's 2002 Honda sedan. Silver Accords were as commonplace in Los Angeles as yoga mats, but this one stood out, its black-primered, driver's-side rear door marking it as the property of Gunner's cheapskate cousin, who'd had the door replaced after a small fender bender but never paid to have it painted. How it hadn't occurred to him before now to look for the car, Gunner didn't know, but he crossed the street toward it thankful it had come to his attention now.

Unlike Zina's house, he found the car unlocked. It was a state Del would have never left it in, Gunner knew, unless he were in too great a hurry upon leaving it to give a damn whether it would be here or not when he got back. The Lakers baseball cap and ancient deodorizer Gunner had grown accustomed to seeing inside Del's Honda—the first sitting on the shelf behind the rear window, the other dangling from the rearview mirror—immediately removed any doubt about the car's ownership.

Gunner looked for a set of keys but, predictably, didn't find any; rifling through the Honda's glove compartment, center console, and door pockets garnered him no greater reward than a case filled with CDs and several rolls of antacid tablets. Between the latter and all the similar medications Gunner had found in his home, it seemed Del had gone nowhere of late without having something he could take to settle a bad stomach.

Gunner popped the trunk and got out of the car to inspect it. Like the Honda's interior, there was nothing to see here he would not have expected to find: road flares, a small tool kit, a set of jumper cables. A spare tire was where it was supposed to be, under the trunk's floor panel, atop a jack.

He closed the trunk and surveyed the street again. Had Del and Noelle arrived here in the Honda together yesterday, or had Noelle driven herself separately? He saw what looked like Noelle's car three houses down—a cobalt blue, late-model Buick Encore. He trotted over and tried all four doors: locked. A woman's red leather purse sat on the passenger seat.

"Shit."

He should have pocketed the spare set of keys he

could now remember seeing hanging on a hook near the utility room door of the Currys' home earlier that day. That he hadn't was more proof yet that his usual attention to detail had suffered greatly in the wake of his cousin's death.

He was headed back to his Cobra, resigned to having little to show for his visit here, when he noticed the old woman in the dingy apron two houses down, still wielding the broom in her driveway like a scythe. He turned and started toward her.

"Excuse me?"

It was only when he spoke that she gave him any clue that his presence had ever been felt. She looked up from her sweeping to face him, her expression neutral, giving him nothing. Her eyes were shiny brown pellets sunk deep into wrinkled, sun-baked flesh. The small boy and girl who'd been riding their bicycles and chasing cats in the yard earlier were no longer around.

"I'm sorry to bother you," Gunner said, "but my cousin was killed in the house there yesterday and I wonder if you'd answer a few questions for me."

"Oh, no, no," the old woman said, shaking her head while waving him away. "I no speak English, sorry."

"No un poco?"

"No, no." She smiled, her head still wagging from side to side.

Before Gunner's disappointment could even sink in, somebody behind the old lady said, "Yo! Can I help you?"

A cholo in his early to mid-thirties had emerged from the house and was stepping off the porch to join them. He wore a short-sleeved, blue plaid shirt and a baggy pair of plaid shorts that fell damn near to his ankles. He had beach sandals on his stockinged feet, and his arms bore more ink than a morning newspaper.

"My mother don't speak no English, bro. What the fuck you hasslin' her for?"

He put himself squarely between Gunner and the old

woman, pausing only for a moment to tell her, *"Volver a la casa, mamá!"*

"I wasn't trying to hassle her," Gunner said. "I was just asking—"

"She's an old woman, she don't know nothin'. Why don't you go ask somebody else?"

It was liquor doing most of his talking—Gunner could tell that much from his breath alone—but he was angry more than he was drunk, and not because some *mayate* he didn't know was annoying his mother. His was an old outrage, something that had been with him for a long time, and all Gunner was was a convenient excuse to let it off its chain for a while, rather than drink another beer to try and suppress it.

"Sure thing. No problem," Gunner said.

"Goddamn right, no problem. Get the fuck outta here, asshole!"

The man's mother was tugging on his left arm, trying to guide him away from Gunner and into the house, pleading, *"Por favor, Gordito! Dejarlo solo, mijo!"* But Gordito wasn't moving, determined to stand his ground until Gunner had bitched up as ordered and skulked away, tail between his legs.

Only a few weeks ago, Gunner would have been happy to comply. His pride would have been easier to swallow, the shame of letting a bully like this think he'd sent Gunner home, crying to his own mother, no great burden to carry. But of late, Gunner wasn't as prone to trade an ounce of dignity for a pound of common sense; his business was going south and his relatives were dying, and every affront to his self-esteem felt like another nail in his coffin.

"What, you didn't hear what I said? Get the fuck off my property!"

The man named Gordito pulled out of his mother's grasp to leap right in Gunner's grille, likely planning to do nothing more than chest-bump him into submission.

And Gunner drove a straight right hand into his face. The blow met his forward momentum head-on, making a sound all three people could hear. As his mother screamed, Gordito dropped to the ground like a ballast bag from a balloon, eyes rolling up in his head on the way down, and he didn't get up.

While Gunner stood there watching, rubbing the knuckles of his throbbing right hand, the old woman fell to her knees to attend to her son, frantically imploring God in Spanish to spare his life. Gunner was certain her prayers were in vain—from all appearances, Gordito was dead—but then the fallen man's eyes began to flutter and a finger on his left hand twitched, allowing both his mother and his assailant to feel a common sense of relief.

The two small children who'd been playing in the yard earlier now stood on the front porch, watching in wide-eyed terror and open-mouthed curiosity. The aged Latina Gunner assumed was their grandmother finally looked up at him, tears streaming down her weathered brown cheeks. *"Vete, por favor! Mi hijo está enfermo! Largáte y déjanos en paz!"*

Her words were lost on Gunner but not her meaning.

"I'm sorry," he said.

He slowly backed away, then turned to make a full retreat.

10

GUNNER DROVE FROM ZINA'S HOME to meet his uncle at Harbor UCLA with the idea they would talk over an early dinner in the hospital cafeteria, but Daniel Curry surprised him.

"To hell with the cafeteria. Let's go get a drink."

Leaving Daniel's wife with Zina—only an act of God could have uprooted her—they found a steak joint with a bar a few blocks away and took the corner table farthest from the nearest patron. Little had been said between them before now, at the hospital or in Lilly Tennell's Tahoe, short of a few words about Del's daughter, whose condition had apparently changed only marginally for the better since Gunner had last checked. His uncle's silence suited him, in any case. His mind was elsewhere, still trying to make sense of the altercation he'd had with Zina's crazed, expansively tatted neighbor, Gordito.

What the fuck had been the fool's problem? What had Gunner done to provoke him to such madness, and how could it have been worth all he had placed at risk? Because nothing less than his life had hung in the balance. It used to be a man could step to a stranger in anger without inviting death; fists would fly and blood would flow, but no one had to die. Those days had passed, however, and Gordito had to know it. Today, in this new America where hate speech was every citizen's first line of defense and violence came right behind it, no insult was too trivial to answer with mere injury, and an argument was just a lead-in to a fatal exchange of gunfire. Restraint was for punks, and tolerance of any stripe—racial, religious, political—was an outmoded concept.

Ultimately, Gunner decided that both he and Zina's deranged neighbor had been lucky. The latter, because one punch had been enough to extinguish Gunner's anger, and the former, because Gordito hadn't come off his front porch shooting, dispensing with conversation altogether.

"Well? What have you found out?" Daniel Curry asked, snapping his nephew out of his reverie.

He was an imposing-looking man under any circumstances, Gunner's uncle, but in the dim crimson light of the restaurant, he appeared almost otherworldly. The temptation was great to tell the old man he hadn't found out a thing, that he, Daniel Curry, had relieved Gunner this morning of all responsibility where Del was concerned. But Gunner wasn't so far gone that this was anything more than a passing thought.

"I've found out Del was in money trouble. Both at work and at home. I don't know how bad his situation was, exactly, but it was bad enough to have him seeing a doctor for ulcer-like symptoms and chewing antacid tablets like candy."

"Never mind all that. Who cares if he had money trouble, we all have money trouble at times. I'm asking you what you've found out about my son's murder."

"Murder?"

"You heard me. All this talk—"

He was forced to stop as the bartender came by to take their drink orders.

"All this talk about him shooting his wife and daughter before killing himself is a damn lie," Daniel Curry continued, the second they were alone again. "Del was murdered, Aaron, plain and simple, and if you can't see that, you're just as big a fool as that idiot police detective I've been arguing with all day!"

Gunner put down the water glass he'd just picked up, lest he do something with it he would instantly regret.

"You think I want to believe it? That Del did what they say he did?"

"No, but—"

"He was more my brother than my cousin, Uncle. I loved him. I can't see him killing himself, let alone trying to kill Noelle and Zina, any more than you can. But what we can see him doing and what all the evidence to this point says he did seem to be two different things."

Del's father dropped a fist on the table like the hammer of Thor. "I don't give a damn about the evidence!"

"Then you're the fool, not me. It was Del's gun. Witnesses say he, Noelle, and Zina were the only three people in the house."

"I don't—"

"Listen to me!"

Their drinks arrived as heads all around turned their way. The two men held their tongues only long enough for the bartender to serve them and disappear again.

"Listen to me," Gunner repeated, lowering his voice. "He called me to say he was sorry and then he took his own life. Whatever happened to Noelle and Zina, Del committed suicide; the coroner's report is clear about that. If he didn't shoot Noelle and Zina, what the hell was he apologizing for?"

He waited for his uncle's answer. The old man merely sat there glowering at him, lips quivering, hands flat on the table.

"It's a lie. You can't make me believe it," he finally said.

"I'm not asking you to believe it. All I'm asking you to do is prepare yourself and Corinne for the possibility. You won't be able to help me find out the truth unless you do."

"The truth?" Daniel Curry gave Gunner a skeptical look.

"I told you. I loved Del like a brother. I've got no reason to think the police aren't doing their job, but I'm not about to take their word for what happened yesterday, either. I'm going to find out for myself how Del died—

how and why. Not because you demand it, but because I demand it. I'm doing it for my peace of mind, not yours. Now, you can help me or get the hell out of my way, I don't give a damn which. What's it going to be, Uncle?"

His uncle studied him, trying to gauge his sincerity, and slowly nodded his head. He wasn't a man for tears, Daniel Curry, but he was on the brink of them now.

"How can I help?"

"Del's financial problems. Were you aware of them?"

"No. Who says he was having financial problems?"

Gunner told him what Del's office assistant Viola Gates had reported about Del's ailing business of late, and the similar story he had read in the family checkbook at Del's home earlier that afternoon.

"Are you sure you didn't know about any of this?"

"Yes, I'm sure. We never talked about money."

"Then he never asked you for a loan of any kind."

"Certainly not."

"What about Corinne?"

"Corinne?"

"Is it possible Del borrowed money from her?"

"Without my knowledge? No. I handle all the finances in our home; my wife gets all her money from me." He lifted his glass of scotch to his lips and sipped from it like a maiden at a church social.

"What about Del's marriage? Were he and Noelle doing okay, as far as you knew?"

"Why ask me? You were the one living out here in California with the two of them, seeing them on a regular basis. Don't you know?"

"I only know what Del let me see," Gunner said defensively. "On the surface, they looked happy enough. But maybe there was more going on between them that he only felt comfortable sharing with you and his mother."

"They had their fair share of troubles, certainly," Daniel Curry said, under obvious duress. "But name me a married couple that doesn't."

"What kind of troubles, Uncle?"

"The usual kind. You know."

"Let's pretend that I don't."

The old man took another sip from his drink, stalling for time. "The boy was getting restless. His eyes were starting to wander."

"Wander how?"

"You know what I'm saying. Do I have to spell it out? He was thinking about other women. Same way we all do, sooner or later."

"You're saying he was having an affair?"

"No. No! He was thinking it about it, I said. Just thinking about it."

"And why was he thinking about it?"

"I just told you. Because we all think about it, eventually. Especially when our wives are leaving us little choice."

"Excuse me?"

"You aren't a married man. You wouldn't understand. Wives are temperamental creatures. Their affections come and go like the wind. One day they love you and the next day they don't. A good woman never rejects you for very long, but sometimes, even a good one will keep her distance for months. Especially if she's going through the change."

He drank some more scotch and Gunner did the same with his bourbon, piecing the puzzle of his uncle's words together as best he could.

"So they weren't having sex because Noelle was going through menopause, and Del was having a hard time coping. Is that it?"

"It is."

"How long had it been? Since they'd last...you know."

"I can't tell you, exactly. And I'm not sure you have any right to know, in any case. But suffice it to say, to my knowledge, it had been a year at least, maybe even two."

"Two years?"

Gunner was incredulous. He'd had no clue. Twenty-four months without sexual intercourse had never proven fatal to anyone, male or female, but it was the kind of drought men still young enough to care took hard. Del had only been fifty-seven, three years younger than Gunner, and as long as Gunner had known him, he had talked as good a sex game as anyone. Of course, talk was cheap, a eunuch could do it, yet Gunner couldn't imagine his cousin doing all the crowing he'd done in Gunner's presence over the last several months, let alone twenty-four, with Noelle rejecting his advances all the while. Del had seemed to love his wife too much to hide that kind of pain so well.

"I know what you're thinking. No wife of yours would have ever done that to you," Daniel Curry said. "Denied you what she promised would be yours for the asking, 'til death do you part, for weeks, months, years at a time. You wouldn't have allowed it.

"Well, that's what we all think in the beginning." He downed the last of his drink in one swallow, finally resembling a man who knew how to handle his liquor. "And then we discover where the real power lies in a marriage."

"Actually, I don't know what I'd do if it happened to me," Gunner said. "I suppose it would all depend on the woman."

"Of course it would. And the woman in Del's case was Noelle. Which should explain, if you knew her at all, why my son was so willing to wait for her to come around. Until very recently, anyway."

"When he started thinking about having an affair."

"Yes."

"Was he angry at Noelle or just hurt?"

"I'd say a little of both. But more than either, he was afraid."

"Afraid?"

"That he'd lost her and might never get her back."

Gunner let a moment pass before asking his next

question. "How ugly did things get between them? Do you know?"

"Ugly? What do you mean by 'ugly'?"

"I mean argumentative. Vindictive." He added pointedly: "Violent."

Daniel Curry recoiled from the word. "If you're suggesting my son ever laid a hand on his wife in anger—"

"He loved her, but she wasn't reciprocating, at least not physically. He was angry and hurt, by your own admission, and no doubt highly frustrated as well."

"Del would never have hurt her. Never."

Gunner interrupted his uncle again. "The idea that she might have some other reason for cutting him off—that she was seeing someone else, for instance—would have had to enter his mind at some point. And if she was—"

"No! Enough!" Daniel Curry exploded. "Del would never have abused Noelle. Not for any reason, in no way, shape, or form. He wasn't that kind of man. He was a good man. A decent man. He was a loving husband and devoted father and..." His voice caught. "...a fine son. A fine son."

The tears he'd been able to hold at bay until now finally came, but only under the old man's silent and stubborn control. He turned his eyes to one side, away from his nephew's gaze, and sucked in a breath, already fast at work reining in his emotions.

"I'm sorry, Uncle. I know this is hard."

Del's father faced him directly again, and said, "I don't understand. It makes no sense. Why my boy? Why?"

"I don't know."

"If things had been that bad for him, he should have told us. Whatever he needed, we would have given it to him."

It was the same thought Gunner had been having, off and on, for almost two days now.

"You're assuming what he needed was something you and his mother had to give. But maybe it wasn't. Maybe what he needed was something nobody could have given him, short of Noelle."

"'Pray,' I told him. 'Pray for strength. Pray for patience. She's a good woman and she loves you. She's just going through a rough time right now; she'll find her way back home. Watch and see.'"

"She bought a gun," Gunner said, putting it out there without preamble to see how his uncle would react.

"What? Who?"

"Noelle. I found it in a kitchen drawer at their place this afternoon."

Gunner's uncle considered the implications. "How do you know it was Noelle's?"

"Because she tried to buy one from a mutual acquaintance of mine and Del's three weeks ago. She must have found another seller when he turned her down."

"I'm not following you."

"The reason he turned her away was the condition she put on the sale: she didn't want Del to know about it."

Daniel Curry said nothing.

"Married women who buy guns they don't want their husbands to know about are very often the victim of some kind of abuse, Uncle. If things between Noelle and Del were as bad as you describe, or worse—"

"It wasn't her husband she was afraid of."

Gunner stopped, surprised. "What?"

"Del and Noelle had been having a great deal of trouble with my granddaughter in recent months. Especially Noelle. From what I understand, she didn't care for the kind of people the girl was associating with and wasn't shy about saying so."

"Are we talking about Zina's boyfriends?"

"The men she was sleeping with. Yes. Noelle described them to my wife as dogs. Parasites who only wanted one thing from the girl."

"And you think that's why Noelle bought the gun? To protect herself from one of those parasites?"

"Like I said, she was in the habit of telling them to their faces what they were. Some took it in stride, but others responded violently. Once, even physically."

"Who was this?"

"I never heard a name. It's possible she gave Corinne one, but I doubt it."

Gunner fell silent, once more trying to absorb something his uncle was telling him. What he would have sworn he knew about Del and his family only three days ago was gradually taking the form of a laughable delusion.

"So Noelle told Corinne all this?"

"Yes."

"What about Del?"

"He admitted it was more or less true, but insisted Noelle was exaggerating greatly. He had a tendency to side with his daughter where she and her mother were concerned, and I think he felt his wife was too protective of the child."

"You call her a child, but Zina is what? Twenty-one, twenty-two? That's a grown woman by almost anyone's standards."

"Agreed."

"Have either you or Corinne told the police about this boyfriend who allegedly attacked Noelle physically?"

"Of course. We both did. But do you think they believed us? Or give a damn if they do? Hell, no!"

"Take it easy, Uncle. We don't know what they believe yet."

"I think their actions speak louder than words. You said so yourself, the only theory they're pursuing is that Del did all the shooting in that house, and we both know that's not possible."

"I never said it wasn't possible. All I said—"

"There was someone else in that house when my son was killed. And you're going to find out who it was."

"Uncle..."

"I don't want to hear any more of your excuses, Aaron."

"For God's sake! All we've established tonight is that one of Zina's boyfriends may have had a motive to harm Noelle. Not Del and certainly not Zina. And there's no evidence such a person was at the scene when all the shooting occurred."

"He was there. He must have been."

"Then why would he leave Del alive?"

"Del wasn't alive! For the last time—"

"Think about what you're getting ready to suggest: that this boyfriend shot Noelle and Zina outright and then what? Faked Del's suicide? After Del called me to all but confess to shooting his wife and daughter himself? It doesn't add up, Uncle. It's ludicrous."

"So you're giving up, then. You're quitting."

"No! Goddammit, you're not hearing what I'm saying!"

"All right, then. Try me again. What are you going to do, Aaron? Since what I'm suggesting is 'ludicrous,' what's your plan?"

Gunner's uncle took up his drink, drew a long sip from it, and then sat back, waiting.

11

ZINA HAD REGAINED CONSCIOUSNESS OVERNIGHT.
Gunner got the word from his uncle Wednesday morning. He warned Daniel Curry that the police would want to try talking to the girl as soon as possible, but between her doctors and both grandparents, he knew it would be hours before Jeff Luckman and his partner would be allowed access to her.

He could foresee how their first interview with Zina would go, in any case. They'd gently break the news to her about her parents, then give her a few moments to absorb the shock. After that, she'd shut down and say nothing, moving the worried hospital staff to order everyone from her room, lest she fall into a dangerous depression. Interview over.

Gunner decided he would go by the hospital in the afternoon, when his chances would be better of catching Del's daughter alert and conversant, and keep to the two things he already had on his morning schedule. The second of these was a trip out to the Twin Towers jail to visit Harper Stowe with Kelly DeCharme; the first was a sit-down with his old friend Matthew Poole.

Poole was a recently retired LAPD detective Gunner had known for many years. As jowly and dawdling as an aged basset hound, Poole had always been an anomaly among his peers, an old-school white cop whose decades of service on the Los Angeles Police Department had failed to leave him with any noticeable disdain for the public he served, most especially Angelenos of color. Over his career he'd moved from one division to another, never straying too far from the inner city, and in the course of their strange relationship, he and Gunner had formed a bond built on respect, cynicism, and a dogged infatuation with the truth.

Officially, the department had no mandatory retirement age, but Poole, made to feel increasingly anachronistic by partners and superiors alike, turned in his badge three years ago, shortly after his fifty-sixth birthday. These days, he worked as a part-time consultant for various private security firms and played poker at the Lucky Lady Casino in Gardena. Luring him away from both occupations with the bait of a free breakfast platter at the diner of his choice had proven as difficult for Gunner as picking up the phone.

"Egg whites, no Tabasco. Really, Poole?" Gunner said, eyeing the ex-cop's plate with open pity.

"You had any sense, you'd be doing likewise. Or don't you want to live to be seventy-five?"

"Define 'live.'"

They were sharing a table at an IHOP on Slauson and Western, in Chesterfield Square. Any other cop, ex- or otherwise, would have insisted this meeting take place at a beachfront restaurant with linen tablecloths and waiters in aprons, but not Poole. Poole was a common man in every way, including the fees he charged for favors.

"Living is living, Gunner. With hot sauce or without, it beats the alternative either way."

"Maybe."

Poole let a moment pass before going on, seeing Gunner's mind had drifted off toward Del again. "Yeah, I know. Kind of hard to see what any of this shit means right now, huh?"

"He should've talked to me, Poole. Before he put that fucking gun in his mouth, he should've talked to me."

"Sure he should have. The same way you would have talked to him, in his place."

He waited for Gunner to explode, thinking he'd gone

too far, but Gunner just ran a fork around in his food instead, conceding his friend's point.

"We're secretive creatures, we men. Anything worth feeling's worth hiding. And no hole's too deep that we don't think we can climb out of it on our own power, without anybody's help."

"He didn't shoot his wife and daughter, Poole. No way."

"You want to believe that. And maybe it's true. But maybe what's true instead is that he was up against something so fucked up, it changed him, just for a minute. A good man gone bad. It happens, partner. About a thousand times a day."

"No." Gunner shook his head. "No."

"Okay. So if you didn't call this meeting to hear my opinion, why did you call it?" Poole shoved another forkful of egg white in his mouth.

"I need you to find something out for me."

"Unlike a lot of words in the English language, Gunner, *retired*'s only got one meaning."

"I'm not asking for any Black Ops action here. You could do this in your sleep."

"The only thing I do in my sleep is sleep."

"I just want to know that these guys on the case are playing it straight. Not mailing it in, not cutting any corners. Del deserved better than that."

"I don't know anybody at Southeast anymore."

"Bullshit. You know somebody everywhere."

It wasn't true, but it was close enough to fact that Poole didn't bother denying it.

"What are the names again?"

"Luckman, Jeff. He's the lead. His partner's name is Yee. Chris, I think."

"I can check in. Get a feel for things. That's all."

"That'll do."

Gunner held his right fist out for Poole to bump.

"Jesus. Let me get my dashiki out of the car."

The white man bumped Gunner's fist with his own and went back to his free meal.

12

FIREBASE RIPCORD had been Hamburger Hill all over again, only in reverse.

They called Dong Ap Bia, aka Hill 937, Hamburger Hill because the battle that took place there in May 1969 had been nearly as bloody as it was pointless. It was a fight for control of a strategically innocuous position atop the A Shau Valley between the North Vietnamese Army, which held it, and US and South Vietnamese forces, who wanted it; and over the span of ten days a lethal combination of tactical blunders, bad weather, and military hubris cost seventy-two US soldiers their lives. Along with the 372 Americans wounded and all the time, manpower, and ordnance "victory" had required, the casualties were a high price to pay for a prize that ultimately held so little value, it was surrendered right back to the North Vietnamese within days of its capture.

A little over a year later, the battle for Firebase Ripcord was no such fiasco, but it was close. This time, it was the NVA fighting to take control of a hilltop position on the eastern edge of the very same A Shau Valley, with an outgunned and outnumbered US Army digging in its heels to defend it. Among the grunts in the latter contingent was SP4 Aaron Gunner, D/2-506th Infantry.

Ripcord was intended to provide artillery and navigational support for a planned offensive on Viet Cong supply installations on Co Pung Mountain, nine kilometers to the south. For the first two months of its existence, the enemy had shown the base little interest, but it was only playing possum. Under cover of the dense jungle

that loomed over Ripcord on all sides, several NVA bat-
talions were methodically working their way down the
hills toward it, constructing a complex chain of tunnels,
bunkers, and firing pits as they went.

On the morning of July 1, the now heavily entrenched
NVA began an assault on the firebase designed to blow
it off the face of the earth. Sixty millimeter and 82mm
mortar shells rained down upon the Americans' heads
like the wrath of God. No amount of return fire or aerial
support could make the barrage stop; the enemy was too
well camouflaged, its defenses too impenetrable. Inevita-
bly, the US forces were left with but a single choice: climb
up into the hills to put the NVA guns to rest or perish beneath the onslaught.

It was a no-win proposition. Outnumbered almost
ten to one, fighting uphill against an enemy lying in wait
within heavily fortified bunkers barely visible to the naked eye, platoon after platoon of GIs marched up the
sides of the A Shau into a hornet's nest of machine gun
and RPG fire. Trying to take the hills back knoll by knoll,
ordered to either mark the NVA bunker positions for an
aerial assault or destroy them outright on the ground, all
the Americans could do in the end was keep coming, to
no discernible effect.

On the seventh day of the battle, it was Gunner's turn
to go.

First Lieutenant Greg Brewer, the greenhorn shake-
and-bake in charge of Gunner's squad, tried to put PFC
William "Jolly" Mokes at point, but Jolly told the white
man to go to hell. Big, clumsy, and anything but jolly,
Mokes had fallen in with a band of knuckleheaded Pan-
ther-wannabes back at Camp Evans and was now treating every order from a white CO like an affront to his
manhood. Gunner understood the impulse—black GIs
in 'Nam caught more hazard duty than mere coincidence
alone could explain. But militant insubordination was all
too easily written off as cowardice, and that was a badge of

dishonor some liked to apply with a broad brush to every brother in uniform.

Still, Gunner was as loath to take point as Jolly was. He did it when ordered, but he never volunteered, and he sure as hell wasn't going to volunteer now.

Left to assign the thankless duty to someone more amenable than Jolly, Brewer ultimately gave the job to PFC Andy "Duke" Wayne, and the kid ambled up to the front without complaint.

Duke was an eighteen-year-old white boy from Myrtle Beach, South Carolina, splattered with red freckles and brimming with cornball, country humor; and he was the closest thing to a real friend Gunner had in the service. Gunner spent more time with Jolly because they'd known each other longer, since their days in boot camp back at Fort Benning, but the truth was, he and Duke had more in common. With Jolly, conversation always turned to women and booze or nothing at all; Duke, on the other hand, liked to jaw about everything from food to politics, movies, and music. Like Gunner, he was a huge fan of Arthur C. Clarke and Raymond Chandler.

It was their mutual love of fast cars, however, that formed the real bond between them. Duke was the son of a Ford dealer back home, and what he didn't know about automobiles Gunner had no interest in learning. He could talk about one subject alone—the fire engine red 1965 Ford Shelby Cobra convertible his father had given him for his sixteenth birthday—for hours on end without losing a minute of Gunner's attention.

When Duke was given point in Jolly's place that day up on Hill 1000, Gunner almost raised an objection. But he didn't feel like dying and Duke wouldn't give a shit about his objections in any case, so he just kept his mouth shut and let the white boy lead the squad forward.

It was a decision he would second-guess for years to come.

Aerial prep had bombed the upper third of the hill

into mulch, making the climb up the last two hundred meters a tedious, backbreaking slog. It was all the GIs could do to keep their balance as they pressed on, boots catching and sliding in the muck. Seventy meters from the knoll that was their objective, Duke's left leg sank knee deep into the pulverized earth and he stumbled trying to pull it free. The mishap saved his life, at least momentarily, as an AK-47 round that would have surely taken his head off ripped through his left arm instead.

The grunts behind him scattered, diving for cover that wasn't really there. Brewer led most of the platoon downward in retreat, taking heavy fire from the gunman above, as Gunner and Jolly scurried sideways across the face of the hill to a shallow depression barely big enough for one. From there, all they could see above them was Duke, well out of their reach, flat on his back behind a fragment of tree stump, screaming and cursing in pain. The gook with the rifle was beyond their range of view.

"We've gotta go up and get him," Gunner said, referring to Duke, curled up in a ball so as to avoid the fusillade of bullets kicking up dirt all around them. Brewer and the others were answering the enemy fire as best they could, but they were shooting at a target they simply couldn't see.

Jolly shook his head. "Man, fuck that."

Gunner propped the nose of his M16 up under the big man's double chin, and said, "You're the reason the man's up there, nigga. You're either gonna help me get him down or die right here. See if I'm playin'."

Gunner wasn't and Jolly knew it. "Okay, G. Be cool, man."

At Gunner's signal, they chucked a pair of frag grenades overhead and used the cover of the explosions to scramble up the hill toward their fallen comrade. When they reached him, the seriousness of Duke's injuries became immediately apparent to both: his left arm was tied to his shoulder by the merest of threads, the Viet Cong

AK-47 round having sheared through his upper biceps to leave a single strand of muscle behind. He was still conscious, but not by much, mumbling nonsense through a thick fog of pain and delirium. Gunner knew he was as good as dead if they didn't get him back to base, fast.

It wasn't going to be easy. The respite from enemy fire the two grenades had afforded them was already over, the NVA rifleman above them once more ringing their position with a heavy spray of lead. In fact, it seemed obvious to Gunner that the Viet Cong soldier was no longer alone; there had to be three men firing upon the GIs now, at least. The mere act of applying a tourniquet to Duke's arm involved a degree of risk tantamount to a death wish; all Gunner or Jolly had to do was raise his head an inch too high to give the enemy a target they couldn't—and no doubt wouldn't—miss.

Brewer shouted up the hill for status, he and the others in no position to be of much help. An uphill charge to the rescue would be suicide; they were too far down the slope, with nothing but open space between them and the three GIs above. Gunner barked an order for them to stay where they were and get ready to lay down a shitload of cover fire. He and Jolly were bringing Duke down.

"How the fuck we gonna do that, G?" Jolly wanted to know. It was clear even to him that it couldn't be done.

And Gunner knew he was right, if success was to be measured by the survival of all involved. There was no plan he could conjure that would allow for that. What he had in mind, in fact, was going to get either him or Jolly killed for sure. There was no other way. Somebody was going to have to play sacrificial lamb for the other two, and that somebody could only be Gunner. Duke was his friend, not Jolly's, and guilt had surely pushed Jolly as close to death for the white boy's sake as he was ever going to go.

"When I tell you, throw homeboy over your shoulder and haul ass down the hill," Gunner said. "Don't stop, don't look back, just run. Understand?"

"Alone? What about you?"

"Don't ask any questions, fool. Just shut up and do what I say. You ready?"

Jolly bit his lower lip, set himself to go, and nodded.

"Go!"

Gunner jumped to one side out of the foxhole, M16 blazing. He could just see Jolly throwing Duke across his back out of the corner of his right eye. For a second, all he could hear was gunfire: his own, the NVA's, and that of the rest of the platoon behind him. Bullets whizzed all around, then something struck him up high in the chest and caromed off: a satchel charge, tossed down by one of the gooks at the top of the hill. The yellow, one-pound blocks of C4 the NVA favored didn't always detonate, but this one did.

He only had time to turn his face away before the explosion blew him off his feet like a paper doll.

He awoke in a hospital bed back at Camp Evans thirty hours later. He'd had the kind of luck a grunt only saw once. Had the satchel charge gone off at his feet, rather than down into the foxhole after bouncing off his chest, he would have lost one leg at the very least. Instead, the blast had merely torn his right thigh open from knee to hip, a flap of flesh and muscle peeled up and back like the lid on a rations can. The army surgeons had simply sewn the flap back on and plucked a pound of shrapnel out of it and the rest of his lower extremities. The result was a lot of pain but no paralysis; when the time came, he'd walk out of the hospital tent on his own two feet, without the aid of crutches or, worse, a wheelchair.

Jolly had been even luckier, though of course, his good fortune had not come cheap. He'd been in the process of scurrying down out of the foxhole, Duke slung over his shoulders like an oversized duffel, when the satchel charge exploded. Without the white boy's body between him and the blast, he would have been decapitated; instead, he was merely dotted with shrapnel and sent flying down the hill. Duke was ripped to pieces, but Jolly's only significant injuries, as near as he or the medics could tell, was a badly sprained right ankle and a laceration of his left ear that required stitches to save the lobe.

The bitter irony stuck in Gunner's craw for a long time. Jolly had been bound and determined to have Duke die that day, and hell if the giant bastard, for all of Gunner's efforts to stop him, hadn't finally gotten the job done, inadvertently or no.

But there was greater insult added to Gunner's injuries left to come. Less than three weeks later, the US military command would capitulate to the NVA and abandon Firebase Ripcord altogether, following up a complete withdrawal of troops with a wave of B-52s that would turn the base back into the rubble from which it had been built. Duke's name was then added to that of the thousands of others who had died in Vietnam to no apparent purpose.

Gunner was back home in the States and out of uniform by year's end. His war was over and his country's would be soon enough. He wasn't the same man coming out of Vietnam he'd been going in, but he was alive and whole and for that he couldn't help but be grateful. He resigned himself to putting the war behind him and, for the most part, was successful. The noticeable limp he would walk with for several years yet was the only vestige of Firebase Ripcord he gave any thought to, until one day in the spring of 1971, when he received a phone call from a man he didn't know. It was Duke Wayne's father.

He said the last letter he'd received from his son before he died had included some instructions in the event of his death, and one of them was to see to it that Gunner got his fire engine red '65 Ford Shelby Cobra. Duke's father wanted to know how soon Gunner could get out to

Myrtle Beach to pick the car up. He was anxious to have the constant reminder of Andy out of the family garage and was prepared to sell it to the first interested party if Gunner didn't come by soon to take it off his hands.

Four days later, Gunner was fireballing west back to Los Angeles behind the Cobra's wheel, the title assigning him ownership tucked into his back pocket. He cried off and on throughout the trip, unable to decide how to feel. The car was a wet dream come true, but it had Duke's blood all over it and always would.

The memory of Vietnam had just become that much harder to outrun.

13

THESE DAYS, OVER THREE DECADES LATER, the only time Vietnam crossed Gunner's mind was when he was in Jolly's company, and then only rarely. The nightmares and the cold sweats, the flashes of sudden recall that used to come upon him with only the slightest provocation, were things of the past. Jolly was even more unscathed, at least on the surface. For reasons neither could fathom, they had been chosen to survive the war relatively intact, a miracle for which Gunner made a point of saying thanks whenever he found it necessary to pray to the Lord above.

Harper Stowe III had not been so fortunate. He had come back from the hostile fields of Afghanistan with the full weight of the war still strapped to his back. Where Gunner had managed to put the memory of Firebase Ripcord behind him, Stowe seemed to live, day and night, in an Arghandab River Valley of the inner mind, haunted by ghosts and wracked with pain. Whether the war had turned him into a murderer or not had yet to be factually determined, but his resemblance to one could not be argued; watching him shuffle listlessly into the visitation room of the Twin Towers jail downtown early Wednesday morning, a uniformed sheriff's deputy guiding him along like a nurse steering an old woman through a convalescent home, Gunner had no trouble imagining him turning suddenly violent. There was just something about the way his eyes darted from one focal point to another that seemed to suggest a permanent—and dangerous—state of fear and unrest.

Wearing the standard orange jumpsuit of a prisoner, Stowe was led into position and deposited into a chair behind the glass barrier of the cubicle where Gunner and Kelly sat waiting for him. The deputy uttered a few instructions to him and stepped away, leaving him to pick up the handset of the phone on his side of the cubicle as Kelly took up her own.

"Who's this?" Stowe asked his attorney as she tried to make preliminary small talk, referring to Gunner.

"This is Aaron Gunner. The investigator I told you about, the one who's been helping me with your case."

Stowe looked at Gunner blankly, overcome with indifference. "Okay."

"How are you doing?"

He shrugged, but one would have had to be forewarned the gesture was coming to notice it.

"Do you need anything?"

"I need to get out of here."

"I know. We're working on it. But we need your help."

"What kind of help?"

"We've been trying to find out where you were at the time of Darlene's murder, since you say you don't remember."

"I don't 'say' I don't remember. I don't fuckin' remember."

"Of course. I'm sorry. You don't remember where you were."

"No."

"And that's still true? Nothing at all's come back to you since the last time we talked?"

"No. Nothing. I've been trying to remember. Don't you think I've been trying?"

"What about the night before? At Tyrecee's apartment?"

"I told you. We hung out, I crashed, that's it. Next thing I know, I'm wakin' up at Pops's."

"Around 2 p.m. the next day."

"Yeah. Somethin' like that."

"And the gun?"

"Gun?"

"The gun that killed Darlene. The one the police found your fingerprints on. You must have handled it at some point, Harper, and we need you to tell us where and when."

"I can't. I never touched that gun. I haven't touched a gun since I was discharged."

Kelly turned to Gunner. He'd only been privy to her end of the conversation, but the lack of value in her client's responses had been easy enough to ascertain. He and Kelly swapped positions in the cubicle and Gunner took the phone, Kelly pushing in close so they could share the instrument's earpiece.

"Listen, Harper. Fingerprints don't lie. You came in contact with that gun somehow and we've got to figure out how. Knowing where the gun came from would be a good place to start."

Stowe just shook his head.

"If it wasn't yours, maybe it was your father's. Is that possible?"

"Hell, no. Pops ain't got nothing to do with this." His voice was loud enough now to carry across several cubicles.

"What about Darlene? Did she keep a gun in her office that you're aware of?"

Stowe paused before answering. "I don't know. I never saw one in the office."

"But?"

"But I saw Johnny get one out of there once."

"Johnny Rivera?"

"Yeah."

Gunner and Kelly shared a look. Stowe had the idea that nothing more needed to be said.

"Go on."

"He got into it with some asshole who was all up in his grille. Johnny went back in the office and came back out with a piece. He told the guy, he didn't get the fuck out, he was gonna put a round in his ass."

"And then?"

"And then nothin'. The guy took the hint and left."

"And the gun?"

"Johnny put it back where he got it. I never saw it again after that."

"Did you get a good look at it?"

"The gun?"

"Yes."

"Nah, not really. Black semiauto, that's about all I could say for sure. I was on the other side of the store with a customer when it happened."

"Any idea who this guy Johnny was beefing with was?"

"Nope."

"Can you describe him?"

It was asking a lot of Stowe, considering his memory lapses, but to Gunner's surprise, he said, "Pissed-off white boy. Dark hair, dark complexion, beard ratty as shit. 'Bout my age, maybe a little younger."

The picture he painted meant nothing to Kelly, but Gunner thought it fit someone he'd seen once to a T: the owner of the emerald green Camaro that had roared into the Empire Auto Parts lot the day before, near the end of his last interview with Eric Woods.

"And you're sure you never touched this piece Johnny had that day?"

"No way. I told you."

"Okay. Let's forget the gun for now," Gunner said. "You told the police and Ms. DeCharme here that it was just you and your boy Eric chilling at Tyrecee's the night before the murder. Is that right?"

Stowe nodded. "Yeah."

"Well, Eric says there was a fourth person there that night. A girlfriend of Tyrecee's who's apparently on the large side."

"On the large side?"

"Fat. Eric said she was fat."

Stowe grew still, his mind reaching for something he could sense, but not yet fully see. "Roxanne."

"You remember her?"

"Yeah. She and Ty go back a ways. Fifth grade, or some shit like that." Stowe nodded, trying hard to piece the memory together.

"Harper—" Kelly started to say, but Gunner waved her to silence. Push Stowe now, he knew, and the man would lose the thread he was working to unravel.

"Yeah, she was there. She gave me a ride."

"From Ty's? When?"

"In the morning. She crashed there, too. We left together. Yeah." He nodded again, more forcefully this time, confidence growing that this wasn't just something he was imagining had happened.

"Where did she take you?"

Stowe gave the question some thought, shook his head. "I don't know."

"Try. Try to remember."

"I am trying! What the fuck you think I'm doing?"

His outburst got a rise out of the guard who'd brought him in. Now standing a short distance away, arms crossed like iron bands across his chest, the deputy had been watching Stowe closely ever since dropping him off, waiting for what he clearly thought was the inevitable disturbance of the prisoner's making that would require his removal from the room.

"Harper, calm down," Kelly said.

"Fuck that. I didn't kill Darlene. This is bullshit. You guys need to get me the hell outta here!"

"We're trying."

"Yeah, well, you ain't tryin' hard enough!"

The deputy took a step forward but Gunner froze him in place, flashing the palms of his hands to indicate he had things under control. But it was a lie that wouldn't hold up long. Stowe was losing patience with all the questions and was showing signs that a major migraine might be looming.

"Just a couple more questions, Harper," Gunner said. "Can you handle that?"

Stowe shrugged in silence on the other side of the glass, petulantly holding his tongue.

"You and Eric went over to Tyrecee's the night of the murder and hooked up with her and this girl Roxanne. You and Roxanne crashed there overnight, but not Eric. Why was that?"

"Why was what?"

"Why didn't Eric stay too? Overnight, I mean."

"Oh. Because Laticia threw him out."

Gunner tried to place the name.

"Ty's mother?" Kelly asked.

"Yeah. She threw his ass out."

"Why?" Gunner asked.

"I don't know. He said or did somethin' to piss her off, but I was asleep when it happened, so I couldn't tell you what it was. Don't take much with Laticia, anyhow. That bitch is crazier than me."

Stowe laughed, and the effort involved twisted his face into knots.

Kelly gave Gunner a side glance: interview over.

He nodded without argument and rose from his chair as Kelly raised a hand, bidding the deputy who'd brought Stowe in to return her client to his cage.

"Well, we didn't get what we came for," Kelly said as they made their way out to their respective cars, "but we did learn a few things we didn't know before."

"This girl Roxanne, for one. If she did give him a ride from Tyrecee's crib like he says, she might be able to give him an alibi for the time of Evans's murder. That, or confirm that he actually committed it."

"I prefer to hope for the former."

"And I need to go back to see Johnny Rivera again, ask how he could threaten a customer with a gun he claimed yesterday he knew nothing about."

"Can I help? Maybe I should talk to Rivera while you talk to Ty."

"No, I'd prefer to do both. Only, I don't think I'm going to talk to Tyrecee this time. I'm going to talk to her mother."

"Laticia? Why?"

"Because I think it's safe to say her daughter didn't want us to know her girl Rox was hanging with her and the boys that night, so she isn't likely to tell me where I can find Roxanne the first time I ask. I'd also like to know what Woods said or did to Laticia that got him thrown out of her apartment."

"Is that important?"

"Maybe. Maybe not. But it'll give me a better idea of who Woods is, and what kind of friend he is to your client. And that info could be important."

Kelly nodded in agreement. They reached her car in the parking lot and discreetly kissed goodbye.

"I take it you're going by the hospital now?" she asked. Gunner had told her about the change in Zina Curry's condition earlier, as they sat in the visitors' waiting room prior to meeting with Stowe.

"Yeah. No sense putting it off any longer."

"You're afraid of what she might say."

"Up to now, I've only had to fear the worst. Having to live with it might be more than I can take."

14

GUNNER REACHED HARBOR UCLA just before noon. By then, LAPD detectives Jeff Luckman and Chris Yee had already come and gone. Zina had been drifting in and out of a thick sleep all morning, and the time she spent awake could be counted in minutes on one hand.

Zina's grandparents were still there, however, though not in line with Gunner's expectations for how he might find them. Corinne Curry was the one stationed in the waiting room, wide awake, when he arrived, while her husband Daniel dozed at their granddaughter's bedside, folded up in a chair like a sock stuffed into a shoe.

Corinne told Gunner that Zina's doctors now expected her to live, and she showed no obvious signs of paralysis, thank you Jesus, but she was still a far ways off from being out of danger.

"Has she spoken to anybody yet?" Gunner asked.

"Said a few words to your uncle and me. That's about all."

"You told her—"

"Yes." The urge to cry was no match for her determination to do otherwise.

"What exactly did she say?"

"She asked where she was. I told her. She asked about her father and that's when...we told her he was gone. Her father and mother, both. After that, she just cried. Cried 'til she fell asleep again."

"You didn't ask her what happened?"

"Daniel tried. I told him it was too soon." She didn't need to explain; Gunner could see it in his mind's eye, his uncle's mouth closing in midsentence as Corinne's withering gaze voiced the order.

"And the police?"

"She didn't say anything to them at all. We tried to tell them she wasn't ready, but they wouldn't listen. We only let one of them see her. The white man. All he did was upset her. They said they'll be back later tonight."

Gunner glanced in the direction of Zina's room. "How long has she been out?"

"Couple hours. But—"

"I need to talk to her, Miss Corinne."

"No. We're gonna let her rest now."

"If somebody other than Del did this, she might know who it was. And the sooner we get a name, the sooner we can run them down for the police."

"Somebody?" Del's mother almost smirked. "There ain't no 'somebody.' My son did this. Nobody else."

Gunner had no words.

"Oh, I know what his father says. Not Del. Not his son. Del would never do such a horrible thing. But he doesn't understand. *I* understand."

"Understand what?"

"What it had been like for him lately. Feeling all alone. Like a failure."

"But he wasn't alone. And he wasn't a failure."

"Not to you or to me. But to him, he was both those things. Noelle didn't love him anymore and his business was about to go bankrupt."

"Who says Noelle didn't love him?"

"She did. She told him so, more than once."

"So he decided to kill her and Zina and then commit suicide?" He shook his head. It felt like he'd been denying this thing every hour, on the hour, for two days now. "No. No."

She slapped him hard across the side of the face, demonstrating more power than he would have thought she could generate. Now the tears she'd refused to shed shone in her eyes. "You think I'd say such a thing if it weren't true? Do you think I could say it if it weren't true?"

Gunner held his tongue, his cheek burning like fire.

"She's awake again," somebody at the door said.

Daniel Curry stood there watching them, attuned to the fact he'd just interrupted something of great import. Gunner glared at Corinne, a warning of intent not to be questioned, and marched past his uncle into Zina Curry's room.

It was dark and cold inside, lit only by the array of machines surrounding the young woman's bed. Walled off from the other patient in the room by a drab green curtain, Zina Curry tracked Gunner's approach toward her with eyes barely open. She looked like a science experiment gone terribly wrong. Had he the luxury of time, Gunner would have taken a moment to pity her.

"How're you doing, Zina?" he said when he reached her bedside.

She blinked at him dumbly.

"It's your Uncle Aaron."

"Who?"

Corinne and Daniel Curry piled into the room, a nurse right on their heels. "She's not ready for this. I told you!" Corinne scolded.

"Zina, we need to know what happened. Please. Who shot you?"

"No. No!" Del's daughter turned her face away from him.

"Sir, you need to leave," the nurse ordered.

"Who shot your mother, Zina? Who was there when it happened?"

"Momma did it," Zina said, turning back around to face him. "Momma did it all."

She began to weep. The nurse took Gunner by one arm and Daniel Curry took him by the other. Corinne Curry just stood at a distance, content to observe his removal from the room.

"Wait!" Gunner said.

But his escorts steered him out into the hallway, empowered by his reluctance to tear himself from the grasp of a man twenty years his senior and a nurse he outweighed by at least thirty pounds.

"Sir, I'll call security if you don't leave. Right now," the woman in the starched white uniform said.

"She's lying. She has to be. She's laying the blame all on Noelle and there's no way Noelle shot all three of them."

"She's confused, that's all. What do you expect?" Daniel Curry said. "The child's near death!"

"And if she does die before she tells us the truth? What then? We've got to find out what she knows while she's still capable of talking to us, Uncle. Otherwise, we might never learn what really happened in that house."

"Sir—" the nurse insisted.

"We're going to leave the girl be for now," Corinne Curry said. "All of us."

She fixed Gunner with a look that said he'd have to knock her to the floor to reach her granddaughter again.

Defeated, Gunner stormed off, caring little if his aunt and uncle heard the curses he was uttering under his breath.

Johnny Rivera wasn't there when Gunner went looking for him at Empire Auto Parts. Eric Woods said he'd had to leave early that morning, something about a family emergency.

"Any way I could get a number for him? Or a home address?" Gunner asked. "This is pretty important."

"I don't know. I don't think Johnny would like it," Woods said. He glanced about for an unattended customer, looking for an excuse to end this conversation where it stood; but the only patron in the place was already being helped by Woods's lone coworker, over at the parts counter.

"He wouldn't have to know it came from you. I could tell him I got it from the boss."

"The boss?"

"The new owner. Sam."

Woods mulled it over. "I think that's a good idea."

"What?"

"You getting Johnny's number from Sam. Ask him, not me."

Gunner could see his mind was made up. "Okay. Will do. Thanks." He turned to leave. "Oh." He came back around, as if he'd almost forgotten something. "I saw Harper this morning. He told me a couple things I found rather interesting."

Woods just stood there waiting.

"First, he said Tyrecee's mother Laticia threw you out of their apartment the night before the murder. Is that right?"

Woods shrugged. "I guess you could say that."

"Would you mind telling me why?"

"No, I don't mind. Me and Ty got into a little argument, and her moms didn't like how I was talkin' to her little girl. So she asked me to leave. The end."

"What kind of argument?"

"I'd rather not say."

"Give me the short version."

Woods sighed. "Ty likes me. Maybe more than she likes Harp. Every time homeboy's got his back turned, she's comin' at me. You follow?"

Gunner did, though he didn't necessarily believe it. He moved on. "The other interesting thing Harper said was that Johnny once threatened a customer in here with a gun. A gun he got from the office somewhere."

"Okay."

"You weren't here at the time?"

"No. Or if I was, I didn't hear it."

"Well, this guy Harper says he threatened, I think

he was here yesterday. He arrived while you and I were talking out in the lot. Drives a trashed green Camaro, looks like a mountain man with a grudge to settle."

"Oh. Pete," Woods said.

"Pete?"

"Pete Burdzecki. His real name's Pyotr, but everyone calls him Pete. He used to work here."

"When?"

"Before Harp hired on. But he quit about a year ago. He and Johnny didn't get along."

"So why's he still coming around?"

"He's a customer. And the rest of us are cool with him. Even Dar liked Pete. Johnny's the only one got beef with him."

"Any idea why?"

"Maybe 'cause Pete's the only one ever worked here Johnny didn't scare. And that includes me."

Gunner was going to ask him to explain, but the reason to stop talking to Gunner that Woods had been looking for had finally presented itself: two new customers wandering the shop's aisles who had yet to be pestered by a uniformed employee.

"Hey, I've gotta go. Sorry I couldn't help you out with Johnny's number."

Gunner didn't know much about Noelle Curry's private life, but he knew she spent a great deal of her time at church. She and Del had been Catholic, and the parish name on the losing raffle tickets he bought from her every year by way of her husband was that of St. Patrick's, the church across the street from the LAPD's Newton Community station on Central Avenue.

"Hello?"

"Is this Iris Miller?"

"This is she. Who's this?"

"My name is Aaron Gunner, Ms. Miller. Noelle Curry

was married to my cousin Del and I understand you and she were very close friends."

Silence. "Who told you that?"

"Monsignor Villanueva at St. Patrick's. I told him how important it was that I contact you, and he was kind enough to give me your number."

Frank Villanueva, whom Gunner had been lucky enough to find at the rectory when he called right after leaving Eric Woods at Empire Auto, hadn't had much to say about Del or Noelle, and Gunner hadn't really expected him to. Anything Noelle, in particular, might have told him in confidence was going to stay that way. But Gunner had pressed him hard nonetheless, and in the end, the priest had seen fit to give up Miller's name and phone number, willing to leave the decision to talk to Gunner or not to Miller herself.

"I'm very sorry for your loss, Mr. Gunner. Noelle was a wonderful person and I'm sure your cousin was too, in his way. But what do you want with me?"

In his way. The words made Gunner cringe. "If it's all the same to you, I'd rather not answer that over the phone. Would it be possible for us to meet over coffee or something in an hour or so? It's a matter of some importance, as I said."

More silence.

"For Noelle's sake. Please."

Iris Miller held out a moment longer. Her conscience successfully turned against her, then let out a little sigh and asked him where he'd like her to be and when.

"I'm not comfortable doing this. Just so you know."

"I understand," Gunner said.

They sat in a big-brand coffee shop on the corner of a strip mall at Crenshaw and Redondo Beach Boulevard, Gunner patronizing a ubiquitous chain he ordinarily avoided as a plague upon the face of the earth. St. Patrick's

Monsignor Villanueva hadn't described her, but Noelle's friend Iris Miller had been easy to spot, so incongruous was her quiet piety in this setting. She was tall and slim, sitting when he found her at a table near the window as taut as a violin string, and the only thing revealing about the blue dress she wore were the mid-length sleeves on both arms.

"Noelle was my friend. She talked to me because she trusted me. If I tell all her business to some stranger now—"

"I'm not some stranger. I was family," Gunner said testily. "I'm asking for your help because I need it."

"Why? Noelle's dead and so is her husband. And poor Zina.... What good can we do any of them now?"

"We can make sure the right people are held accountable for what happened to them. All of them."

"But we already know that."

"Do we? The police think Del shot everyone, and maybe he did. But if someone else shot Noelle and Zina, they're out on the loose somewhere while my cousin takes the heat."

"But who else could have shot Noelle?"

"That's what I'm hoping you can help me figure out. Noelle had been afraid recently. Afraid enough that she thought she needed a gun to protect herself. When she couldn't get one on the street, her only other option would've been to ask a friend. Someone she could trust not to tell her husband or anyone else."

Miller just stared at him.

"Where did you get the gun, Ms. Miller?"

"I didn't—"

"Where?"

"From my brother. I told him it was for me." She began to choke up. "If I'd known what he was going to do with it—"

"That wasn't the gun that killed her."

Her eyes went wide. "Pardon?"

"The gun you gave Noelle was in a kitchen drawer at her home. I found it there yesterday afternoon."

"Oh, thank God." She put a hand to her heart.

"Yes. I'm sure that comes as a great relief to you. But you just said 'he.' If you'd known what 'he' was going to do with it. I take it you meant Del?"

"Yes. Who else?"

"You're saying he was the reason Noelle thought she needed a gun?"

"No. I just thought when I heard how they'd all been shot, and that he was the one who did it—well, I just assumed that that was the gun he must have used."

"All right. So if Del wasn't the reason she wanted a gun, who was?"

Iris Miller hesitated, still unsure that she was doing the right thing by Noelle in telling this man all her secrets.

"I don't know his name. She never gave me his name."

"Who?"

"She made a mistake. That's all it was. Noelle loved her husband."

"You're telling me Noelle had an affair?"

"No! It wasn't an affair. She only had relations with the man once, and only then because he took advantage of her." She saw the look come over Gunner's face, rushed to correct the impression she'd left him with. "I don't mean she was raped, exactly. I just mean…. He knew that she was just looking for attention. That she was vulnerable. He could've stopped her from getting so close at any time. But he didn't. He let her come ahead."

"Who?"

"I swear I don't know. She was too ashamed to tell me who. I asked and asked, but she wouldn't tell me."

"I'm sorry, Ms. Miller, but I don't believe you."

"I have a name, that's all. Buddy. And the only reason I have that is that she let it slip once. Buddy. As God is my witness, that's all I know about the man."

"She must have told you something else about him.

Where they met, and how."

"I only know what she said after it happened. She never mentioned him before that."

"So?"

"She said he was a friend of a friend. That he liked to flirt and she'd flirted back. One thing led to another and she had sex with him, once. Once. She regretted it immediately and had no intention of doing it again. But he kept coming back for more. He frightened her."

"And that's why she needed the gun?"

"Yes."

"Why didn't she go to the police?"

"Because she couldn't do that without her husband finding out. And she dreaded that. She loved Del, Mr. Gunner. She only did what she did because she thought she'd lost him, that he didn't love her anymore."

Gunner fell silent, trying to take in all that he was hearing. Noelle had been unfaithful to Del, given cause to believe he no longer loved her. It seemed there was nothing he once took for granted about the pair that could be trusted as the truth anymore.

"Did Del ever find out?"

"Not that I'm aware of. If he did, she never told me. But...like I said, when I heard about what happened, I assumed he must've found out. What else could make him do such a thing?"

Gunner lacked the will to suggest his cousin's innocence again. He changed the subject instead. "Tell me about Zina."

"Zina?"

"Noelle's father-in-law says she and Zina had been fighting quite a bit lately. Over Zina's choice in boyfriends, for the most part."

"It's true. The girl was driving poor Noelle crazy."

"Well, 'the girl' regained consciousness this morning and claims it was her mother who shot her and her father, not Del."

"What?"

"It's not possible, at least not in regards to Del, and the police understand that. But I'm curious to know why she would say such a thing about her mother."

"You just said it. She didn't like Noelle interfering in her business. She resented it."

"And her boyfriends? Del's father says Noelle was in the habit of getting in some of their grilles."

"When they moved her to, yes."

"Anyone in particular?"

"Well, I can think of one. He used to work for Del. I think his name was—"

"Glenn Hopp?"

"Yes. You know him?"

"No." Gunner's head began to swim. Zina and Hopp?

"He and Zina were fooling around," Miller said, "so Del fired him. But even after that, he wouldn't stay away. Noelle caught them together at least twice afterwards and raised holy hell."

"And Del?"

"I don't think she ever told Del. She was afraid of what he might do if she did."

Gunner thought it all through, struggling to see where and how the pieces could possibly come together. "Could Noelle have wanted the gun to use against Hopp?"

"I wondered about that. But I don't think so, no."

"Why not?"

"Because he didn't scare her like this man Buddy did. Noelle said the whole thing was just a joke to Glenn, that all he ever did when she got in his face was laugh."

"Maybe she thought he'd take her more seriously with a gun in her hand."

"Maybe. But I still don't think so. She didn't want the gun just for show, Mr. Gunner. She wanted it to protect herself from somebody. Somebody who had her scared half to death."

He questioned her for a few minutes more, but he'd

heard all she had to relate that could be qualified as useful. He thanked her for her time and gave her a business card.

"I feel horrible about what happened," Miller said. "But I didn't know what to do. She was in trouble and I was her friend. If I'd refused to help her and that man had killed her...." She looked to Gunner for approval. "You understand what I'm saying?"

"Sure. I understand. The gun you gave her?"

"Yes?"

"Where'd it come from? Just curious."

She went back on the defensive. "You won't—?"

"Just between you and me. Promise."

She blushed, on the verge of opening herself up to this man more than she'd ever intended. "It was mine. My brother gave it to me a long time ago, when I was being stalked by an old boyfriend who liked to put his hands on me."

"He wouldn't be a cop, by any chance? Your brother, I mean."

"In Long Beach. County Sheriff's Department before that. How did you know?"

Gunner smiled. "Lucky guess."

Fucking Little Pete.

15

"YOU AGAIN?"

"Yes, but this time I'm not here to see your daughter. I'm here to see you."

Tyrecee Abbott's mother Laticia, striking the same inhospitable pose at the threshold of her Panorama City apartment she had the day before, looked genuinely surprised. And flattered. "Is that a fact?"

"May I come in?"

Her unit was a revelation, a staggering departure from the prison riot leitmotif of the complex's exterior. The furniture was simple and spotless, arranged with taste and common sense, and everything from the carpet to the light fixtures was equally devoid of ostentation. It all appeared lived in but shown great respect, like something borrowed she would soon have to return to its rightful owner.

Laticia Abbott herself was almost equally surprising, in that the strong resemblance to an idle sloth she had struck the day before was no longer evident. Today, her hair was brushed back neatly and her mode of dress would have met most any occasion without drawing a sideways glance. She was still as big as a grizzly and nearly as imposing, but to find the gruff beneath the surface now, you had to look deep.

They ended up in the dining room, on opposite sides of a glass-topped table with a loaded fruit bowl as its centerpiece. Off an open door to one side, a kitchen smelled more of lemon-scented dish soap than bacon grease.

"Is Tyrecee here?" Gunner asked.

"No. I thought you were here to see me."

"I am."

"So? I was on my way out when you showed up, Mr...?"

"Gunner."

"Mr. Gunner. I've got some errands to run and I'm kind of in a hurry. I don't mean to be rude, but—"

"This should only take a minute. Two at the most."

"Okay." She clasped her hands on the table in front of her and waited. A bank officer primed to reject a loan applicant at the first wrong word.

"You remember why I'm here?"

"You work for Harper's lawyer, you said."

"That's right. We don't believe he killed Darlene Evans and, among other things, we've been trying to prove he was elsewhere when her murder was committed. But his memory's a mess in general, as I'm sure you know, and it's even worse in regards to the morning of the murder and most of the evening before. That's where you and Tyrecee come in. We hope."

"Yeah?"

"He spent the night before Evans died here, with your daughter, and then left before dawn. Were you aware of that?"

"Sure. Reesie's a grown woman, she wants to have a man in her room to keep her warm at night, that's her business. I guess that makes me a bad mother."

"Not particularly."

"That's what you were thinking."

"Actually, I wasn't. I was thinking about my next question."

"And what's that?"

"Were you here all that night yourself?"

"Mostly. I ran out to see a friend for a while, but I was back a couple hours later."

"Then you know Ty had more company that night than just Harper."

"Are you talking about that little bitch friend of his, Eric?"

"Eric Woods and Roxanne, yes."

He'd struck a nerve; Laticia Abbott actually twitched in her chair. "Roxanne?"

"Then I guess you didn't know. Remind me what her last name is again?"

"Niles." The name was like poison in her mouth. "Roxanne was here that night? Says who?"

"Harper and Eric both. Tyrecee, I guess, forgot to mention. You have a problem with this Roxanne?"

"You could say that."

"And the problem is?"

"Reesie can do better, that's the problem. She only comes here to eat and sleep, like this is her second home or somethin'."

"Sleep?"

"Personally, I think Reesie found her on the street. If she's got a home of her own, I've never heard about it. I don't want my daughter associating with people like Roxanne. Or Eric, for that matter."

"And what are your issues with him? Aside from the fact he's a little bitch?"

"He's two-faced. Harper thinks he's his friend, but Eric's only friend is himself."

"Why do you say that?"

"'Cause I've seen how he acts with Reesie when Harper's around, and I've seen how he acts when he's not. That's why."

Gunner could not have been less surprised. "You mean he's got a thing for Ty."

"She thinks it's funny, but not me. Only a dog sniffs around another man's girlfriend the way he does with Reesie."

"Is that why you tossed him out that night?"

A secret she would have preferred had remained as such. "He told you about that, huh?"

"He admitted it. But it had to come from Harper first. And his version of things was a little different from yours."

"Is that right?"

"The way he tells it, Ty has a thing for him, and he was putting her in check when you intervened."

Laticia Abbott threw back her head and laughed, the feckless joke that was Eric Woods too funny to be believed. "Ain't that some shit!" When she was done, she pushed herself up from the table and said, "I've gotta go. Come on."

"Hold on a minute. About Roxanne—"

"No, I'm done. Let's go."

Gunner followed her outside and watched her lock the front door, purse in hand. "Roxanne. Where could I find her?"

"No idea. Sorry." She started off toward the parking garage and her car. Gunner scurried after her.

"Guess I'll have to come back and ask Tyrecee, then."

Tyrecee's mother slammed on the brakes, spun on her heels. "No. Leave Reesie alone. Leave us both alone!"

"Where can I find Roxanne?"

She jingled the keys in her hand, trying to decide how badly she wanted to throw them in his face.

"She works in the mall sometimes. Sellin' cell phone accessories at one of them little booths."

"Which mall?"

"The Westfield in Sherman Oaks. All right? Are we done?"

When she marched off this time, Gunner just let her go.

The game was called Slaughterhouse Alley 2, and as near as Gunner could tell, its object was to kill as many olive-skinned, flesh-eating, undead "terrorists" as you could before your thumbs went numb. Gallons of blood spilled did not appear to be a factor in scoring, but Gunner could only imagine that this had been an oversight, because the game's developers had clearly devoted hundreds of man-hours to building a constant flow of 3-D crimson into every minute of play.

Befitting his status as a man who held a video game controller in his hands about as often as he rode a horse, Gunner was getting trounced by the bespectacled preteen boy standing beside him in front of the giant flat-screen TV, when the Mega Buy salesman he'd come here to see finally turned up.

"Were you looking for me?" Glenn Hopp asked.

He was a young black man in his mid-to-late twenties, his voice as smooth as a polished gemstone and his body too finely chiseled to waste on the Mega Buy uniform of green polo shirt and tan slacks he was wearing. His face was that of a male fashion model who'd done all his early posing in the joint.

"Some say all this pretend killing is cathartic," Gunner said, continuing to blast away at the steady onslaught of slavering, bloodthirsty pseudo-Islamists on the screen, "but all it does for me is make me nostalgic for the days of Pong."

"Pardon me?" Hopp glanced behind him, confused. "My manager said—"

"Aaron Gunner." He finally set the game controller aside and held out his hand for Hopp to shake. "Viola Gates told me where to find you." Though she'd acted on the phone as if she would have preferred to chew glass. "You don't remember me, do you?"

"No. I mean...." Hopp went through the motions of shaking his hand. "You look a little familiar, I guess, but.... Remind me."

"You and Viola both used to work for my cousin. Del Curry. We met once or twice at the office, I think."

"Oh. Yeah, yeah. Okay." He started to grin, but then it hit him: Del. "Fucked up—I mean, real sorry to hear about what happened to Del, man. It's a shame."

"Yeah, it is. You been by the hospital to see Zina yet?"

"Zina? No. But I've been prayin' for her. How's she doing?"

Christ, Gunner thought. This boy's good.

"It was touch and go there for a while, but things are looking up. She regained consciousness this morning and the doctors say the worst is probably over."

Now Hopp let the smile come as he nodded his head. "Good, good. I'm happy to hear that."

"Are you?"

"Of course. What do you think?"

"I think you were doing the boss's daughter and that's how you ended up here. When was the last time you saw Zina, Glenn?"

"Whoa there, old man. Take it easy. I wasn't *doin'* Zina, and if she told you that, she's lyin'."

Gunner let the "old man" crack pass and said, "We should probably find someplace else to talk about this. Unless you're down with all these people going home with the idea you're a suspect in a murder investigation."

"Murder? Hold on." He threw his hands up, sufficiently cowered. He measured Gunner's face for mercy but saw nothing coming back but a blank stare. "Okay, okay. This way."

They ended up outside in the back of the store, where employees drifted off to smoke and eat lunch. Having the space all to themselves, they sat at a patio table beneath a darkening sky and a red-and-white metal umbrella cocked to one side on its pole like an old hat.

"You a cop?" Hopp asked.

"No. But I know a few."

"What do you want? I didn't have nothin' to do with no murder, man."

"But you were doing Zina."

"I was. Not anymore. I partied with her a few times a while back, that's all."

"So when was the last time you partied with her?"

"Three, four weeks ago, maybe more. She got me

fired, just like you said, and I ain't had nothin' to do with her since."

"That's not the info I was given, Glenn. I was told you were seeing her even after Del fired you."

"Who told you that? Viola?"

"Viola?" Gunner was thrown, finding the accusation an odd one. "No. But it doesn't matter who told me. What matters is whether it's true or not."

"Did I see Z after I got fired? Yeah, man, I seen her. But I didn't do nothin' with her. Can I help it if she kept comin' around?"

"She's got a jones for you, is that it?"

"Damn straight that's it. You think I went lookin' to do Del's daughter? You think I wanted that kind of trouble? I had a good thing goin' with Del. He liked me and I liked him, but Zina's been sniffin' my leg since day one, and I just finally gave in. Bad mistake. I'm a man, what can I say?"

"You can say where you were Monday between 10 and 11 a.m."

"What?" He caught on. "Ah, hell no. I already told you—"

"If Zina's feeling you as much you say she is, it hasn't been weeks since she last tried you. I'm thinking the last time might've been Monday morning at her crib, either before all the shooting started or during it."

"No. Fuck that. I wasn't nowhere near Zina's crib Monday!"

They were no longer alone in the break area, and a couple of Hopp's fellow employees, standing nearby, set their cell phones aside to turn their way. Hopp paid them no mind.

"Can you prove it?" Gunner asked.

"Can I—?" He thought about it, took things down a notch. Being careful now. "Yeah, I can prove it. If I have to."

"I'm guessing you're gonna say you were with a woman."

"That's right. And if the cops wanna know the lady's name, I'll give it up. But I ain't givin' it up to you." He stood up from the table. "Like I said—I'm sorry about what happened to Del and his family. But I didn't have nothin' to do with it."

He hustled back into the store, leaving Gunner where he was. Something he'd just said had a trigger in it, and it took Gunner a few seconds to nail it down. Give up the "lady's" name, Hopp had said, when "girl's" would have been more in line with his vernacular. Perhaps implying his friend was older and more deserving of respect than a mere "girl."

Gunner raced off after Hopp, scanning the aisles until he spotted and caught up with him.

"Viola. You weren't just doing the boss's daughter, but his office clerk, too."

Hopp tried to play it off, twisting his face up as if simply incredulous, but he wasn't fooling anybody. "Say what?"

"She grew horns at my suggestion your firing might have been for cause, and you assumed she was the one who had to have told me you were still seeing Zina afterwards. If anybody's got a jones for you, it sounds like it's her."

Hopp just stood there burning, until the initial shock of being found out wore off and he could find his swagger again. "So what?"

"So if she's your alibi for Monday morning, she's about to get tested. Better pray she's up to the task."

Hopp had no answer to that and it was just as well, because Gunner was all done listening.

16

NOT MUCH HAD CHANGED in the six hours plus since Gunner had last seen Zina at the hospital. She'd spent most of the day drifting in and out of sleep, her grandfather said when Gunner called to check in, and she'd done little in the way of talking to anyone, especially to Detectives Luckman and Yee of the LAPD, who had paid her a second visit upon learning from her doctors that she'd regained consciousness.

"Did she tell them what she told us? That her mother did all the shooting?" Gunner asked.

"Yes. But they didn't believe her any more than we did."

"Of course they didn't. It's a lie, Uncle. It's impossible."

"The girl's still heavily sedated. She doesn't know what she's saying."

"Maybe. Maybe not. What reason does she give Noelle for shooting both her and Del? Even if they didn't believe her, the police would have asked her for a motive."

"She said her mother was angry, that's all. That Noelle was a—I won't use the word she used—an evil so-and-so who hated her and wanted her dead."

"And Del?"

"He got shot trying to stop her from shooting Zina."

"It's bullshit. All of it. She's either trying to protect herself or somebody else."

"Yes, but who?"

"Did she say anything else? Has she asked for anyone by name?"

"No. She asked for her cell phone once and got upset when we told her the police have it. We asked who she wanted to call, but she wouldn't say. Who do you think she's trying to protect, Aaron?"

Gunner knew he was asking for trouble, putting this bug in his uncle's ear, but he couldn't see his way around it. "Glenn Hopp. Del's old assistant. Zina's the reason he lost his job."

"Zina? I don't—" But then he did. "You don't mean he was seeing my granddaughter?"

"Apparently so. Noelle learned about it before Del did, but once he found out, Del fired him immediately."

"And that's why he killed my son? Because he got fired?"

"Hold on, Uncle. You're jumping the gun again."

"I'm doing nothing of the kind!"

"Having a motive to kill Del doesn't magically place Hopp in Zina's house Monday morning. Nor does it explain why he would want to kill Zina and Noelle, as well."

"That's for the police to decide. Have you told them about this man yet?"

Here it was: the headache he'd brought upon himself. "No. Not yet."

"Why in God's name not?"

"Because there's somebody I want to talk to first. Somebody who might be able to give Hopp an alibi for the time of the shooting. There's no point dragging him into this if his involvement was a physical impossibility."

"Who is this person you're referring to? I want a name."

"I'll give you her name after I've spoken to her. And if she can't prove Hopp was elsewhere when Del and Noelle died, I'll turn Hopp over to the police myself. Personally." In the space of his uncle's hesitation, he sealed the deal: "You have my word."

Another moment of silence. "The funeral will be held Monday," Daniel Curry finally said. "Holy Cross Cemetery at 11 a.m. Corinne will want your help with the invite list."

"Of course. Anything I can do."

Johnny Rivera's first question was the one people always asked Gunner, under similar circumstances: "How'd you get this number?" Like that wasn't how private investigators spent half their time, figuring out how to reach people who didn't particularly want to be reached.

Rivera had sounded annoyed. Gunner told him he'd gotten the number from Rivera's new employer, Samuel Evans. "If it makes you feel any better, I had to ask more than once."

It didn't make Rivera feel any better at all. Over the last three hours, Gunner had called his cell twice and sent him a garbled, all-thumbs text, and Rivera had every right to assume the barrage would continue until he broke down and hit Gunner back. Having Gunner insist on a face-to-face, rather than simply ask his questions over the phone, only nudged Rivera's petulance closer to the edge.

"This can't wait until tomorrow at the shop?"

"It could, but I'd rather it didn't."

"All right. But you're gonna have to come to me. Wife's got the car right now."

Gunner drove out to his home, a little two-bedroom cottage in Highland Park that sat behind a low cobblestone wall, at the crest of a tall berm of well-tended grass. Night had fallen as he drove and he took the winding steps up to the front door with care, nothing but a single light in one front window to show him the way. The porch was dark and inhospitable. Gunner pushed the doorbell button once, twice, and heard only silence on the other side of the door each time. He knocked instead.

"Yeah?"

It sounded like Rivera, but Gunner couldn't be sure. He gave his name and the deadbolt was tripped, the door pulled open.

"Come on in," Rivera said. He had slippers on his

stockinged feet and a can of Coors in his hand.

He led Gunner back to the source of the only light on in the house, a ceiling lamp hanging over a dining room table strewn with playing cards and cash. Two other middle-aged Latinos sat at the table, cards in hand and beers at the ready, watching Gunner enter the room like something that had slithered in on its belly. They were different physical types—the bald one was built like a lifelong gym rat, and the man with the goatee cast the same rotund shadow as a snowman—but either could have made a good living playing members of the Mexican Mafia in the movies. Perhaps, Gunner thought, because that was exactly what they were.

"I didn't know I was interrupting poker night," Gunner said.

"Hey, don't worry about it," Rivera said. "We were just fucking around. Hector, Joe, this is the guy I was telling you about. The detective who's working for Harper."

Hector and Joe mumbled equally apathetic greetings.

"You want a beer?" Rivera asked.

"No, thanks. Look, if this is a bad time—"

"You said it was important. That it couldn't wait until tomorrow." Rivera retook his own seat at the head of the table. "So let's hear it."

"It might be better if we spoke in private." He addressed Rivera's friends. "No offense."

"I've got nothing to hide and these are my boys. Whatever you want to ask me, ask."

Gunner didn't like it, but the man who owned the house made the rules. "I saw Harper today. He says there was a gun in Darlene's office and that you knew about it."

Rivera tossed a bill into the kitty, picking up the game as if he'd never left it. "Raise." To Gunner: "Is that right?"

"He said you threatened a man with it once. Pete Burdzecki."

The game went on, cards and money crossing the

table in their turn, Rivera and his boys mumbling their plays. It was as if Gunner had never come to the front door. "Pete? Why would I want to threaten Pete?"

"That's a good question, but not the one I came here to ask. What I want to know is, why did you lie about the gun?"

Rivera didn't flinch but Hector and Joe both looked at him at once, each conveying the same unequivocal message: Gunner had crossed the line. Which of course had been his intent. There was nothing else to call a liar but a "liar," and he couldn't do his job and worry about Rivera's honor at the same time.

"Look here, home—" the fat man with the goatee started to say.

"Joe. Go get some more chips for the table," Rivera said, cutting him off. "And bring me another brew." Joe didn't move, so Rivera added, "Do it."

The fat man finally went, disappearing into the kitchen, but not until he'd held his glare on Gunner as long as he could without walking into a wall.

Rivera put his cards down flat on the table. "That was very rude, Mr. Gunner. Come into a man's house and insult him in front of his friends. You could get hurt doing that kind of shit."

"My apologies. But I'm not getting paid to show off my people skills. I'm getting paid to keep Harper out of prison, possibly for the rest of his life. If there was a gun in Darlene's office before she was murdered and you flashed it once at Burdzecki, I owe it to Harper to ask why you played dumb when I asked you about it yesterday."

"Maybe I played dumb because I didn't want you jumping to any false conclusions. Like, if Johnny knew about the gun and liked to wave it around at people, he must've been the one who shot Darlene with it."

"You saying that's a reach?"

"I'm saying it's bullshit. I had no reason to hurt Darlene. Harper's the one who threatened to kill her, not me."

Gunner was beginning to wonder what was taking Rivera's large friend Joe so long to get chips and beer from the kitchen.

"So if you had no reason to kill her, why bother to lie to me about the gun? What the hell do you care what I think?"

Rivera didn't have a ready answer. He and the man named Hector just sat there, trying to see who could glare a hole between Gunner's eyes first. And there was still no sign of Joe.

"It wasn't Darlene's gun," Gunner said, because no other explanation would come to mind.

Rivera's silence held.

"Admitting you handled the gun that killed Darlene would have been one thing. But copping to it being yours would have been something else entirely."

"Okay, so the piece is mine. What does that prove? Darlene was getting jammed up by some crazy fuck in the shop every day, so I brought something in for her to defend herself with. Fuck me. I risked getting violated to help the lady out, and this is the thanks I get. *Chingado!*"

Rivera and Hector addressed each other in a rapid burst of Spanish. What little Gunner could understand was clear enough: What should we do with this black motherfucker?

He tried to remember the last time he'd seen a full kitchen with only one way in or out and came up empty. If Joe eased up behind him now to put a knife to this throat, having slipped out the kitchen by an unseen door, Gunner wouldn't spend the last moments of his life being surprised.

"You didn't have to admit the gun was yours. All you had to do was tell the police Darlene kept it in the office. They've been trying to pin its ownership on Harper from the get-go and it would've done wonders for his case for them to know it wasn't his."

"Fuck Harper's case. I did what I had to do. I tell the

cops the truth about the gun, I become suspect number one, and everything I've worked for for the last nine years goes to shit."

"Not necessarily."

Rivera jumped to his feet, kicked his chair to one side. "Bullshit!"

Gunner watched Rivera's ese Hector to see how far south things were about to go. If the bald man with all the muscles followed Rivera's lead and got to his feet, the Ruger pressing against the small of Gunner's back would have to come out. He usually fought the urge to carry the weapon, but tonight he'd gone with it, still feeling the aftereffects of his unnerving encounter with Zina Curry's neighbor Gordito the day before. What would happen now, if he had to flash the Ruger for these two men to see, would be anyone's guess.

Hector remained seated at the table but there was still no sign of Joe. Gunner wasn't going to wait any longer for him to show. He started to reach for the Ruger...

...and heard a distant toilet flush. He left the gun where it was.

"I think I'll ask one or two more questions and then go, before somebody loses their head," he said.

"That would be a good idea," Rivera agreed. "Ask your questions and get the fuck out of here."

"Burdzecki. Why did you draw down on him that day at the store?"

The fat man named Joe finally reappeared, entering the dining room the same way he'd left it, a beer bottle in one hand and a bag of potato chips in the other. Rivera paid him no mind. "Because he's crazy as fuck, that's why. And I don't like him doing business in my store. He can do whatever he likes out in the lot, but not inside. I'm a parolee, I can't be around that bullshit."

"What kind of bullshit?"

"Drugs, man. What do you think? Pete's a fuckin' dope peddler. He's been slinging shit out of Darlene's shop for years." He saw the look of surprise come over Gunner's face but put it to rest before it could lead to anything: "Happy now? You asked your question and I answered it. Now get the hell out of my house."

He sat back down at the table and picked up his hand. "Joe, where the fuck is my beer?"

17

"YOUR HANDS ARE SHAKING," Lilly said. "Your hands don't ever shake."

Gunner just nodded and sipped his drink. He hadn't really wanted to end one of the longest days of his life here at the Deuce, knowing how conversation would be pressed upon him, but family obligations made Kelly DeCharme unavailable to him and he wasn't yet up to spending his last waking hours alone.

"What happened?"

"Nothing happened. Leave me be, Lilly."

"Last time I checked the news, Zina was still alive. She didn't pass, did she?"

"No. Step off."

The bartender held her ground, looming over him from her side of the bar like a grizzly that had learned to cross its arms. Gunner was only one of four customers in the house tonight, so it wasn't like she had other things to do. Purdee Abellard and her latest girlfriend were lost in each other at a table, and a somnolent white man in a plumber's uniform, whom Gunner knew only as Owen, sat to his left at the bar. Were Lilly to walk out the door and not come back until morning, none of them would have noticed her absence in the least. Even the music Lilly usually had going during business hours had given way to a disinterested silence.

"You had a mother or a wife, I'd let their asses worry about you," Lilly said. "But since you ain't got either, it's left to me. So you're gonna talk to me or get your behind off that stool right now."

Gunner drew the Ruger from his pants and slapped it down hard on the countertop of the bar, drawing a sideways glance from Owen and a flinch from Lilly, who usually reacted to things that startled others exactly as a glacier might.

"I almost drew this on three men tonight. And if I had, there's a good chance I would have used it, whether I had a choice or not. Three men." He faced Lilly directly. "You get it?"

"I get it."

"A man wakes up one morning just a man, goes to bed that night a murderer. Three lives on his conscience forever. And what the fuck for?" He slammed the rest of his drink down, shoved the empty glass toward the bartender. "Because somebody got insulted. One man didn't show another the respect we all think we deserve, and he did it in the presence of other men. Men who would remember who got punked and who got served, and would judge the other two accordingly."

He watched Lilly refill his glass. "My hands are shaking because there's a part of me that wishes I'd emptied that gun in all three of those motherfuckers."

"But you didn't. That's what's important."

Gunner nodded, unconvinced, and took the shot glass up in his hands again.

"You're in a bad way, Gunner. What happened to Del's got you all shook up. Hell, I'm a mess, myself."

"It's not just what happened to him. It's everything I've found out about him and Noelle since."

She wasn't his therapist or his priest, but she was the closest thing he had to either. And she wasn't going to let him out the door now without hearing the rest of what he had to say. So he told her. All of it.

"The great detective," he said when he was done, mocking himself. "My own cousin, my best goddamn friend, and I didn't have a clue about any of it. His finances, his marriage. All the shit he and Noelle were going through with Zina. I thought the sonofabitch was good."

"That's what we all thought. That's all we could think. That's how he wanted it."

"But why? Why carry all that shit around alone if he didn't have to?"

"'Cause that's what you dumb asses do. Carry your troubles around all by yourself, like 'I got this, I'm good.'" She snorted. "Men. You would've done the same damn thing."

She gave Gunner space to offer a rebuttal but he offered none.

"So you think what Zina says is true?" Gunner said. "It was Noelle shot her and Del?"

"No. Not a chance."

"Why not?"

"Because Del killed himself. I've been trying for two days now to prove he didn't, but I can't. Whoever else may have shot Noelle and Zina, Del's death was a suicide."

"Why's the girl tryin' to blame her mother, then?"

"She's protecting somebody. Hopp, most likely. He had a legitimate motive to harm Del, and maybe even Noelle. Del fired him and Noelle was trying to keep him away from their daughter. Hopp was at the center of all their family drama. But he wasn't the one who did the shooting. Zina's covering up for him for some other reason."

"Why can't he be the shooter? If he had a motive—"

"Nobody saw him go in or out of the house that day, Lilly, and Del never said a word about him when he called me on the phone. Del put everything on himself, the same way Zina's putting it all on Noelle, and it's for damn sure he didn't do it for the same reason: to protect Glenn Hopp."

He sounded convinced but was anything but. Hopp had a hand in the deaths of Gunner's cousin and Noelle, and Zina's shooting, in one form or fashion. He was too integral to the crossfire of emotions that had sparked the violence not to have played some vital role in it. But what, exactly, that role had been, Gunner could not fathom.

Because there was no way to reconcile the presence of a fourth person in Zina's house that day with Del's failure—or refusal—to mention it. The same question that had presented itself in the immediate aftermath of Monday's unthinkable tragedy remained, two days later, as unanswerable as ever: why would Del take the blame for shooting his wife and daughter if he hadn't in fact been responsible?

His glass empty again, Gunner offered it forward until Lilly poured him another shot.

"Tell me about Noelle," he said.

"Noelle? What do I know about Noelle?"

"She was seeing somebody. A man named Buddy, her girlfriend said. I'm thinking Del finding out about it is what set all this shit in motion."

"So?"

"So he might not have told me about it, but he could have told you. Friday night, when the two of you were in here reminiscing about J.T. Remember?"

"I already told you what he said that night. He didn't say nothin' about no man named Buddy."

"Are you sure?"

"Yeah, I'm sure. My middle name is Sure."

"Fuck the comedy tonight, Lilly. I don't have the time or the patience. I need you to think about it again, hard: Are you sure Del didn't say anything to you about Noelle having an affair?"

It was the second time in three nights he had dared to get in the big woman's grille, in her own place, with others around to hear it. By rights, he deserved to be tossed out on his ass, after she'd wasted what was left of the bourbon he'd been draining by breaking the bottle across the side of his face. But Lilly's capacity to forgive the reckless blathering of fools, thrown off course by liquor and personal crisis, was a vastly underrated aspect of her character, and tonight she was of a mind to let Gunner's effrontery pass. If barely.

When she was sure he understood his good fortune, receiving the benefit of her mercy, she said, "He asked me about J.T. Did I ever miss him? He said he didn't know how I do it, go on livin' without him. And then he said he'd never make it without Noelle." She paused to find his exact words, as she had the night before. "'I'd never make it, it was me,' he said. And then I said—"

"God willing, he'd never have to."

"Yeah. But he said somethin' right after that, before he gave me that funny smile." She let it come to her. "I remember now. He said, 'We'll see.'"

"'We'll see'?"

"Yeah. That's all. 'We'll see.' And then he smiled." She pieced it together, grew cold with the sudden dawning. "Oh, Lord."

Del's insinuation was clear: Noelle's absence in his life was already a fait accompli. He either viewed his wife's leaving as an inevitability, or had made up his mind to make her go away.

Gunner dug some bills out of his pocket and scraped them across the bar, climbing from his stool onto legs that felt like strands of putty. "I need to find this asshole Buddy that Noelle was fucking around with. Get the word out. I want to know who he is, and where I can find him."

Lilly took the money up in her hand and watched him push away, a drunk doing a yeoman's job of walking like he hadn't had a drink in days.

"You try her cell phone?"

Gunner interrupted his retreat to take one last look at her. "What?"

"A woman's sleepin' with a man, his name and number's usually in her cell phone."

He nodded, sufficiently impressed with the barkeep's head for police work, then turned to complete his exit from the bar.

The great detective.

18

GUNNER CALLED KELLY DECHARME before bedding down for the night to inform her of his visit to Johnny Rivera's crib, and of Rivera's admission that the gun that had killed Darlene Evans was his.

"Wow. That's fantastic."

"I don't know about fantastic. But it is big."

"It's a game changer. He's the owner of the murder weapon and he lied about it to the authorities. Assuming he's got no alibi for the time of Evans's death, he's now just as viable a suspect as our client."

"Or he would be if he had a motive, you mean."

But Kelly would have none of Gunner's guarded pessimism, nor his sympathy for Rivera who, if innocent, was about to get violated for what amounted to the crime of chivalry. Kelly vowed to alert the D.A.'s office of this latest development first thing in the morning and made Gunner promise to check in with her by noon, at the latest.

He lay in bed for six hours afterwards, but nothing he did could have accurately been described as "sleep." Sleep was out of his reach. As the minutes ticked slowly away, inching toward dawn the way a shadow crawls from one side of the earth to the other, he peered into the dark reaches of his bedroom, closed his eyes, and drifted off into a fevered dream, then awoke to start the cycle all over again, exhaustion and anxiety mounting in equal measure. He had much to do the next day and he could barely imagine where to start.

As it happened, Matthew Poole made the decision for him.

Gunner was making coffee in the kitchen, barefoot and only half-dressed, when his phone rang. Poole's name was in the caller ID window.

"You awake?" he asked.

"It's damn near six. What kind of fool would still be in bed before dawn?"

"I'll take a shot: the kind with a life?"

"State your business, Poole."

"No need to worry about Detectives Luckman and Yee, Gunner. They're both straight shooters doing a righteous job on your cousin's case. Which, by the way, is all but a formality at this point."

"Meaning?"

"Meaning sometimes, what looks like a duck and quacks like a duck turns out to be exactly that: a fucking duck. Del had a gun, there was a struggle for it, and his wife and daughter got shot. You know what happened after that."

Poole waited for Gunner to say something.

"I know this wasn't what you were hoping to hear. Del was a good guy, and you loved him. But there's no mistake here. He was the lone shooter; there wasn't any other."

"There couldn't have been anyone else in the house?"

"They can't rule that possibility out completely. There's always a chance somebody chose the exact moment they could slip in and out without being seen. But they found no evidence of such a person, in or out of the house, and the daughter makes no mention of anyone else being there."

"She also suggests her mother did all the shooting. If she's lying about that, she could be lying about a fourth person being in the house."

"Again, there is that chance, but it's slim at best. Did you have somebody in mind?"

Gunner told him what he'd learned the day before about Glenn Hopp, and his romantic relations with both Del's daughter Zina and his assistant, Viola Gates.

"Sounds like quite the Romeo," Poole said, "and asshole, to boot. But unless he can turn invisible and leave no trace of himself behind wherever he goes, I wouldn't count on him being anything more than that."

"Neither would I. I'm just reserving judgment on his innocence until after I've spoken to Gates again."

"Suit yourself. If there's anything else I can do—"

"Noelle's cell phone. I want it."

"Say again? Her cell phone?"

"She had a one-night stand with somebody and I think Del may have found out about it. I want to see if his name and number's in her phone."

"And if it is? How does that change anything?"

"Most likely, not at all. But I still want the phone."

"I get it. This guy's to blame for your cousin going off the rails, so you'd like to find him to convey your thanks. Forget about it, Gunner. Not gonna happen."

"It's not about that, Poole."

"No? Then what's it about?"

Gunner had known the question was coming because he'd been wrestling with it himself for hours now. The truth was, his interest in his cousin's death had long ago ceased to be rooted in the possibility that someone else had killed him, and what was left of his doubt that Del had also shot his wife and daughter was rapidly diminishing.

"Answers. I just want answers," he told Poole.

A sparse crowd of the usual do-it-yourself garage monkeys was spattered around the parking lot at Empire Auto when Gunner showed up around 7 a.m. As he'd hoped, Pete Burdzecki's green Camaro was already there, but it was sans any obvious signs of its owner. Gunner eased Lilly's Tahoe into a space alongside and got out, then went hunting for the man he'd come here to snare.

He found him hidden at the back of the lot, well

around the rear corner of the store, engaged in conversation with two other men. One was a black man of indeterminate age, dressed in the oversized, incongruous clothing of the dispossessed, and the other was a teenage white kid with a skateboard under his arm and a cigarette pressed between his lips. Neither man resembled anyone with the slightest interest whatsoever in auto parts.

Yesterday, Gunner might have paid the trio little mind, but now that Johnny Rivera had shown him the light, he could see the true nature of Burdzecki's business here. The tightly packed huddle he and his mismatched friends were forming, as if to deflect the cold, was the same one buyers and sellers always used to shield an exchange of money for little packets from the prying eyes of strangers.

Gunner ducked out of sight before Burdzecki could take note of him and went straight back to the green Camaro, drawing the Buck knife he always carried from one of his pockets. He snapped the six-inch blade open, waited until he was sure no one was watching, then hunkered down in the space between Burdzecki's car and Lilly's SUV to slice a giant gash in the sidewall of the Camaro's left-rear tire. As the tire silently went flat, he placed a note he had prepared earlier on Burdzecki's windshield, got in the black Chevy Tahoe, and drove off.

Del's office hadn't noticeably changed in the two days since Gunner had last seen it. He had come here halfway expecting his key would no longer fit in the door, so unwelcome had Viola Gates found his last visit, but he got inside without any problem and went straight back to the PC on his cousin's desk. He had promised his uncle he would help Corinne Curry assemble a guest list for their son's funeral, and the contact list on Del's office computer seemed like an obvious place to start.

Of course, Gunner now had his own reasons to acquire a list of Del's contacts, and the info on one lady in particular: Viola Gates.

Had Del been the kind of man to value such things, a more than rudimentary password on his PC might have stopped Gunner cold, but Del had always treated computer security like a chore. Once when Gunner was still working for him, Del had sent him to the bank with his ATM card to withdraw some emergency cash, and Gunner had entered his PIN number, 0987, wondering how long it would be before somebody robbed his cousin blind. Today, 0987 didn't do the trick—but 5432 did.

Pete Burdzecki was already blowing up his phone, but he let all the dealer's calls go straight to voicemail, focused only on opening up the appropriate software on Del's PC and printing out two copies of Del's contact list, one for Corinne and one for himself. When he was done, he closed up Del's office and drove out to the address given for Viola Gates, who apparently lived in a ground-floor unit of a two-story apartment building in West LA, where script on the face read Sandbar Estates above a gold starburst that had lost two of its pointed tines.

"Sorry to bother you," he said when Gates opened the door on his second knock. If she'd found other employment since Del's death, her relaxed mode of dress did not betray it, and only a bible salesman could have drawn a more withering look from her.

"Yes?"

"Del's funeral is Monday. Holy Cross Cemetery, eleven o'clock. I'd like to ask you a few more questions if I could."

"You already asked me some questions."

"These questions are different. They're about you and Glenn."

She hadn't thought he'd be so direct.

"I haven't said anything about you two to the police yet, but then, neither of you has done anything to this point to make me think I should. Can I come in?"

She made him wait to save face, then beckoned him inside, her expression as firm as bedrock. She walked him into the living room but didn't offer him a seat or take one for herself, giving him no excuse to assume he had more than a few minutes to speak his piece and get out.

"Look. I don't know what Glenn told you, but our relationship has nothing to do with what happened to Mr. Curry and his family."

"Your relationship? Describe that for me, exactly."

"It's none of your business, but if you must know, we're friends. Very good friends."

"Lovers?"

He wasn't sure: Was that a smile? "Yes. Something wrong with that?"

"Not particularly."

"Not particularly? Say what you mean, Mr. Gunner. You think he's too young for me. A big, strong buck like Glenn's got no business foolin' around with an old heifer like me."

"Actually, if I had a problem with it, it would have more to do with ethics than age. Or haven't you ever heard the old adage, 'Don't shit where you sleep'?"

"Things happen. Sometimes, two people are just drawn to each other. You said you wanted to ask me some questions." She crossed her arms, a reminder he was on the clock.

"Where were you when Del died?"

"Monday? I was here. It was my day off."

"Were you alone?"

"Yes."

"Glenn wasn't with you?"

"No."

Gunner thought he knew why she didn't ask if it was Hopp who'd told him they'd been together: she had already heard Hopp's account of his conversation with Gunner at Mega Buy yesterday.

"You didn't see him at all that day?"

"No. But I didn't have to be with him to know he didn't kill Mr. Curry and his wife. Glenn could never do anything like that."

"Maybe it wasn't Del and Noelle he was really after. Maybe they only died because they were in the wrong place at the wrong time."

"What are you talking about?"

"I'm talking about Zina. She's the reason Del let him go, not any downturn in Del's business. He was doing her at the same time he was doing you. Don't tell me you didn't know?"

"I know that Glenn did everything he could to put that little bitch off him before she finally broke him down. I know that. She waved her ass in his face until he had to fuck her just to make her stop."

"Only, she didn't stop."

"No. Hell, no! She just kept coming, even after she cost the poor man his job."

Her rage was like a stoked furnace, blowing heat in waves that Gunner could practically feel on his face. She hadn't killed Del or his wife, that was a possibility too remote to ever add up, but if she had nothing else, she most definitely had the temperament for murder, providing Zina was her intended target.

"So maybe that's why he tried to kill her," Gunner said, referring to Del's daughter. "And her parents just got in the way."

"No. He didn't!"

"Did Del know about you and Hopp?"

"No. Of course not."

"Because you knew he wouldn't approve."

"He would have felt the same way about us you do. We've got no business being together. So we were discreet. But Mr. Curry wouldn't have known the difference even if we hadn't been."

"No?"

"No. He was too deep into his own problems to see

anything else. He thought his precious—"

She drew up short, her anger having taken her to the very edge of saying something that would have clearly pained her later.

End of interview. Gunner knew it. And for once, having been ordered out of enough homes over the past twenty-four hours to last him a lifetime, he walked out of this one on his own terms.

From the parking lot of the Westfield Fashion Square in Sherman Oaks, where he hoped to catch up with Tyrecee Abbott's best girl Roxanne Niles, Gunner finally made the call back to Pete Burdzecki the dealer had been begging for for well over an hour.

"Hello?" It was only one word, but Burdzecki made it sound as bitter as strychnine.

"Is this Pete?"

"Yeah, that's right. Who's this?"

"I'm the guy who left the note on your windshield at Empire Auto. Sorry about the tire, man, I was loading up the ride and dropped a—"

"Never mind being sorry. I've been calling your ass all morning. You gonna buy me a new tire, or what?"

"Of course. Why else would I have left the note?"

"All right. So when are you coming back?"

"Back to Empire Auto? I won't be back that way at all today. But I can meet you somewhere out here around noon if you want."

"Out here? Where the fuck is 'out here'?"

"Watts. I'm getting my hair cut at twelve; why don't you meet me at the shop? I'll have your money then. Say, a hundred even?"

"Nah, fuck that. I ain't drivin' out to Watts to meet you at no goddamn barbershop."

"Well, it's either that or wait 'til next week, when I get back from Spokane. My flight leaves at four and I won't have another free minute until then."

"Shit! This is bullshit!"

"Hey, partner, I'm just trying to do the right thing here. I didn't have to leave you a note at all, I could've just driven off and kept my hard-earned money."

"Okay, okay. Fuck it. Where's this barbershop at?"

Gunner gave Burdzecki the name and address of Mickey's shop, working to keep the grin on his face from showing in his voice, and promised to meet him there in a little over an hour.

The stars were all aligned to make Roxanne Niles easy to find. The early morning hour, the encroaching death of the shopping mall as the great American meeting place, and the young woman's supposed girth. How hard could she be to spot in such a sparse crowd if she were as big as Eric Woods described her? But, in the end, Gunner's eye would have been drawn to Tyrecee Abbott's girlfriend had she been sixty pounds lighter and seated in the loge at a sold-out Dodgers game.

It was her hair.

Gunner had seen blond black women before. And he had even seen a few redheads. But this was the first time in his life he had seen a black woman who was both, and in equal measure. The wig Niles wore—and he would not allow himself to believe it was anything but a wig—was divided front-to-back right down the middle of her head, platinum blonde hair to the west, lipstick red hair to the east, with nary a curl to be found in either region. Sitting on a stool beside the cell phone accessory kiosk he had been told to look out for, tipping the scales at two-and-a-quarter easy if Gunner's talent for measuring such things without a scale could still be trusted, she was the human equivalent of a white flare against a midnight sky, as impossible to ignore as a penguin in a lion's den. But it was the yin-yang hair that most did the trick.

"Are you Roxanne?"

She raised her eyes from her phone to look at him with the rapid-fire reflexes of a dying house cat. He realized with some surprise that she was pretty beneath the wig and glittering eyeshadow.

"Yes. Who are you?"

"Tyrecee's mother told me where to find you. Can I ask you a few questions?" He showed her his license, but he may as well have put a Chinese bill of lading under her gaze.

"So you're a cop?"

"Of a sort." She was flashing a level of intelligence her appearance completely belied, demanding he alter the approach he'd planned to take with her. This lady was no dummy. "It's about Harper. I'm working with his attorney and we think you might be able to help us."

"Me? How can I help?"

"You were with Harper at Tyrecee's the night before he was arrested. Remember?"

"What if I was?"

"The woman he's accused of murdering was killed the next morning. We're hoping to prove he was somewhere else at the time. With you, maybe."

"Did Harper tell you that?"

"No. Between the time he went to sleep that night to late the next afternoon, his memory's a total zero. He doesn't know where he was or who he was with. That's why I'm here, talking to you."

She glanced about the mall, searching for an excuse to send Gunner on his way. "I'm working right now."

"I realize that, so I'll make it quick. Were you with Harper that morning or not?"

She turned her gaze back in his direction to study him, measuring his worth as a confidant and taking her sweet time about it.

"Yeah, I was with him."

"You two left the apartment together?"

"That's right. He asked for a ride so I gave him one."

Gunner took a deep breath. One huge hurdle down. "What time would that have been, do you think? When you left the apartment?"

Where someone else might have shrugged, Roxanne Niles thought about it. The coroner had placed Darlene Evans's time of death in the area of 4 to 7 a.m., and Johnny Rivera had reported finding her body at 6:45. If Niles and Stowe had been together at Tyrecee Abbott's crib as late as 6:30, it was game over, the case against Stowe all but eviscerated.

"Around five. Everyone else was asleep."

"Are you sure it wasn't later than that?"

"Yeah, I'm sure. I set my alarm to wake me at 4:50 and we left right after. Harper couldn't sleep and I didn't want Ms. Abbott to know I'd slept over. She's got a problem with me." She smiled with pride.

She had a car and she had a job, and what was far more impressive to Gunner than either, she had a real head on her shoulders. Whatever Laticia Abbott's "problem" with Roxanne was, it had nothing to do with her being homeless or beneath Tyrecee Abbott's level. Maybe she was just too damn smart for Laticia's tastes?

"So where'd you guys go after you left Tyrecee's?"

"We didn't go anywhere. I dropped him off at his crib. Or a bus stop near his crib, really."

"A bus stop?"

"He said he wanted to talk to the driver who threw him off the bus the day before and got him fired. He was loaded and pissed and said he wanted her to know how she'd fucked him up."

Stowe lived with his father somewhere in the Mid-Wilshire district, approximately sixteen miles from Empire Auto. No one had seen the need to do the math prior to this, but Gunner estimated now the bus ride one way was probably around twenty minutes, traffic permitting.

"So what time did you drop him off?"

"I don't know. About 5:20, 5:30?"

"And that was the last time you saw him?"

"Yes, sir."

Gunner saw no reason to hide his disappointment. He and Kelly had the alibi witness they'd been hoping for, except that she wasn't. She'd parted ways with Stowe too early to do them any good.

"Did I say something wrong?"

"Wrong, no. Just unfortunate. But thanks for your help." He handed her a business card, strictly out of habit. "If you can think of anything else that might be helpful to Harper's case, please give me a call."

She looked the card over, like a tip for services rendered she found insulting. "I don't have to call you. I can think of something right now."

"You can?"

"Well, I don't know if it'll help. But I think I know where he got the gun. The one that woman was shot with."

"You saw Harper with a gun?"

"Not Harper. His boy. Eric. I saw Eric with a gun, that night before we left."

"I'm listening." Damn right he was listening.

"It was late. I fell asleep on Ty's bed but everyone else crashed in the living room, watching a movie. I got up to go to the bathroom and saw Eric putting it down his pants. Ty and Harper were on the couch, still asleep. I'm the only one who saw him."

"But I was told Ty's mother threw him out of the apartment that night."

"She did. But once she bounced, he came back."

"Okay. You saw him with a gun. Did he see you?"

"No."

"Then you never asked him about it?"

"What, so he could shoot me, too?"

"You thought he was going to shoot Harper and Ty?"

"Not Ty. Just him. Harper."

"Because he wants girlfriend for himself."

"And girlfriend wants him back. Yeah. You know about that, huh?"

"I heard rumors to that effect. You said he was putting the gun in his pants when you saw it. How do you mean? Like he was putting it back?"

"Yeah. Like, he had it out and he was putting it back."

"And Harper was asleep? You're sure?"

"He looked asleep to me."

Gunner nodded, satisfied. "Your phone have an internet connection?"

She couldn't help but smile, so ludicrous was the question. "Of course."

"Do me a favor and search for an image. Taurus PT-Three-Eight-S."

He thought he'd have to spell it out for her, but she found a decent photo just fine without any help.

"Is that the gun you saw?"

"I guess." She took a closer look. "Yeah, I think so."

"But you never saw Harper with it. Just Eric."

"Right."

"You've been a great deal of help, Ms. Niles. Is there a number I could call you at, in case I need to reach you later?"

"Sure." She recited it for him and he wrote it down in his little notebook, leaving her to find the outdated practice quaint as opposed to pathetic. "Next time you see Harper? Tell him I said hey."

"I'll do that. Thanks again."

19

FOR OBVIOUS REASONS, he hadn't let Mickey cut his hair in years. What hair his head deemed to sprout had long ago been reduced to fuzz a wet razor at home could easily shave away, so a barber's professional hand was no longer necessary. But every now and then, he longed for a sharper look than he could produce himself, staring into his bathroom mirror, so he'd sit in his landlord's chair and let the old man do his thing.

That's how Pyotr Burdzecki found them when he showed up at Mickey's shop that morning, the investigator sitting in the first barber's chair, sheathed in a striped apron, the first barber himself turning Gunner this way and that, using clippers to shape the hair on his face the way a carpenter might wield a rasp to sculpt fine lines into a sconce. No one else sat waiting for their turn in the chair, and the classic soul and jazz that usually provided a soundtrack to the barber's work and endless chatter were strangely absent.

Burdzecki walked in looking like a mouse braving a cage full of owls, his eyes wild with suspicion and resentment for having had this trip into the unknown forced upon him. Gunner had made a point of not giving Burdzecki his name, so all the white man could say by way of introduction was, "I'm supposed to be meeting a man here."

"That would be me," Gunner said.

"Good. You got my money?"

"Sure. But I've got a few questions for you first." Mickey kept right on shaving his face, treating Burdzecki's presence like a buzzing he could barely hear.

"Questions? I ain't got time for questions. Just pay me for my tire and let me get the fuck out of here."

"I think you're going to want to make time for these questions. They're about the murder of Darlene Evans and whatever part you played in it."

"Darlene?" His scowl went to the next level, suspicion turned to fury. "What the fuck is this? Who are you?"

"My name's not important. What is is that I spoke to a young woman this morning named Roxanne Niles. You don't know her, but she knows a friend of yours—Eric Woods—and she says she saw Eric with the gun that killed Darlene the night before she died. I think he was placing Harper Stowe's fingerprints on it while Stowe slept."

"So? What's that got to do with me?"

"Maybe nothing. Except that there isn't much that goes down at Empire Auto that you don't know about, considering the nature of your business there and how often you're there to conduct it. If anybody was in position to see Eric coming or going that early in the morning, either before or after killing Darlene, it was you."

"I didn't see anything."

"No? Then I'm sorry I bothered you. Enjoy the rest of your day."

"What about my tire?"

"Fuck your tire."

Burdzecki hesitated, undone by the choice Gunner was forcing upon him: leave before any real damage could be done, or stay to find out exactly how much this smart-ass nigger really knew? He walked right up to one side of the barber's chair, putting less than an arm's length between himself and the man sitting in it.

"Why the hell would Eric wanna kill Darlene?"

"I don't think he planned to kill her. I think he only planned to rob her. But something went wrong. Either Darlene put up a fight or refused to cooperate, something, and she wound up dead."

"So if you already know so much, asshole, what the fuck do you need me for?"

"I need you to tell me why. Eric's got a thing for his boy Harper's girl, so the robbery had to be motivated at least in part by his need to make Harper go away. Framing him for an armed robbery he didn't commit was the endgame, but I wonder if there wasn't more to his jacking Empire than that. Like the most obvious, for instance: money."

Burdzecki didn't say anything.

"The first time I talked to Eric down at Empire, you pulled into the lot like a man who was overdue to get paid. And Eric went running after you like maybe he was the one you'd come there to see. I didn't make the connection at the time, but now it seems hard to miss."

"So he owes me money. What's that prove?"

"How much is he into you for?"

"That's my business."

"Forget I asked. The answer's obvious. It's got to be well over five bills to have caused so much drama."

"Hey, I didn't cause any goddamn drama. Like I keep tellin' you, whatever Eric did, it don't have shit to do with me."

"You mean, unless you put him up to it?"

Finally, Burdzecki had his answer: this nigger knew just enough to be dangerous.

"I want my money," he said. "Right fuckin' now."

Gunner didn't move.

Mickey finally turned his clippers off. "I think you'd better leave," he told Burdzecki.

"Shut the fuck up, old man. Nobody was talkin' to you."

"This is my shop. I tell you to leave, you leave."

Burdzecki slapped the barber hard across the face, nearly knocking him off his feet. Gunner was out of the chair in a flash, apron flying. He clamped his left hand around Burdzecki's throat and threw a punch with his right, sending the white man crashing to the floor. Gunner moved in to follow before he could rise, but Burdzecki scrambled out of reach, right hand seeking something hidden at the back waistband of his pants.

Gunner pounced, frantic, knowing all was lost if he couldn't stop Burdzecki from drawing whatever weapon he was reaching for. The two men tumbled across the checkered floor, cursing and grunting, each one grasping for any part of the other he could get a hand on. But it was a struggle destined to be brief; Burdzecki was younger and stronger, and Gunner quickly realized it was only a matter of time before Burdzecki's right hand finally found the gun at his back.

"You wanna slap me now, son?"

Burdzecki froze as if struck by lightning. Mickey was holding a gun of his own to the white man's head. He'd run to the back office and retrieved Gunner's Ruger P-85.

Gunner struggled to his feet, trying to catch his breath, but Brudzecki remained on the floor, motionless, eyes locked on the Ruger and the angry old man holding it.

"Thanks, Mick. I can take it from here," Gunner said. He held out his hand for the Ruger.

But Mickey paid him no mind. "Wants to come in my place and treat me like one of his bitches. Hit me with an open hand like somebody he ain't gotta worry about hittin' back." There was a tremor in his voice and his eyes were damp.

"Give me the gun, Mickey."

Again, Gunner's landlord ignored him. His only point of interest in the room was Burdzecki.

"How about it, boy? I look like a bitch to you? Speak up!"

"No," Burdzecki said. Like Gunner, he understood this was no game Mickey was playing.

Gunner reached for the Ruger once more, and this time, Mickey turned to face him.

"I'm a grown man. I might be old, but I ain't too old to

deserve some respect!"

"He's a fool, Mick. Fuck him. Come on."

Like a melting ice floe, Mickey slowly gave in, reason taking hold. He came up from his crouch to place the Ruger in Gunner's outstretched hand. The exchange was the chance Burdzecki had been waiting for. He finally got his own gun free. Gunner snatched the Ruger from Mickey's grip just seconds before Burdzecki could fire, and put a single bullet in the white man, just under the left eye.

"Jesus!" Mickey cried.

Burdzecki's body crumpled to the floor and grew still. Blood began to spill across the black and white linoleum beneath the dead man's head.

Gunner kicked the black Hi-Point .45 out of the corpse's hand, then stepped forward to check the body for a pulse. He didn't find one.

"You might want to put up the 'Closed' sign," he told Mickey, starting toward his back office, "while I call 911."

Hours later, when a relentless LAPD was through with him, Gunner met Kelly DeCharme for a late lunch out on the plaza of the LA County Courthouse building downtown, where a vast, roiling sea of attorneys and jurors was taking in the sun. At a table near the running fountain, he told the attorney about his busy morning, working his way backward from his killing of Pete Burdzecki. Any other time, he would have admired the woman's understated beauty, the way she made this charcoal business suit look like a skin-tight evening gown—but not today.

"Oh, babe, I'm so sorry," DeCharme said.

She worried over him as he relived the scene at Mickey's in detail, the incident having left a mark upon him she understood would only grow over time. But when he got around to offering his report in full, shorthanding his recent interviews with Eric Woods and Johnny Rivera, she couldn't help but let her excitement show.

"We have to have Woods picked up before he disappears," she said, glowing. "If he finds out Burdzecki's dead and how he died, he might put two and two together and take off."

"He might."

She dug her cell phone from her purse and made her second call today to the D.A.'s office, this time to schedule a meeting with the ADA assigned to Harper Stowe's case. As luck would have it, she was told the ADA was in the county courthouse now, so she asked for a call back as soon as the attorney was out of trial. Then she went back to her half-eaten salad.

"I wish we had more. All we had on which to base a case against Woods were Burdzecki and the girl. Now that Burdzecki's dead—"

"Now that he's dead, I'm not."

"Of course. You only did what he forced you to do. It's just...." She took a deep breath and laid a hand on his. "I just wish there'd been some other way."

She was echoing the very doubts he held himself. But there had been no other way. "I drew him out to Mickey's to talk, that's all. I thought he'd be more forthcoming outside his comfort zone. Nothing would have happened had he just walked away. But he came in there with a Hi-Point .45 in his pants and slapped a sixty-eight-year-old man with an open hand hard enough to spin his head around. If I hadn't killed the sonofabitch, Mickey would have."

Kelly gave in with a nod and a smile, but it was obvious she still had her reservations.

"Can you come with me to talk to the ADA?"

"Afraid not. I'm going by the hospital to see Zina, try to get her to talk to me one more time."

"Really?" She seemed surprised.

"You don't think I should?"

"It's not that. I only...." She was on shaky ground, and she proceeded with the care of someone who knew it. "Her mother was having an affair. A daughter takes that sort of thing very hard, Aaron. As would her father. If they both knew and, in a fit of jealousy, Del did what the police say he did—what the evidence suggests he did—is it really that hard to see Zina defending him after the fact by blaming it all on Noelle?"

If he were willing to be honest about it, his answer would be no. It was the way all the pieces were finally starting to form a whole. But all he said now was, "I have to hear it from her. She knows the truth and she owes it to her grandparents to tell it. She owes it to me to tell it."

The attorney in Kelly wanted a better answer than that, but she let him go without asking for one, much to his relief.

With their granddaughter no longer at death's door, Daniel and Corinne Curry had finally left her unattended at the hospital, if only temporarily. Gunner called his uncle on his way to Harbor UCLA and discovered Del's father and mother had Ubered to their hotel room in Inglewood, intending to be there just long enough to shower and change clothes. It was Corinne's first such respite since their arrival in Los Angeles and only Daniel's second.

"Wait for me there," Gunner told his uncle. "Both of you. We need to talk."

"We can talk when we get back to the hospital."

"No. We need to talk now. Away from Zina."

"How far away are you?"

"Ten minutes. Wait for me, Uncle."

Daniel Curry didn't like it, and Gunner knew his wife would like it even less, but Del's father said, "We'll wait ten minutes. Then we call for another ride. If it gets here before you do, we're leaving."

Gunner agreed to his uncle's terms and hung up the phone, then drove straight out to Harbor UCLA, where his niece finally had no one around to protect her from his questions.

Zina was sitting up, sipping juice through a straw, when Gunner walked into the room. A tray of untouched food sat on a stand beside her. Sleepy-eyed and listless, the crown of her head wrapped like a cocoon, she was still strung up like a Christmas tree with wires and tubes, but this seemed more precautionary now than necessary to keep her alive.

"You're looking good, Zina," Gunner said. He set down the flowers he'd brought along as a peace offering on a chair.

"I don't wanna talk to you," his niece said, her voice as coarse as a gravel path. Her left hand groped for the nurse's call button at her side, but Gunner found it first.

"Take it easy. Nobody wants to hurt you. I just want to ask you some questions."

"No. Leave me alone!"

"I'll leave you alone when you tell me what I want to know."

"I already told the police everything." What little voice she had started with was already half-gone.

"You told them a lie. Your mother didn't shoot your father, Zina. He killed himself."

"No." She shook her head.

"His wife was having an affair. His business was in the toilet, and his only employee was doing his office assistant and his daughter, both." Zina's eyes lit up the room. "Oh, yeah, I know all about you and Glenn. And I know Del didn't like it any more than your mother did. What I don't know is why he took that gun to your crib Monday morning. Something set him off. What was it?"

"Nothing. I don't—"

Gunner leaned in close, his patience for the girl's lies, and all the others he'd been fed over the last four days, completely exhausted. "Listen to me. If you don't tell me today, you'll tell me tomorrow. Or the day after that, or the day after that. Because I'm not going to stop asking. Not ever."

She tried to call out for the nurse, but the sound she made had no chance of reaching the door, let alone the nurse's station beyond.

Gunner bore down. "He'll take the blame for everything, do you understand? If you don't tell the truth, they'll put Del in the ground Monday morning thinking they're burying a murderer. Is that what you want?"

Her head swung side to side. "No!"

"Then tell me what happened. Why did your father bring that gun to your crib?"

"He didn't! I brought it!"

It was the kind of confession that should have come with tears, some show of anguish or remorse, but all this was was fury. Bitter, unrepentant fury.

"Daddy didn't have nothin' to do with it. He shouldn't have even been there!"

"What's that supposed to mean?"

"It means I called her, not him!" She had to stop to catch her breath. "If Momma'd just stayed out my bus'ness, let me see whoever the hell I wanted to see, none of this would'a happened. But she had to ruin everything!"

"So you killed her?"

"No! It was an accident. Daddy tried to take the gun away. He thought I was gonna use it, but I just wanted to make Momma say it. What she did."

"You mean her affair with Buddy."

The name took her aback. "What?"

"Your mother's lover. Somebody in a pos⋅ion to know told me she'd had a one-night stand with a man named Buddy."

Surprise turned to something else as he watched, a smile slowly making its way onto the young woman's face. She would have laughed outright had the pain not become too much. "You don't know anything," she said, her voice dripping with pity for his ignorance.

"Everything all right in here?"

The nurse who stood at the open door was not the same black woman who had forcibly removed Gunner from the room the day before; this one was white and more formidable. She had posed the question for Zina to answer, but her eyes were on Gunner and the call button remote he still held in his hand.

"No!" Zina said, expending the last ounce of voice she had left. "Make him go away!"

A brief stalemate held them all at bay, the question of how much Gunner cared to chance his second eviction from the room in twenty-four hours hanging in the balance.

The nurse started toward him. "Sir—"

"It's okay. I'm leaving." He turned to Zina, tossed the remote call button into her lap. "But I'm not done with you."

20

"I TOLD YOU HE WAS GOING TO DO THAT. Didn't I?" Corinne Curry said. Her lips were trembling with rage.

"Yes, you did." Daniel Curry stood toe-to-toe with his nephew in the middle of the Currys' hotel room, no less infuriated by Gunner's insolence than his wife. "You lied to us, Aaron. You played us for two old fools. But I tell you what—it'll be the last time."

"Uncle—"

"If you go out to that hospital again without our permission, I'll have you thrown in jail. So help me God, I mean it."

"It's not my lies you should be worrying about. It's hers. Zina hasn't told the truth about a damn thing to anybody—me, you, the police—since she came out of that coma. And I'm sick of it. I wasn't going to wait any longer for her to come correct."

"You don't know what's correct!" Corinne said, both hands balled into fists at her sides. "And neither does she."

"You're wrong. She does know. And now, I think I might know, as well." He turned to his uncle. "Are either of you interested in hearing it?"

Corinne wanted no part of what Gunner had to say, but her husband overruled her. He had been riding Gunner to find the truth behind their son's death since he and his wife stepped off the plane at LAX three days ago, and now that Gunner thought he knew it, Daniel Curry could hardly turn a deaf ear. So Gunner sat Del's parents down and told them how he thought it had all played out, a mixed bag of what he knew to be fact and what he yet could only surmise. It was a pathetic and lurid story of a man caught in a downward spiral on all sides: the wife he obliviously neglected and forced, at least momentarily, into the arms of another man; and the pair's daughter, a self-absorbed woman-child who, stung by her parents' constant interference in her sex life, somehow learned of her mother's infidelity and became so enraged by the hypocrisy of it that she sought to rub her mother's nose in it at the point of a gun. A gun that eventually went off, as guns were so prone to do, in terrible and unpredictable ways.

At least once, Corinne Curry tried to put a stop to Gunner's account—"No, no, no," her head swiveling from side to side in denial—but Daniel Curry shut her down with a look, paving the way for Gunner to make it through to the end. He took it all in without having uttered a single word himself. Wringing the life from a white handkerchief clutched in his right hand, Del's father had no greater desire to believe what he was hearing than his wife, but this was the puzzle he had charged his nephew with piecing together, and he was bound to receive it with an open mind.

"So you're saying Noelle and Zina were shot in a fight over the gun, and then Del used it on himself? Why would he do that?" Daniel Curry asked.

"The struggle for the gun started with him. Noelle was dead and it probably looked as if Zina was, too. He thought he'd just lost the two most important people in his life and that he was the one responsible."

"But he wasn't responsible!"

"No, of course not. But, in his mind, Noelle's adultery and Zina's affair with Hopp were both a direct result of his failure as a husband and a father, respectively, so what happened in that house was ultimately on him."

"That's plain foolishness," Corinne said.

"Of course it is. But that's how Del would have seen it, nonetheless."

"And this man Buddy that Noelle was seeing?" Del's father asked. "What about him?"

"I still haven't identified him, and I'm not sure there'd be any point in my continuing to try. Because he played no part in what happened at Zina's home Monday, whoever he is, and from all indications, he and Noelle were together on only the one occasion. He's a sleeping dog. We should probably let him lie."

"Yes, but—"

"Zina likely knows who he is and I suspect she'll let us all know, too, eventually. There's nothing to be gained by giving him a name now other than to have one more person to share some part of the blame for all this."

They all fell silent for a moment, Gunner feeling suddenly and thoroughly exhausted. Del's mother returned to shaking her head, the movement muted this time as she wiped tears from both eyes. Her husband, meanwhile, continued to strangle the handkerchief clutched in his hand, fingers biting down on the cloth to exorcise the anger he was desperately trying to contain.

"Glenn Hopp," Daniel Curry said, bringing them all back to the present.

"Yes," his wife said bitterly. "Are we supposed to treat him like a 'sleeping dog,' too?"

"Well, he's certainly less innocent than the other," Gunner said. "In fact, you could argue he bears more responsibility for Del's and Noelle's deaths than Del did himself. But there'd be no way to prove that in court, and there's nothing illegal about what he did, in any case. Sleeping with a man's office assistant and his adult daughter, both, may be highly unethical, but there's no law against it, no matter how much damage he causes."

"We could sue," Del's father said.

"Yes, Uncle. You could try. But based on what? Most of what I've just told you is conjecture. I'm fairly confident it's accurate, but the reality is, we'll never know what's true until Zina gives a full account of what happened, and there's no guarantee she ever will. Especially if she thinks the truth will interfere with her future relationship with Hopp."

"'Future relationship'? You don't mean to say the child expects to go on seeing him?" Corinne Curry asked.

"I'm afraid that's how it sounded to me at the hospital an hour ago. As far as Zina's concerned, Hopp didn't cause her to do what she did Monday—Noelle did. Noelle's the villain here, not Glenn Hopp."

The thought was appalling, even to him. Zina had lured her mother into a trap. Whether she planned to use the gun or not was almost immaterial; her intent was to point a loaded weapon at Noelle and let whatever happened, happen. All because she didn't want to be told who to sleep with by a woman who was herself an adulteress. An adulteress whose infidelity had come at the expense of Zina's beloved father.

Had Del not shown up without his daughter's invitation at her crib Monday—either by chance or at the urging of his wife—perhaps things would have turned out much differently. But as it was, both of Zina's parents were dead today, and the events leading up to their deaths could be traced straight back to her decision to draw an unarmed woman into a heated argument while she herself was armed to the teeth.

Again, silence was threatening to overwhelm them when Corinne Curry stood up from the hotel sofa and said, "We have to go. Zina's waiting for us."

Her husband and nephew both turned to give her the same look of disbelief.

"Corinne. I can't. Not right now," Daniel Curry said. Pleading.

"You can and you will. We must. No matter what she's done, the child's still our granddaughter, and you and I are all she's got left."

"You go. Let Aaron take you."

"We're both going."

"No!" Gunner's uncle erupted, and for a moment Gunner thought he might have to put himself between Daniel Curry and his wife to keep him from taking her in hand. "Not tonight. If I go to that hospital tonight, I don't know—I don't know what...." He dared not speak the rest. He shook his head, determined, and one more time, told Corinne, "You go."

But his wife had lost her tongue.

Gunner rose to his own, unsteady feet. There was nothing for him to do but what he most wanted to avoid. "Come on, Miss Corinne. I'll take you."

21

FRIDAY MORNING, Gunner allowed Kelly DeCharme to cajole him into joining her for a meeting she had set up with Harper Stowe III's father, Harper Stowe Jr. She had briefed the elder Stowe on the latest developments in his son's case over the phone the night before, and now she wanted to do so in full, in person. But not without Gunner riding shotgun. Despite the good news she was bringing him, the old man was nearly as mercurial as his son and twice as large. Kelly didn't care to be in a room with him alone if he chose to turn their conversation sideways.

They arrived at Harper Jr.'s tiny but clean Spanish-style home in Hyde Park at the agreed upon time of 11 a.m., sharp. Green lawns cut as flat as a tabletop lined the block, and a leaf blower growling several yards away made the only sound on the street as they left Kelly's car.

Harper Jr. opened the door for them before they could ring the bell, as if he'd been watching out for them for hours. Gunner had never met the man before but had been warned by Kelly what to expect, and still Stowe made an impression. He looked like an ill-tempered, sixty-year-old triathlete. His hair was as white as dried-out driftwood, pulled back into a single cord of dreadlocks, and he was dressed for a yacht party out at Marina del Rey: blue silk shirt, tan slacks, and brown closed-toe sandals. The brown leather belt cinching the slacks to his waist might have last fit Gunner twenty years ago.

"You're late," he said. Making an accusation that only held merit if one measured punctuality to the nth degree.

They paused in the foyer just long enough for Kelly

to make introductions, then Stowe led them through the house and out to the back patio, a simple red brick affair dotted with potted plants and a single reclining deck chair. The view was of a backyard lawn as green and immaculately trimmed as the one out front, interrupted only by a lemon tree rising from its center. Stowe waved his guests into seats at a round wrought-iron table and took one for himself.

"Just made a pot of coffee," he said, a cup in his hand. "Or I can get you water, if you prefer."

Both Kelly and Gunner declined the offer. Getting down to business, the attorney said a few words to lay the groundwork for him, then gave Gunner the floor to describe at length the previous day's events, which she'd only briefed Stowe on the night before. Harper Jr. listened intently, anger building, and allowed Gunner to finish before speaking his piece.

"You know where they'll find him, don't you?" he asked.

The question wasn't directed at him, specifically, but Gunner volunteered to answer it. "Woods?"

"He'll be with Tyrecee. At her mother's place, or a friend's. Wherever he is, she knows about it."

"It's certainly possible."

"It's more than possible. They were in this together. She's no less responsible for what Eric's done to my son than he is."

"You're saying Tyrecee put Woods up to framing Harper for murder?" Kelly asked.

"Of course. Don't sound so surprised."

"I'm sorry, Mr. Stowe, but I haven't seen anything yet to suggest that's the case," Gunner said. "In fact, depending on who you believe—the girl's mother or her girlfriend—Woods's infatuation with Tyrecee might be strictly a one-way street."

"Don't be ridiculous." He chuckled derisively. "They stabbed my boy in the back. Both of them. But they aren't going to get away with it."

They waited for him to go on, curious to hear what he was inferring, but he just sat there staring back at them.

"Mr. Stowe," Kelly said, "I think we should just wait to see what Woods has to say when he's taken into custody before we make any assumptions about Tyrecee."

"Oh, I'll wait. Not much else I can do. But I'm not going to wait long. If that little bastard doesn't turn up soon, I'll go out and find him myself."

"That wouldn't be a good idea," Gunner said.

"You think I give a damn whether it's a good idea or not?" The old man turned all his ire Gunner's way. "Harper's been through hell. Fought in a goddamn war we shouldn't even be in, for a cause no sane person could explain, and he came back less than half the man he was when he left. Can't sleep, can't eat, can't go four hours straight without the pain in his head and his legs driving him to madness.

"And for what? How do people show their thanks for all his service and sacrifice? By treating him like a dog, that's how. A sick, mangy dog unworthy of their time or pity!"

He stood up from his chair, tossed the remainder of his coffee into the yard. When he turned back around, his eyes were filled with tears. "He used to be beautiful. There wasn't anything he couldn't do. And now...."

He paused, shifting from morose to furious in the blink of an eye. "He loves that girl, do you understand? And he looks upon Eric as a brother. When he finds out what they tried to do to him, how they murdered that woman just to be rid of him, it's going to tear him apart. They may just as well have put a bullet in his head!"

Gunner and Kelly shared a glance, neither wanting to be the one to warn Stowe again that any assumptions about Tyrecee Abbott and Eric Woods being coconspirators in Darlene Evans's murder were as yet premature.

"Mr. Stowe—" Kelly said.

"No." Harper waved a hand to cut her off. "Don't. I'm all done talking. Justice is going to be done for my boy, and words aren't going to do it. How soon before he can be released?"

"That's hard to say. But certainly not before Woods is found and questioned."

"And Tyrecee? What about her?"

"I'm sure the police will want to talk to her, as well. But—"

Stowe broke in on her again. "I want to thank you both for all you've done for my son. And I appreciate your coming by."

And just like sheep, Gunner and Kelly were herded out to the front door.

Nothing about funerals distressed Gunner more than the wait leading up to them. The space of time between a person's death and their eventual internment always felt endless to him, and the relief of having all the pomp and circumstance of a traditional service behind him—the vehicular procession, the halting obituaries, the graveside ceremony drowning in real and fake tears—could not come soon enough.

This time, however, it was Del he was waiting to see set deep in the ground, which only made his impatience that much more acute.

The final two days leading up to Del and Noelle's Monday morning funeral passed in relative lethargy, one empty hour leading to the next. The dual tracks of work he'd been doing for Kelly DeCharme on the one hand, and in the service of his cousin's memory on the other, were all but done. Suddenly, Gunner had little to occupy his mind but grief.

He might have joined the search for Eric Woods, whom the cops had yet to find, or continued to press his niece Zina for more details about the fate of her parents, but he lacked motivation for the one and the will for the other. Woods would turn up eventually, with or without Gunner's help, and Zina—as Gunner had fully expected she would—had shut down again, even in the face of her grandparents' intensified questioning. Once Del and Noelle had been laid to rest, Gunner would share with the LAPD the girl's confession that she, and not Del, had provided the gun that killed her father and mother, and whatever truths she had yet to tell would be forced from her. But for now, as a gesture to Zina's own sense of loss, he was content to leave her be.

For her part, Kelly did what she could to preoccupy Gunner until Monday could come. He spent all three weekend nights in her company and most of the day Sunday. Otherwise, Gunner waited for Monday's arrival as a recluse, either shutting himself up in his office at Mickey's or in his living room at home. The thought of visiting the Deuce barely crossed his mind.

Lilly Tennell was left with no choice, then, but to bring the Deuce to him.

When she showed up at his door early Sunday afternoon, Gunner immediately recognized the moment as an unprecedented one. The barkeep had never been to his crib before, uninvited or otherwise.

"You finished with my car?" she asked the instant Gunner answered her persistent ringing of his doorbell.

She hadn't come about the car, and had only halfheartedly told the lie, but they both played along as if Gunner were too dumb to know better.

"You want it back? I'll get the keys." He turned as if to do so.

"Ask me in first, fool. Where the hell are your manners?"

She stepped inside his home like the new owner and didn't stop until she was sitting in the living room, the full freight of her giant frame taxing the cushions on his couch to the limit.

"What do you want, Lilly?"

"Somethin' to drink, to start. Water's good, but ice tea would be better. You got ice tea?"

He went to the kitchen and filled a glass with tap water, taking care to make it as tepid as possible, just for spite. He put the glass in her hand and she sipped at it without complaint, taking her damn sweet time, stretching his patience out like an elastic band she was testing for it's breaking point.

"What do you want, Lilly?" he asked again.

She put the glass down on his coffee table, made a face he'd never seen her make before. "We were gonna have a baby."

There had to be more. He waited for it. But that was all she said.

"Say what?"

"Me and J.T. Nineteen sixty-eight, same year they murdered Dr. King. I was nine weeks on in August but lookin' like I was fifteen." A smile crossed her face. "It was gonna be our first; we talked about having four whenever the subject of kids came up. But J. changed his mind. When the time came to put up or shut up, the nigga got cold feet. So—"

"Lilly, why are you telling me this?"

"So I killed it. I went to a doctor like he said and killed my baby, 'cause that's what he wanted and I never wanted anything he didn't want."

Gunner tried again: "Lilly—"

"Shut the fuck up and let me finish!" She wiped her eyes dry with the palms of both hands. Her cheeks shone wet in the darkness of Gunner's living room. "I cried for four days straight. Hadn't cried like that before and I ain't cried like that since. And when I stopped cryin' I got mad. The kind of mad you can hardly see through, or move with it inside you. I hated everything and everybody, I wanted to make the whole world pay for what I'd done. But I didn't hate nobody more than I hated J.T. I hated his ass most of all."

Finally recognizing his place in this exchange, Gunner just let her go, all the way to the end.

"So one night while he was asleep I got out'a bed and got the gun he used to keep in his nightstand drawer. And I put the barrel of that motherfucka right up against his head"—she demonstrated with her hand—"and waited 'til he opened his eyes to pull the trigger." She held the pose, arm out, finger twitching inside the invisible weapon's trigger guard....

"I wanted to do it. Jesus Lord, I did. But somethin' stopped me. I just stopped. To this day, Gunner, I don't know why." Her arm fell loose to her side.

"I thought he was gonna kill me. Hell, I wanted to die. But he didn't. He just took the gun away from me and tucked me back into bed. Like nothin' had even happened." She chuckled, met Gunner's gaze straight on. "Ain't that some shit?"

Gunner nodded. It sounded just like the John Tennell he remembered.

Lilly wiped the tears from her cheeks again, picked up her empty water glass and held it out for him to take. "Get me some more water. And let it run cold this time."

He did as he was told. When she was finished drinking, she took in a deep breath, exhaled it luxuriously. Decompressing.

"You understand what I'm tryin' to tell you?"

"I think so," Gunner said. Sitting down in a chair now because he wasn't sure he could stand. "You could have been Del."

"That's right. I could've. And if I'd'a killed J.T. that night, what would that have made me? Somebody else? Somebody different? No. I would've been the same person I've always been. No better and no worse."

She stood up. He didn't.

"I got pushed. Taken somewhere I don't ever wanna go again. And when that happens, you push back. Hard.

Sometimes too hard. Del pushed back, Gunner. That's all. It don't change who he was."

"No. But it doesn't bring Noelle back, either," Gunner said. "Does it?"

The big woman shook her head—why did she bother even trying?—and left him sitting there without taking the car she claimed she had come for.

Because it had no other choice, Monday eventually came, bringing Del and Noelle's funeral along with it. The weather was mild, the sun in a pale blue sky bearing down on the earth with all the intent of a lit match. Still, Gunner squirmed around in his suit like it was a bear skin, necktie and closed shirt collar making him work for every inhaled breath. He sat at the edge of his bed, elbows on his knees, for nearly an hour after he dressed, dredging up the energy for what lay ahead, but he never shed a tear. Tears would only come, he knew, when his pride could least afford the embarrassment.

When there was no more time left to avoid it, he and Kelly DeCharme picked Daniel and Corinne Curry up at their hotel and drove them out to Holy Cross Cemetery, where both the funeral service and internment would take place within minutes of each other. It was a relief not having to endure the joyless ritual of a funereal motorcade, but no one inside Lilly's car seemed to feel relieved. Del's parents, sitting together in the back seat, were as somber and silent as Gunner was numb.

The chapel at Holy Cross was already half-full when they arrived. Gunner had to guide Del's parents past a gauntlet of mourners to get them to their seats at the front. Among those in attendance, Gunner saw his old friend and attorney, Ziggy Zeigler; Lilly and a host of Acey Deuce regulars; Mickey and his second-chair, Winnie Phifer; Noelle's girlfriend Iris Miller; and Viola Gates and Glenn Hopp, situated conspicuously separate from each other, Hopp standing at the back as if he didn't expect to be there for the entire service. Gunner gave him a small nod: I see you. I know what you've done. This is partly on you. There was no sign of Noelle's brother Lavar Long, who would have been easy enough to spot, by way of his sheriff's deputy escort, had he been granted release from Lancaster State Prison to attend his sister's funeral. Gunner wondered if he'd even asked permission. Zina's absence, understandable as it was, left a noticeable void in the room.

For the first time in Gunner's recent memory, a eulogy was given by a man of the cloth who actually seemed acquainted with the deceased. Monsignor Frank Villanueva, Del and Noelle's priest at St. Patrick's Church, did the honors, and talked about the pair not simply as two good people who had died before their time, but as friends he knew more than superficially. It was a refreshing departure from the generic, one-size-fits-all dissertation that had become the norm for such speeches of late.

Not surprisingly, no mention was made of murder-suicide, nor any blame assessed to either the living or the dead. Instead, Villanueva spoke with eloquence and grace about the arbitrary nature of life, and how a man or a woman's faith is not always up to the challenge of overcoming its most debilitating turns. Sometimes, he said, the darkness wins out and people are moved to do its bidding. Decent people, loving people, people who have simply grown too tired or too lonely to bear the weight of their pain a minute longer. So they break down and, on occasion, deliberately or otherwise, they take others down with them.

Asking God for reasons is pointless. God can only offer comfort to those left behind, not answers.

Withhold your judgment, the monsignor beseeched the congregation. Condemn the act, but neither the man nor the woman whose lives were lost as a result of it. Because they took their truth with them, Del and Noelle, and with it the right of others to say what they would have done differently, under the same circumstances.

It was a moving eulogy. Villanueva stepped down from the podium to the sound of women softly sobbing and men clearing their throats, the latter in a vain attempt to choke back tears of their own. But Gunner was not among them. Gunner felt only anger. Del could go to hell. None of this had to happen. He could have sought some other way out, or given Gunner the chance to help him find one.

Fuck Del.

It was only upon taking his cousin's casket up in his hands, as one of six pallbearers tasked with removing Del to his final resting place, that Gunner finally broke down and cried.

Del and his wife were buried in adjacent plots, side by side as in life, on a rising slope of grass where headstones cast the only shade. The same band of mourners who had filled the cemetery chapel circled the gravesite to hear Villanueva bid the pair one final farewell, some cried out, others only now moved to weep in earnest. Gunner stood behind the two white folding chairs in which his aunt and uncle sat, at the limit of what he could quietly endure, and measured the faces around him. All were grim and ashen, but two, in particular, were unique. Viola Gates was glaring daggers at Glenn Hopp, who remained at the same remove out here he had established inside the chapel. It was a silent exchange similar to the one Hopp and Gunner had engaged in earlier, with one notable exception: this time, Hopp was glaring back.

"Amen."

Villanueva's closing jolted Gunner's attention back to the ceremony. The funeral party repeated the priest's call, and just like that, it was over. As the congregants kissed and hugged and dispersed to leave, pausing to shake

Villanueva's hand or hover around Del's parents to pay their final respects, Gunner looked back to find Hopp again and saw that he was already gone, walking off in the distance among the parked cars lining the access road. He had stopped at the door of a burgundy sedan when Gunner's attention was drawn away.

"We're all going over to your place now. Right, G?"

Gunner turned to see Mickey standing at his elbow, bursting out of a blue suit that was the first Gunner could recall him ever wearing.

"That's right. Everything's already set up." Lilly's part-time bartender Pharaoh Doubleday had offered to organize the funeral repast and was waiting at Gunner's crib now for their arrival.

As Mickey moved off, Kelly DeCharme approached, bringing Del's parents along with her. The crowd had thinned, and the four of them were nearly the last people still at the gravesite.

"I think we're ready to go," Kelly said, and Gunner understood her meaning immediately. Daniel and Corinne Curry looked worn and tired, as if this day had wrung every ounce of life from their bones.

Gunner helped Kelly rush the pair to Lilly's SUV, which stood at the curb close by, and gently closed the doors behind them. He drove them all out of the cemetery with great care, the black Tahoe joining a long line of cars flowing toward the exit, and passed Glenn Hopp's burgundy Honda Accord on the way. Only it wasn't Hopp's Honda, at all. It belonged to Viola Gates, who sat behind the wheel now, weeping into both hands.

Either mourning the death of Del and Noelle Curry or the deep, meandering scar someone had carved all along the side of her car, from its nose to the very tip of its tail.

22

THE POST-FUNERAL REPAST for Del and Noelle's mourners was uneventful. Neither Viola Gates nor Glenn Hopp attended. Gunner was not surprised.

He walked through his own house those three hours like an uninvited guest, taking part in conversations he had no interest in, looking past people as if they weren't really there. Later, he knew he must have eaten something because he wasn't hungry, but pressed to describe what he'd put on his plate, he wouldn't have been able to recall.

The irony was, the event was precisely the kind of social affair Del would have helped him suffer through. Like spies on a mission, they would have come together again and again to trade jokes and observations, sotto voce, about everyone in attendance, laughing in secret one minute, openly and without shame the next. They would have had too much to drink and raised too many eyebrows. But Del was gone and he wouldn't be coming back. The vital role he had played in Gunner's life over the last twenty-six years—confidant, advisor, voice of reason—was vacant now and was likely to remain so until Gunner himself was laid to rest.

Near the end of the evening, when most of the guests were gone and Del's parents, sitting next to each other on Gunner's couch, could barely expend the effort it took to speak anymore, two late arrivals appeared at the door: Jeff Luckman and his partner Chris Yee.

"We don't need to come in," Luckman said when Gunner answered their knock. "We just wanted to offer the department's final condolences to the Currys."

"That's a classy move. And I'm sure they'll both appreciate it." Gunner glanced over his shoulder at his aunt and uncle, saw the same cold, empty look on both their faces. "But maybe another time."

"This was a mistake," Yee said, giving Luckman a disapproving side-eye. "Our apologies."

"It's not like that. It's just..." Gunner tipped his head toward the living room behind him. "It's been a long day and I'm not sure seeing you guys would end it on the right note."

Luckman nodded. "Sure."

"But I meant what I said. It was good of you to come. And as long as you're here..." Gunner stepped out on the porch and closed the door behind him. "I may as well tell you something I was going to put off until all this was over."

He told them about Zina and Glenn Hopp, and everything he believed he knew about their roles in the deaths of Del and Noelle. Luckman took it all in with a physician's cool, but not so much Yee.

"So you were gonna tell us all this when?" he asked.

"As soon as I had the funeral behind me. Tomorrow, Wednesday at the latest. I had enough on my plate and didn't see any point in rushing it."

"You didn't?"

"No. Why would I? Your case is closed, isn't it?"

"Not officially. But even if it were, what difference would that make?"

"It would make a lot of difference if you're not going to reopen it without sufficient cause. And I was guessing this info doesn't qualify." He turned his attention to Luckman. "Or maybe I was mistaken?"

When neither cop answered fast enough to suit him, Gunner said, "Of course not. You're all about the physical evidence, you've been telling me that from day one, and knowing it was Zina who brought her father's gun to the party wouldn't have changed that evidence a whit."

Yee started to protest. "Even so—"

"No. The man's right," Luckman said. "It would have been nice of him to share it, but it doesn't change anything. We already knew the argument was over the girl. That they were arguing about Hopp, in particular, is barely relevant."

"She lied to us, Jeff," Yee said. "Why would she do that unless she were hiding something?"

"We just found out what she was hiding: she put the gun in her father's hand. Which isn't a prosecutable offense without intent, but it could be she's unaware of that detail."

"Still—"

Luckman looked to Gunner, all done quarreling with his partner. "It's like this, Mr. Gunner: We could keep our investigation open another month, and two things would remain the same—Hopp wasn't at the scene and our shooter was Mr. Curry. All we'd have to show for our efforts would be a better understanding of what led your cousin to do what he did, nothing more. But hey, we're just servants of the people. If you want me and Chris to hold off another week to close our case, we'll start it back up at the hospital tomorrow morning. Just say the word."

It wasn't a choice Gunner wanted to make. It was his uncle's place to make such decisions, not his. But Gunner knew what Daniel Curry would decide, and he knew that Luckman was right: in the end, they'd all be right back where they started, and where they were right now: with the finding that Del had killed his wife and himself and narrowly missed killing Zina. Everything else was just noise.

The front door opened behind him. Kelly had noticed his conspicuous absence inside the house and come looking for him. She eyed the cops suspiciously.

"You okay?"

"I'm fine. These are the detectives who've been looking into the shooting at Zina's." He briefly introduced them. "They just came by to offer their condolences and let me know they're wrapping up their case this week."

"Oh. I see."

A meaningful glance passed between the three men, sealing a deal unspoken, and Kelly smartly pretended not to notice.

"We were just saying goodbye," Luckman told her. "We just need another moment, if we could."

"Of course." She gave Gunner one more chance to escape, but he nodded to decline it and she left them alone again.

"Matt Poole says you and him go back a long ways," Luckman said.

"That's true."

"He says you can be trusted, and we understand he didn't say that about too many people when he was on the job," Yee added.

Gunner just shrugged. Where was this going?

"We only found two phones in the house," Luckman said. "Mr. Curry's and his daughter's. We can't release them to you or anybody else until our investigation's officially closed, tomorrow at the earliest." He reached into his inside jacket pocket and withdrew a folded sheath of paper. "But here's the call logs and contact lists we pulled off both. I'm afraid that's the best we can do."

He held the lists out for Gunner to take and Gunner obliged.

"Thanks."

"Forget about it. Please give our best to your aunt and uncle for us, will you?"

Without waiting for Gunner to answer, Luckman gave his partner a nod and the two cops went on their way.

23

GUNNER LANDED A NEW CLIENT Tuesday morning. Robin Kraft was a twenty-four-year-old adoptee from Portland who'd found her birth mother living on the streets in Compton one month ago, then promptly lost track of her again, after having searched for her for over a year. Homeless missing persons were a bear to trace and Gunner had tried to put Kraft off when she'd first approached him about the gig, but his caseload was wide open now that his work for Kelly DeCharme was essentially over and the lady was a referral. Referrals begat referrals. He had her in and out of his office at Mickey's to sign his standard service agreement by 10 a.m.

Afterward, he spent the next two hours in a chair at the front of the shop, vaguely listening to Mickey parry and thrust with new customers and old as his clippers hummed away, hair piling up on the floor like falling snow. It had been over a week since he'd done this, a force of habit that almost always brought him peace and amusement. These were his people, his friends and his neighbors, and the things they filled the place with—stories true and false, laughter and tears, history lessons and heartfelt confessions—ordinarily warmed him to the core. But today, it was all just a din. A distraction from the melancholy he'd been engulfed in since the last guest at Del and Noelle's repast had left his home the night before.

And yet, like a drug seeping into his bloodstream, the old, familiar ambiance at Mickey's began to penetrate his mood. How could it not?

"Any nigga watches a show like that don't deserve

a damn TV," his landlord was saying now, the "show" in question being a new cable channel, alternative history drama about a Confederacy that had won the Civil War. Three episodes had aired so far to critical acclaim, and Cal Ebbitt, a retired Marine who leaned further right than most of Mickey's regulars, had just risked expulsion from the premises by daring to ask if anyone besides himself had given the show a look.

"How can you say that if you ain't never watched it?" Cal asked.

"I don't have to watch it. The South won the war, didn't it? And the slaves remained slaves, didn't they?"

"Yeah, but—"

"Did Lincoln get shot?"

"Of course."

"Then what the hell's the 'but'? Shit, man, that ain't a TV show, that's a Southern Republican's wet dream!"

Hobie London, who was sitting under the edge of Mickey's razor getting a shave, laughed and stomped his feet on the footrest of Mickey's chair. Mickey laughed, too, and used his free hand to bump Hobie's offered fist. It had taken a while, but the barber was finally coming out of the funk he had been in since Pete Burdzecki had taken him to the very edge of murder.

Cal Ebbitt was unmoved.

"I don't know why I bother with these Negroes," he said to Gunner. "They got minds as closed as a fireworks stand on the fifth of July."

Gunner had just started to look over the printout of contacts and calls Jeff Luckman and Chris Yee had pulled off Del's and Noelle's phones for the first time, when Cal drew him into this latest Trueblood dialogue of the absurd.

"You liked the show, huh?" he asked Ebbitt, trying to examine the printout and come out of his shell at the same time.

"I don't know if I'd say I liked it. I just think the idea's kind of interestin'. I mean, ain't you ever wondered about what your life would be like if the South had won the war and all of us were slaves today, just like our ancestors?"

"I've thought about it."

"Hell, we've all thought about it," Hobie piped in.

"You gotta be dead not to think about it," Mickey added.

"And?"

"And I'm not so sure what we've got is all that different," Gunner said.

"What? Man, be serious!"

"I couldn't be more serious. Oh, whatever we are now, we aren't slaves. Not by a long shot. But we aren't freemen, either. We're something in between. The poorest among us are trapped in a limbo state of perpetual poverty and institutionalized neglect, and you could almost make the argument that keeping them in bondage would have been more humane."

He was voicing a gross exaggeration of how he really felt, of course, but such was the state he was in today, emotionally depleted and desperate for someone to blame. The white man was always an easy target, too easy and too hackneyed, but the habit white folks in the entertainment industry had of foisting their most racially insensitive daydreams upon the general public under the facade of "speculative" storytelling held a special place on Gunner's list of pet peeves.

"Preach, G!" Hobie called out.

"I'm not preaching. I'm just talking. You can watch any damn thing you want, Cal. I'm sure the writers will fill that show with some very smart and honorable slaves. But me, I've got zero interest in the South rising again, on TV or anywhere else."

Sufficiently shamed, Cal fell silent, and Mickey and Hobie did the same, suddenly feeling sorry for him. In the awkward hush that followed, Gunner's phone rang. The number for the incoming call was blocked from his view.

"This is Aaron Gunner."

"You've gotta find Reesie quick. Before that crazy old fool finds her first."

The female voice was breathless, fear and agitation riding on every word.

"Who is this?"

"This is Laticia Abbott. Reesie's mother. Please, Mr. Gunner, you gotta find her for me. I think he had a gun."

"Who?"

"Harp's father. He just come by here looking for Eric. He thinks Tyrecee's been hidin' him somewhere."

"Has she?"

"Hell, no. At least, not in my house she ain't. She knows better."

"Where is Mr. Stowe now?"

"Out lookin' for Reesie. Ain't you heard a word I been sayin'?"

He called Roxanne Niles the minute he got in the car. If anyone knew where Tyrecee was, it was her. She wouldn't want to be a snitch, but Niles had the smarts to understand the danger her girlfriend was in if Harper Stowe Jr. was really out on the street looking for her and Eric Woods, armed with a gun.

"I think I might know where she's at," Roxanne said over the phone, without a moment's hesitation. "But I've gotta take you there."

Gunner didn't want the company but she wasn't going to be dissuaded. He picked her up at the mall where he'd met her before and followed her directions as she offered them.

"Where are we going?"

"My father's house," she said, issuing an admission that pained her. "He lets me and Ty hang out there when we need a place to chill. I think he loves Ty more than he loves me."

"And Eric?"

"Daddy wouldn't care if he was with her or not. He doesn't care much about anything, to be honest. Especially when he's been drinking."

It was a long drive. Roxanne's father lived at the north end of Long Beach, in a staid, boxy apartment building in the shadow of the Long Beach Memorial Medical Center just south of the 405. Gunner had suggested early on that they call ahead, but no one answered when she tried her father's number. "They probably shut his phone off again," Roxanne said. "He forgets to pay the bill all the time."

The two-story complex they arrived at was the perfect complement to the man she was describing, unkempt and past its prime, living on the razor's edge of civilized society. Two trash bins that looked like they hadn't been moved or emptied in ages sat at the curb, as cracked and broken as a pair of stale cookies.

Roxanne turned to get out of the car, but Gunner held her back. "What unit is he in?"

"Fourteen."

"You need to wait here."

"No. I told you."

Gunner drew the Ruger from the shoulder holster under his jacket, gave her a good look at it. "Listen. If Eric's in there, this could get ugly fast. I don't want you getting hurt."

"You don't have to worry about that. I can take care of myself." She hustled out of the car before he could stop her and proceeded to enter the building, giving him no recourse but to follow.

Inside, she led the way to unit fourteen, on the second floor, above an empty swimming pool stained unsettling shades of brown. She knocked on the door and waited, Gunner standing to one side with the Ruger pointed earthward behind his back.

"Daddy, come get the door! It's Rox!"

She knocked again. Music thudding from a downstairs apartment made it difficult to tell if anything was stirring inside number fourteen. Roxanne was fishing a set of keys from her purse to open the door herself when a short, wiry black man with a head of wild, gray hair on the other side of the threshold beat her to it.

"Little girl," he said, two eyes red and wet as marbles smiling at the sight of his daughter standing there. "How you doin'?" He seemed to take no notice of Gunner.

"Daddy, we're looking for Tyrecee. Is she here?"

Her use of the word "we" tipped him off that he'd missed something, and now he glanced to one side to register Gunner's presence. "Who's this?"

"He's a friend. We've got to find Tyrecee. Is she here, Daddy?"

The question perplexed him on some level. "I dunno." He blinked to clear his head, genuinely unsure. Gunner couldn't smell the alcohol on his breath from where he stood, but he imagined it had to be intense. "I think so."

Roxanne turned to Gunner for direction, made a small move toward the door. He shook her off.

"Eric! This is Aaron Gunner! Are you in there?"

Nothing. The girl's father just stood there in the doorway, utterly confused.

"Eric!"

"Go away!" Tyrecee Abbott shouted back. It sounded more like a plea than a demand.

Roxanne barged inside, Gunner moving too slow to stop her for the second time in ten minutes. He pushed past her father into the apartment and gave chase, cursing under his breath, the gray-haired man at the door lagging behind them both. The small apartment was dark and thick with the smells of hard liquor and spoiled food. Roxanne carved her way through it to a back bedroom and stopped abruptly at the open doorway.

Inside, Eric Woods stood wide-legged alongside an unmade single bed, Tyrecee Abbott clutched tight to his chest, the blade of a large carving knife pinned to the girl's throat. Feet bare and naked from the waist up, Woods looked disheveled and tired, as if he hadn't slept in days, and aside from her usual petulant air, Tyrecee appeared to be only slightly better off.

"Get the fuck outta here, bitch," Woods snapped at Roxanne. Then, catching sight of Gunner: "You too, man. I'll kill her, I mean it!"

Unfazed, Roxanne started to plunge into the room, but this time Gunner moved first, stepping forward to block her path to Woods and assert himself as the person Woods was going to have to address. Roxanne's father, meanwhile, hung back behind his daughter and Gunner, his sense of puzzlement growing.

"Hey! What's goin' on?" he asked, befuddled.

"Put the knife down, Eric," Gunner said. "It's over." The Ruger was still in his right hand, down at his side but out in the open where Woods was meant to see it.

"Ain't nothin' over!"

"Yes. It is." Gunner lifted his arm and fired a single round into the bed, at an angle intended to keep the bullet inside the room if it passed straight through. Woods and Tyrecee jumped as one at the sound. He let the gun fall back down to his side. "I'm in a real bad way. This past week has been one kick in the teeth after another. If you hurt the girl, I'm going to kill you."

It wasn't an idle threat. He didn't want to do this, take the Ruger in hand yet again to gamble with Tyrecee's life in this way, but there was nothing else to be done. Two weeks ago, he would have had the wherewithal to play this thing out, to give Woods room to surrender on his own terms, in his own time. But not today. Today, Del and Noelle were still fresh in the ground, and over the last six days, Gunner had suffered all the fools he could take. Burdzecki. Gordito. Johnny Rivera. Burdzecki had tested his patience and lost.

Now it was Woods's turn.

"Put the knife down, son. Live to see another day."

"Hey! Hold up a minute!" Roxanne's father said, alarmed.

His daughter spun on her heels, threw a hand up to silence him. "Daddy, hush!" She looked back at Gunner again, realized with some trepidation that she and everyone else in the apartment aside from Woods might as well have been a thousand miles away, for all Gunner cared about them as witnesses.

"Please, Eric! Do what he says!" Tyrecee pleaded.

But Woods wasn't ready to believe Gunner was serious. He had to study the man with the gun a full minute longer before the truth, as unvarnished and uncomplicated as Gunner had stated it, became obvious to him: he wasn't walking out of here in possession of either his hostage or the knife he was holding to her throat. If he tried to do either, he would draw his last breath on the floor of this apartment, in this room.

"Fuck it," he said, and tossed the knife down at Gunner's feet.

He fell into a sitting position on the edge of the bed, spent, as Tyrecee snatched up the knife and joined the others at the door. "You fucking bitch! I hope your ass gets the death penalty!"

"Call 911," Gunner told her, as much to shut her up as anything else.

For a moment, she looked as if she might argue, questioning why she should be assigned such a task and not her girl Roxanne, but then she gave Gunner's face a closer look and decided to do as she'd been told. As Tyrecee moved off, Roxanne's father still standing mute behind them, Roxanne subjected Gunner to an inspection of her own and said, "You weren't really—"

"Yeah. Yeah, I was."

She had nothing more to say to him until the police arrived.

24

"SO, HOW YOU HOLDIN' UP?" Lilly asked.

"I'll live."

"I know you're gonna live. I'm askin' how you're doin'."

The Deuce was packed with people tonight, bodies and voices competing for every inch of real estate, so it irked Gunner that, despite everything else she could be doing, the bartender was here, towering over his little table, sweating him. He took another swallow of Wild Turkey, his throat burning, and said, "I feel like shit. But compared to yesterday, probably a little less so." He looked up to meet Lilly's gaze directly. "How's that?"

"Well, you ain't gettin' worse, so I'll take it as an encouraging sign. I heard they caught that boy. The one they think killed his boss at that auto parts place."

Nothing escaped the woman. Gunner had never spoken to her directly about his work for Kelly DeCharme, and had only discussed it here with Kelly herself out of the barkeeper's hearing, yet Lilly somehow understood his connection to the news reports of Eric Woods's apprehension this afternoon. He knew she came by this knowledge honestly—it was only her alacrity for gossip at play, not magic—but he still found it cause for wonder.

"Yeah."

"So that other boy—the one your lawyer friend represents—I guess they'll be letting him go."

"They should, yeah. Eventually." According to Kelly, who'd been monitoring the status of his interrogation by the LAPD, Woods had already issued a confession to

Darlene Evans's murder, so Harper Stowe III's eventual release from jail seemed all but a certainty.

"You want another?" Lilly nodded at Gunner's near-empty glass.

He did, but he shook his head forlornly. "Del's father is meeting me here any minute. I think I'd better slow my roll a little."

"He and the wife goin' back home to Atlanta?"

Gunner winced. "No. They've decided to stay a while, or at least until Zina's back on her feet. They're moving out of their hotel into Del's crib tomorrow." He emptied his glass. "I'm sure she'd prefer they didn't bother, but they've got their minds made up."

Were he his aunt or uncle, he would have let the girl rot, happy to let her recover from her injuries alone, as best she could. But Daniel and Corinne Curry were good Catholics, and their threshold for granting forgiveness was far lower than that of their nephew. They did not find Zina beyond redemption for all the hell she had put Del and Noelle through just to be with a man like Glenn Hopp. They wrote her insolence off as the work of the devil, playing on the insecurities and raging hormones of youth. Just as they had hope her body would heal over time, so too did they believe her soul could be similarly rehabilitated.

Gunner held no such belief.

He was still too angry for that, and imagined he would remain so indefinitely. Zina was old enough to have known what Hopp was, and all the trouble she was asking for by sleeping with him. She shouldn't have needed her parents to tell her. But they had told her, both of them, and in Noelle's case, even ridden her like a pack mule trying to steer her out of harm's way. Had she heeded their advice early on and let Hopp go, her mother's own indiscretion might not have enraged her to the extent that it had, and the argument over it that took place in Zina's home eight days ago, culminating in the death of two people and the near-death of another, might never have occurred. But Zina had held on to Hopp instead, recklessly and foolishly, and everything she had put at risk in doing so, other than her own life, had been lost in the bargain.

Gunner didn't much care that she lacked the clairvoyance it would have taken to see just how tragic her selfishness would ultimately prove to be. She should have changed course regardless, if only to spare her parents the indignity of having their place in Zina's life assumed by a jackass like Glenn Hopp.

"Did you hear what I said?" Lilly asked, miffed.

"I heard you."

"Bullshit. I said you owe me a half tank of gas."

It wasn't a half tank, it was only a quarter. His aunt and uncle having declared their independence by renting a car of their own, Gunner had returned the big woman's ponderous Chevy Tahoe to her earlier in the day, cleaned and washed but with less than the full tank of gas he had promised her.

"Put it on my tab."

"Nigga, you ain't—"

"Here he comes now, Lilly," Gunner said, eyeing the bar's front door. "We'll have to settle this later."

Lilly's head swiveled around on her massive neck to give her a view of Daniel Curry, working slowly through the crowded house toward them, dodging outthrust derrieres and sloshing drink glasses on every side as he came. He looked as out of place as he obviously felt, too stern and sober for a dive like the Deuce by a mile; but he was meeting his nephew here of all places at his own request, so Gunner had no reason to feel for him.

Gunner stood from his chair to greet the older man. "Uncle, this is Lilly Tennell. She owns the Deuce. You should remember her from the funeral and the repast yesterday."

"Yes, of course." Daniel Curry held out his hand for

Lilly to shake. "It's good to see you again, Ms. Tennell."

"It's good to see you, too, Mr. Curry. But if you don't call me Lilly, I'm gonna have to ask you to leave."

Del's father smiled, then laughed uneasily. "Lilly it is."

"Please, sit down." Both Gunner and Daniel Curry did. "Can I get you anything to drink? On the house, of course."

After much hemming and hawing, Gunner's uncle ordered a whiskey neat, and off Lilly went, willfully neglecting to ask if Gunner had reconsidered his decision to remain dry. In her absence, Gunner watched Daniel Curry survey the place with two parts awe and one part horror, the sights and sounds of all these poor, loud, unruly black people overwhelming his senses.

"You sure about this?" Gunner asked. "We can go somewhere else a little more quiet if you like."

"No. You said this was a place where my son spent a lot of his time. I wanted to see it for myself, find out who his friends were."

Gunner nodded. He hadn't yet grown a soft spot in his heart for Daniel Curry, but he was beginning to understand him. "You want me to introduce you to a few?"

"Not right now. Maybe later."

"How's Miss Corinne?"

"Corinne is fine. Better than her husband, anyway. She's stronger than I am. Always has been."

"And Zina?"

"She's coming along. Still in a lot of pain, and she sleeps five, six hours at a time. But she'll be okay. Doctor Low says they plan to move her out of the ICU tomorrow."

"That's great news." It rang laughably false, even to him.

"She's our granddaughter, Aaron."

Gunner just nodded.

Lilly appeared with Daniel Curry's drink and moved off again as soon as she set it down before him, summoned back to the bar by a short, heavyset man with blue-black skin and an almond-shaped head who'd been haranguing her most of the evening as only this Acey Deuce regular could.

"Who's that?" Gunner's uncle asked.

"The one doing all the shouting? That's Beetle Edmunds."

"'Beetle' like the bug?"

"Yeah. You don't see the resemblance?"

"And those two?" Del's father pointed at the pair of men sitting at the far end of the bar to Beetle's right, dominoes splayed all across the countertop between them. They were fussing over the basketball game on TV like two hens arguing over the choicest spot in the yard for pecking.

"The older man in the blue work shirt and Dickies, making all that noise about the Lakers, is Howard Gaines. He knew Del well, and was also at the funeral yesterday. The other brother, the youngster with the beard, I don't really know. I've seen him in here a few times, but I haven't caught his name yet."

"You mean Rip?" somebody walking by asked. It was Evelyn Claremont, a short and lean, thirtysomething veteran of the US Navy who popped in and out of the Deuce for weeks at a time as her family here and in Longview, Texas, permitted. She was cute and smart as a whip, and could put a man in his place both figuratively and literally without breaking a sweat, but Gunner was occasionally put off by her interest in bad hair extensions and other people's business.

"The boy sitting next to Howard. Yeah," Gunner said.

"Yeah, that's Rip." She smiled at Gunner's uncle, who was obviously smitten. "I mean, his name's really Robert, Robert Jackson, but we've been calling him Rip ever since Pharaoh said he looks like Rip Black Winkle." She started to laugh. "On account'a that beard, right? Rip Black Winkle!"

She threw her head back and let the laugh go, too amused to do anything else. Jackson's black beard was indeed a marvel, long and pointed and unruly, but Gunner wasn't sure the moniker Pharaoh Doubleday had saddled him with was deserving of this much mirth.

"And what do they call you?" Daniel Curry asked.

"Me? I'm Evelyn. But some people call me Evie."

"Evie? That's all?"

"What do you mean, is that all?" She propped a hand on a hip and grinned, ignited by the old man's flirting. "What do you think they should call me?"

"Evelyn," Gunner cut in. Partly out of embarrassment for his uncle and partly because something about this conversation had just become vitally important and he needed to figure out what it was. "This is Del's father Daniel Curry. He and his wife came down from Atlanta for the funeral."

Evelyn's face fell. The exact reaction Gunner had been hoping for. "Oh. I'm so sorry. I loved Del. We all did."

Properly deflated, as was also Gunner's intent, Daniel Curry took her proffered hand. "Thank you."

Gunner gave the woman a look, distracted to the point of annoyance now, and she caught its meaning instantly. She eased her hand free from the grasp of Gunner's uncle and said, "Well, it was nice meeting you. Have a pleasant evening."

She hurried off.

"That was rather rude, Aaron."

"Why did you ask her that? What people call her?"

"It was an innocent question." Del's father sipped his drink. Gunner waited for him to finish. "Beetle. Rip. Pharaoh. Seems like everyone in this place has one nickname or another. I just thought, someone as attractive as that young woman is—"

"Wait." Gunner raised a hand to silence his uncle in mid-sentence. "Hold on a minute."

He withdrew the printed contact and call log lists he'd had in his pocket all day and began to pore over the one the LAPD had downloaded from Zina's phone first. He was looking for one name, in particular, and he found it.

"Shit."

Del's father leaned in, trying to see what it was that had his nephew so agitated. "What is it? What's wrong?"

Gunner moved on to the second list, the one the cops had taken off Del's phone. The name was different here, but the phone number was the same.

He dropped his head, riding the fine line between astonishment and disgust. The contempt he'd been reserving for Zina alone over the deaths of her parents had just changed hands.

"Aaron," Daniel Curry tried again.

"Sorry, Uncle. But I can't explain right now." He stood up from the table, jammed the printouts back into his pocket. "Looks like I've got some midnight oil to burn."

Later that night, he went back to Zina's, armed with the spare set of keys he had neglected to take from her parents' home nine days ago. Noelle's Buick Encore was still on the street where he last saw it, her purse undisturbed on the passenger seat within.

With one eye open for an ambush should his friend Gordito spot him rooting around in the dark, he used the key on the chain emblazoned with a Buick logo to unlock the Encore's doors, then slipped inside the car. He turned on the interior dome light, reached into Noelle's purse, and pulled out a large Motorola smartphone in a rubberized pink case. He tried to turn it on, hoping his luck would hold, but it wasn't to be: the battery was dead. He'd have to recharge it to complete the object of his mission here.

He fumbled around in the Encore's center console, found Noelle's charger and cable, and beat a hasty retreat.

The next morning, Viola Gates parked her car in the open lot of Del's office building to find Gunner waiting for her. She'd received a call an hour earlier from someone who identified himself as a Detective Richardson from the LAPD, asking her to come, but that had just been Mickey Moore doing Gunner a solid.

"He really put his heart and soul into that, didn't he?" Gunner asked, nodding at the scratch Glenn Hopp had inflicted upon Gates's Honda at Holy Cross Cemetery two days before. He had planned his approach so that she wouldn't see him coming, and she visibly jumped at the sound of his voice.

"What are you doing here?"

"Detective Richardson won't be coming. He sent me in his place."

She started to get back in the car, but he barred her way, setting his feet to deliver the clear message that he wasn't going to be moved. "I know what you did, Viola. And I can tell it right here with just you listening or I can put it on blast. Is that what you want?"

"I didn't do anything."

"You did plenty. Starting with falling for a man who couldn't keep his joint in his pants if his fly were sewn shut."

She tried to push past him. "Let me go!"

He grabbed her by both arms, his grip a vise, prepared to make this as ugly as she wanted it to be. "Somebody set Zina off last Monday by telling her that her mother had been sleeping around on her father. She got Del's gun from the office and called Noelle down to her crib to confront her about it."

"Let go of me!"

"She didn't expect Del would show up, too, but he did, probably because Noelle urged him to come, thinking Zina intended to commit suicide, not murder. And you know what happened after that."

"I don't know anything! Let me go, I said!" She managed to pull one arm free. An old man stepping out of a blue Ford he'd just parked nearby gave them a long look, then went on into the building.

"You were the one who set Zina off, Viola. You told her about Noelle's affair. Because it wasn't just some random stranger she slept with, was it? It was your man Glenn. He wasn't happy just doing Del's daughter and office assistant, he had to fuck his wife, too."

Gunner had only become sure of this himself last night, after all of Daniel Curry's talk about nicknames at the Deuce had inspired him to look for and find one among the list of contacts the LAPD had pulled from Zina's phone: Bunny. Not Buddy, as Noelle's girlfriend Iris Miller had mistakenly recalled, but Bunny—as in rabbit. As in Hopp. Someone whose phone number matched that of Del's former assistant in Del's own cell phone contact list.

"You don't know anything," Zina had told him at the hospital, laughing at his stupidity, when he'd asked her who Buddy was. But now he was in on the joke.

Davis ripped her other arm loose and staggered back a step, trembling with rage. "Yes, he fucked her. Once! Because her husband wouldn't touch her anymore and he felt sorry for her. He only did what she practically begged him to do."

"And is that how you saw it that Monday, when you called Zina to tell her all about it?"

"What call? I didn't call anybody."

"Get off it. I've got Noelle's phone and the call logs off Zina's. You don't think I recognize your number when I see it?"

"So what if I called her? How was I supposed to know what that little bitch would do?" Her eyes grew wet and her voice started to quaver. "All I wanted was for her to leave us alone! She's the one to blame for what happened, not me. All I did...." She choked on the denial, tried to offer it again. "All I did was tell her the truth."

"The truth? What, that the man she's in love with is a dog?"

"Yes! He's a dog who doesn't love her, or me, or anybody else. We're all just meat to his sorry ass, and so was her mother!"

She saw the look come over Gunner's face and realized what she'd said, what kind of monster she sounded like. "Oh, no. I didn't...." Gunner just glowered back at her. "Please. I never meant Mr. Curry or his wife any harm. I was angry and I didn't think. If I could go back—"

"You can't," Gunner said, his words a hammer striking a nail. He stepped aside to clear her path to the car. "All you can do is live with it. If you can."

He doubted that she could, and the thought gave him the strength to walk away without doing to her what he'd done to Glenn Hopp, less than an hour before.

25

IT ALL CAME POURING OUT of Zina eventually, as Gunner had known it must. She was selfish and immature, and just dumb enough to convince her uncle that Glenn Hopp would not be the last sexual sociopath she would trust with her heart; but she wasn't a monster. She had feelings, and love for both her departed parents, and she had borne the guilt of what she'd done to pave the way for their deaths until she couldn't bear it in silence any longer.

Her grandmother was the first to hear the story in full. Daniel Curry was still keeping his distance from the girl, not trusting himself to remain calm in the face of any more of her lies, so he wasn't in her hospital room when she finally came clean.

By her own account, things had gone down pretty much as Gunner suspected.

She had received a phone call Monday morning from a livid Viola Gates, who had taken much pleasure in informing her that the man they both loved had slept with Noelle Curry. It was an outrageous claim, surely a falsehood invented by Gates to drive a wedge between Zina and Glenn Hopp; but to Zina's astonishment and outrage, her mother could not convincingly deny it when Zina called her to pose the accusation. And neither could Hopp.

Half out of her mind with jealousy, Zina retrieved her father's gun from his office and demanded a meeting with Noelle at Zina's home, intending to both terrorize the truth out of her mother and rub her face in her incredible hypocrisy. The thought that their exchange might end in someone getting hurt, let alone killed, never entered Zina's mind. And the last thing she expected was for Noelle to invite poor Del to the party.

By the time Zina's father arrived, his wife had confessed all to their daughter and was pleading for her forgiveness. Beside herself with anger and grief, Zina was still holding the gun and threatening to use it, on herself if not Noelle. Del tried to force the issue and a struggle for the gun—first between him and the two women, then between the two women alone—ensued. The weapon went off three times, two bullets striking Noelle and one wounding Zina....

And that was the last thing Zina could remember, prior to waking up in the ICU at Harbor UCLA Hospital a day later.

The immensity of the tragedy she'd triggered, inadvertently or otherwise, was becoming clearer to her by the day. There was no way of getting around it. But it wasn't her decision to steal Del's handgun from his office to use as leverage against her mother that she regretted most. It was calling Noelle to her home that fateful morning, rather than Hopp. He was the one she should have threatened at gunpoint, not her mother, and if the man she called Bunny had lost his life that day, in the same way or worse....Well, that would have been poetic justice.

As for Del, and why he'd tried to shoulder the blame for everything that happened that day, Zina could offer little insight, other than to second what Gunner had been saying all along: that that was simply who Del was. A good and kind man who would have gone to any length to protect his wife and daughter. Their lives, their reputations. Maybe it had been his hope that, in confessing to a crime he didn't commit, then taking his own life, he'd be closing any inquiries into the shooting before Noelle's affair with Glenn Hopp, or Zina's role in her mother's killing, could be revealed to the world. Why would the police look past the obvious, put his family's darkest secrets out there for all to see in a search for suspects and motives, if he gave them their killer from the jump? Just one more crazy nigger with money problems gone off the rails. In the present state of the nation, what could be more believable than that?

The irony was not lost on Gunner that Del would have very likely had his way were it not for his cousin. Detectives Luckman and Yee of the LAPD had been well prepared to start and stop their investigation into the shooting at Zina's home last Monday with Del; Gunner was the only one determined to dig deeper. He now had all the answers to the hows and whys of Del's death he'd been seeking, but they had come at the price of knowing his cousin surely slept no easier as a result of his meddling.

Ignorance was never bliss, but sometimes, it was the far lesser of two evils.

Early Friday morning, Gunner went down to Venice Beach to watch a seventy-four-year-old Jewish white man surf. He pulled his shoes and socks off, walked down to the edge of the water, and sat in an old beach chair to enjoy the show, the sun still in hiding behind a shield of gray. The ocean spray felt cool on his face and he couldn't help but laugh, seeing the old man ride the modest two-foot waves as easily as a child riding a bike, his black wet suit fitted to his wiry frame like a second skin.

Again and again, the old man climbed atop his board and rode a churning wave inland, then dragged it back out to catch another, until Gunner closed his eyes and nearly drifted off to sleep, the rise and fall of the surf providing a gentle lullaby.

Finally, Ziggy Zeigler came in out of the water, dwarfed by the eight-foot surfboard at his side.

"You should come out with me sometime, Aaron.

There's nothing else like it in the world."

"Aerialists say the same thing about the trapeze. I think my time has passed for both."

"Nonsense."

"Was there some other reason you called me out here today, other than to encourage me to take up water sports?"

His lawyer set his board down and sat cross-legged in the sand, striking a pose befitting a Hebrew Gandhi. "I need you to tell me again what happened to our friend Glenn Hopp Wednesday."

"I told you. I went to his crib to ask him some questions. He was reluctant to answer them, so I offered him a strong inducement to do so."

"You kicked his teeth in."

"Actually, I made it a point to leave his teeth intact, but a physical altercation did take place, yes."

"Can we make the argument that he threw the first punch?"

"Not with a clear conscience, but there's no one but Hopp to refute that assertion, and I'm pretty sure he's not what most juries would call a reliable witness. I take it you've heard from his attorneys?"

"He only has the one. She called me late yesterday. I'm supposed to see papers by early next week."

"They're bluffing, Ziggy."

"Maybe. Hard to make an assault case stick when no police report was filed. But I'm going to keep an eye on my mailbox Monday, just to be on the safe side."

"And if they do file?"

"We'll do what we always do. Pull your sorry ass out of the fire."

Ziggy had spoken to him like that since the day they met, twenty-six years ago. He had only been forty-eight back then, and still it had sounded funny as hell, this old Jew from Encino, built like a steel I-beam, talking like a black cop ten years on the Compton beat.

"I'm worried about you, kid."

"You're always worried about me."

Gunner had closed his eyes again. The sun was starting to melt through the haze and the sand felt soft and smooth between his toes. Ziggy let him have his little moment.

"Yeah, but this time it's different. Mickey and Lilly do what they can, but Del was the one I could always count on to keep you from falling into every open grave you dig for yourself. He was your friend and he was family, and the truth is, I'm not sure how much longer you can stay in the game without him around to watch over you."

"So maybe it's time I got out of the game."

"If I thought you could, I'd suggest it. Seems to me I already have, and more than once. But you don't know anything else besides being a P.I., and it gives you too much perverse satisfaction to walk away from it."

Gunner opened his eyes again. "You sound like a man arguing with himself, Ziggy."

"I'm not arguing with anybody. I'm just saying: I don't know what happens to you now that Del's gone. So I worry about you. Call me an old softy."

Gunner smiled, touched as always by the old man's list toward sentiment. Ziggy was a softy. And he was right. Del's death was a game changer. Gunner's relationship with Kelly DeCharme, should it build on the momentum already being generated, would be a stabilizing force in his life, to be sure, but it wouldn't replace the one he'd shared with Del. It couldn't. In his role as friend and brother, confidant and counselor, Del had been free to tell Gunner things his woman never could, and he'd never failed to meet that responsibility. Who could Gunner speak the unspeakable truth to now, or rely on to deliver a needed reprimand when commiseration was all he wanted?

No one came to mind.

"I'm going to be fine, Ziggy," he said. "I'm going to take

it one day at a time and see how it goes."

Ziggy nodded. "Sure, kid."

"I've got a new client. I start work for her Monday. Did I tell you that?"

"No. That's great." The lawyer got to his feet and tucked his surfboard under one arm. "You coming?"

Gunner shook his head. "I don't think so. I kind of like it here. LA born and raised, and I get down to the beach two, maybe three times a year. Is that crazy, or what?"

Ziggy smiled and pushed off, dragging the tail of his board behind him. Gunner sucked in a lungful of sea air and gazed out at the churning Pacific, seagulls wailing as they raced across the horizon. A pair of elderly women walked in bare feet through the low tide, sun hats big enough to cast a sailboat in shade, as a pot-bellied Asian man in a Speedo he had no business wearing jogged past them in the opposite direction. Out on the water, a woman in a black two-piece bathing suit dipped in and out of waist-high waves like a seal, smoothing her brown hair back every time she brought her shapely body up to the surface.

Venice Beach, Gunner thought. The forgotten Los Angeles.

He closed his eyes again, and this time allowed sleep to overtake him. When he awoke, almost fifty minutes later, the gray sky over the ocean had turned a pale blue and the cell phone in his pocket was humming. Roxanne Niles was calling him to say she had just quit her job at the mall.

"And?" Gunner asked.

"And I was wondering if I could come work for you."

He started to laugh straight up, no filter, struck by both the absurdity of the idea and the brazen, misplaced confidence with which she'd suggested it. Instead, much to his surprise, he said, "Doing what, exactly?"

"Doing what you do. Asking people questions. Finding out things. Learning the truth when nobody else cares what the truth is."

Again, he almost laughed. She made it sound so poetic, like something out of a pulp novel. But it was what he wanted to believe about himself, now more than ever. That his work had some meaning, and that the good he occasionally did for others in the course of it wasn't all in his head. Del used to keep that hope alive for him whenever the need arose. With his cousin gone, he was going to have to find such reassurance elsewhere.

"My office address is on my card, same as my phone number. Come by next Tuesday around ten and we'll talk about how hard you're going to work and how little you're going to get paid."

The next morning, Gunner received an unexpected visit at Mickey's from the two Harper Stowes. The younger had just been released from jail and he wanted to offer Gunner his thanks in person. Or so Harper Stowe Jr. said. To Gunner's eye, the trip had been more the old man's idea than that of his son.

Gunner ushered the pair into his office and offered them both a seat, but Harper Jr. declined it. "We can't stay." He looked at his son, a not-so-gentle nudge to carry his part of the conversation.

"Ms. DeCharme told us what you did. I owe you." The words were sincere but his delivery was forlorn. Dressed in the shabby, oversized clothes he was probably arrested in, he looked tired and distracted, like being a free man might take more effort than he had to give.

"Just doing my job. You all right?"

"Yeah."

"Headaches?"

"Some. Nothing I can't handle."

"It'll probably take a while. It did for me. But eventually, the headaches pass and the nightmares stop, and you find your groove."

"My groove?"

"Your place in the world, away from the war."

The younger Stowe gave him a look. "You were in Afghan?"

"Vietnam. A lifetime ago. Same shit, different day."

The younger Stowe nodded. Something passed between him and Gunner that required no more words.

"I owe you a debt of gratitude myself," Harper Jr. said. "As you may have heard, I'd lost my mind there for a while. If you hadn't found Eric when you did—"

"Forget it. I don't think you would have hurt him, in any case. You aren't the type." Gunner turned back to his son. "So what are your plans now? Besides finding yourself another girl?"

At first, it seemed the joke had gone right over Harper Stowe III's head. But then he laughed, and the other two men felt free to laugh right along with him.

Later that day, Gunner ran his uncle over to Zina's to get Noelle's car. The police had officially closed their investigation into the deaths of Zina's parents late the previous afternoon, so Daniel and Corinne Curry were now free to exchange their rental car for one of the three family vehicles parked at their granddaughter's residence. Gunner suggested they take the newest of the trio, their late daughter-in-law's Buick Encore.

He made no mention of his own visit to Zina's home three nights before. There wasn't any point. Hearing how he'd made one final, midnight intrusion into Noelle Curry's affairs, to secure her cell phone and cement the connection he had already made between her illicit lover "Buddy" and Glenn Hopp, could only open wounds for Del's parents that were just starting to heal.

Instead, he simply delivered his uncle to Zina's doorstep and settled in to wait. In addition to retrieving the Buick, Daniel Curry had been charged by his wife to run into the house and come out again with a small list of items for Zina, and Gunner didn't want to go without seeing his uncle safely away. Zina's belligerent neighbor Gordito was still heavy on his mind. The hotheaded cholo could be lurking about, looking for another excuse to spew hate and spittle in a black man's grille, and it was Gunner's preference that that black man be him and not Daniel Curry.

But hell if the old man wasn't taking forever to reappear from his granddaughter's crib.

"Yo, hom'."

Gunner jerked around in his seat, found the man he'd assaulted ten days ago standing in the street right outside the red Cobra, close enough to put a bullet in Gunner's left ear without fully extending his arm. He'd come up on the convertible from Gunner's blind side, from the other side of the street, and if his intent were to do Gunner harm, the time to stop him had long since passed.

There was no gun in his tattooed hand, however, nor a knife. There was just a brown paper bag in his left, bearing the distinct contours of the six-pack he'd apparently left his mother's house to retrieve. Gunner sat there in the open car, afraid to move, Gordito staring down on him with the one good, unswollen eye the black man had left him with the previous week.

"You remember me, right?" he asked.

Gunner nodded once. "I remember you."

"You fucked me up pretty good. I owe you one, bro. But my mother, she says let it go. 'Cause I drink too much and sometimes I fuck with people for no good reason." He took a deep breath, bounced on the heels of his feet. Recharging his nerve and his will to go through with this, both. "I got a lot of anger in me and, y'know, sometimes the shit gets out. Understand?"

"Sure."

"So like, I'm sorry. You didn't do nothin' I didn't bring on myself. And that's all I got to say. Except, you ever touch me again, I'll fuckin' kill your black ass."

He hurried off before Gunner could extend his misery by saying a word of thanks. Gunner turned and watched as Gordito climbed the steps of his mother's porch and reached the door, where the old woman stood waiting for him with a hug he had to fold himself in half to accept.

A good man gone bad, then good again. At least for a moment.

It was miracle enough for Gunner.

ACKNOWLEDGMENTS

I have been blessed to have an abundance of friends and colleagues in my life who not only made this book possible, but my career as well. Belief in self is everything in this business, and these people have given me that in spades, often at the most critical moments. God bless you all.

And a special shout-out to Doug P. Lyle, MD, whose vast medical expertise has once again lent an air of authenticity to my work that would be sorely lacking otherwise. He's a damn fine writer and the best doctor to ask, "Where does it hurt? And why? And..."

ABOUT THE AUTHOR

GAR ANTHONY HAYWOOD is the Shamus and Anthony award–winning author of twelve crime novels, including the Aaron Gunner series and the Joe and Dottie Loudermilk mysteries. *Booklist* called Haywood "a writer who has always belonged in the upper echelon of American crime fiction." Born and raised in Los Angeles, he now makes his home in Denver, Colorado.